CORRUPTION

EDEN WINTERS

ROCKY RIDGE BOOKS

Corruption © Eden Winters 2013

Cover art by LC Chase

Edited by Jerry L. Wheeler

ISBN-13 978-1-62622-057-7

Published by:

Rocky Ridge Books
PO Box 6922
Broomfield, CO 80021
www.RockyRidgeBooks.com

Praise for the first two Bo and Lucky novels:

Diversion is one of the strongest gay romance novels I have read... It maintains a perfect balance between romantic comedy and hot sexual tension on the one hand and a solid, fascinating, complex plot about prescription drug smuggling on the other...

—Val, ARe Cafe

Forget sleep, I had to find out how this worked out. With a fast paced and tense external plot plus a relationship moving to a new level, *Collusion* kept me turning the page until I got to the end. *Diversion,* the first Bo and Lucky book, did the same thing to me, and this is a more than worthy followup.

—Cryselle, Reviews by Jessewave

So many things go on in [*Collusion*]. Some good (Bo and Lucky), some bad (Lucky in the children's cancer ward), but there's never a dull moment. Some smiley, happy ones (Lucky's confrontation with the neighbor from hell), some tear-jerking ones (the cancer ward), but you *need* to know what's going to happen. The story pulls you along to the ultimate, beautiful conclusion.

—Mrs. Condit Reviews

Diversion snuck up on me, which, given its title (and its author) is something I should have anticipated a bit more. Like Lucky, Eden Winters isn't afraid to go for the emotional jugular and she seems to nick mine pretty much every time.

—Lisa, The Novel Approach

Other titles by Eden Winters:

The Diversion Series

Diversion (Diversion #1)
Collusion (Diversion #2)
Manipulation (Diversion #4)
Redemption (Diversion #5)
Reunion (Diversion #6)
Suspicion (Diversion #7)

Novels

A Matter of When
The Angel of Thirteenth Street
Fallen Angel
Settling the Score
The Telling
The Wish
Duet
Naked Tails

Novellas and other shorts

The Match Before Christmas (Match #1)
Fanning the Flames (Match #2)
A Lie I Can Live With (Match #3)
Galen and the Forest Lord
Summer Boys
Tinsel and Frost
Highway Man
Almost Mine
The Pirate's Gamble

Many thanks to Pam, John, Lynda, Doug, Feliz, Z., Jerry, and Will, for handholding and critique.

CORRUPTION

EDEN WINTERS

PROLOGUE

Another night in Hell.

Simon "Lucky" Harrison paid the cover charge at Armageddon, or whatever the fuck they called this gussied-up bar. The pretentious crowd the club catered to made the place close enough to Hell in his book. And nobody even frisked him. He shifted the holstered department-issued gun beneath his jacket. Damn, but he missed his own weapon, and damn the son-of-a-bitching bastards who'd swiped his .38.

The bouncer waved him through. Wasn't much use in finally having an honest-to-goodness Southeastern Narcotics Bureau badge if he didn't get to flash the shiny gold shield once in a while to get his way, but going high profile would blow the whole undercover thing to kingdom come.

Heavy bass pounded against his skull before he'd even gotten properly inside the door. These assholes called this racket music? If he wanted to bust somebody, he'd definitely come to the right place—they had to be taking some weird-assed shit.

Tonight wasn't about taking down the bad guys, though. Tonight merely laid groundwork, Lucky showing himself off as another run-of-the-mill club-goer. The better to lull the sheep in the presence of a wolf. A drink or two, some mingling, then home to bed. Alone, damn the luck.

Fuck this off-duty, keep-your-hands-to-yourself recognizance, he could see half a dozen people who needed a tap on the shoulder from the long arm of the law. Was the guy in the holey jeans reaching for his wallet or a baggie? The mullet-haired asshole should be reaching for the door, 'cause he sure as hell didn't fit in with a crowd where *casual* meant *lose the*

1

tie. What a huge pocketbook on that lady's arm. A whole kilo would fit in there. And one big-assed alligator gave its life to make the thing.

A trip to the bar yielded a club soda with some kind of green vegetable sticking out of the glass. Seemed a man couldn't even drink without finding greens. Bad enough they made their way onto dinner plates. The guy standing two feet too close turned away. Lucky took the opportunity to shove the offending stalk into the man's glass of orange liquid.

To the club's credit, he'd been in the place a full five minutes and hadn't witnessed a fight, and no peanut shells littered the floor. His elbows hadn't stuck to the bar when he'd waited for his drink, either. The bartender'd been hit with a few ugly sticks, but he controlled the booze, giving him an automatic upgrade from a three to an eight. He seemed friendly enough and kept his fingers away from the top of the glass—all Lucky needed in a bartender.

Now to find a vantage point on the second floor, the better to see and be seen. The nooks and crannies near the balcony also provided discreet enough venues for drug dealing. His scouting mission didn't mean he couldn't tag someone dumb enough to mistake him for a buyer.

Lucky sipped his drink, staring down at a writhing mass of humanity, folks who didn't have anything better to do than waste their hard-earned money on watered-down drinks and spine-rattling dance tunes and go home with someone they'd deny knowing the next day. Huh. And to think he'd dressed up for this. He scratched his leg through the unfamiliar stiffness of a pair of dress slacks. Hell, he'd even ironed a shirt for the occasion.

Nothing much seemed to be happening on the main club level, except for one couple hanging on the fringes, pushing the envelope of public decency. A table in the far corner provided entertainment when two women kissed their male dates and disappeared toward the ladies' room. Their dates waited a full thirty seconds before pouncing on each other like starving wolves. They'd better come up for air before the ladies returned.

2

A woman's scream jerked Lucky's attention away from the two men in need of a room. "Get away from me!"

Lucky grasped the railing, leaning over for a better view of the packed floor below. There, in the red dress. The woman screamed again, "Go away!" She swatted at the air above her head.

Oh hell. Let the crazy begin. Fighting with shit that wasn't there was never a good sign.

"'Scuse me," Lucky muttered, squeezing through the on-lookers. "Get the fuck out of my way" worked better, but the department frowned on the direct approach. They should stick with what worked.

The woman's shouts carried over the throbbing beat from the DJ booth, and Lucky lost sight of her a time or two while struggling to get past a couple who didn't want to move. A hand landed on his ass from behind. "Wanna keep that hand?" he snapped. The hand disappeared, and the couple jumped out of the way. Fuckers.

He caught sight of the screaming woman again a few yards to the left. Her friends stood back, creating some space. "Can't you see them?" she shrieked, staring toward the ceiling.

"Move, dammit!" Lucky pushed against a wall of gawkers four or five inches taller than him. They didn't budge. All hell was about to break loose. "Get the fuck out of my way!" bought Lucky enough space to slither through.

A man grasped the woman's arm about the time Lucky got within grabbing distance. She pulled back for a swing. Lucky jerk-ed back. *Crack!* She bypassed Lucky and slammed her knuckles into the man's jaw. He fell with a thud. *Better him than me.*

Two uniformed security guards approached, middle-aged men who huffed and puffed by the time they reached the ruckus. *Here come Doofus and Dipshit.* 'Bout time the fuckers got here before Lucky blew his cover. Back in his day, clubs employed muscle-bound gym bunnies to work the crowds. They didn't make bouncers like they used to. "Ma'am, you need to settle down," the first one said, stand-ing outside the woman's reach.

Doofus. Was he for real? *Settle down?* Did he have any fucking idea what he was dealing with? She might appear a

3

sweet young thing in a red dress, but whatever she took/snorted/shot up had definitely taken control of the wheel.

"Make them stop!" The woman ducked beneath her arms, batting away invisible attackers.

"There's nothing there, ma'am," Doofus said, while the other guard rolled wary eyes upward.

"Maybe you better come with us." This time Dipshit spoke. He must have gone to the same training program as his partner. Didn't they at least watch some outdated training video on the warning signs of drug use and dealing with folks on their way 'round the bend?

The woman straightened, eyeing the guard. "Ahhh! You're one of them! Get away, get away!" Flinging another woman to the side, she charged toward the exit, screaming and swatting. The guards trotted behind her.

"They better pay me extra for this." Lucky stepped on a couple of toes and bumped a drink or two while zigzagging in pursuit.

He burst through the front door and followed the screams down an alley. The ankle he'd broken during an investigation last summer squealed in protest at being forced into a run.

Doofus and Dipshit had the woman cornered by the time Lucky caught up. Damn fucked-up leg. *Heal, you sumbitch, heal! Six months should be long enough.*

"Stay back! Stay the fuck back!" the woman squawked. She grabbed a hank of her not-found-in-nature-red hair, and jerked the strands out of her head with nary a wince. Holy shit. That had to hurt. Her breath turned to fog before her face, adding another layer of creepy to the moment.

She took a few wobbly steps back, a high-heeled shoe on one foot and the other bare. A sleeve hung from what had likely been an expensive designer dress. Eyes wide, she pressed against the brick wall of the club. Lucky shivered, wrapping his jacket tighter around him. Late October, close to midnight, and the woman didn't appear to feel a lick of cold.

"Easy, ma'am, we don't want to hurt you," Dipshit said, empty hands splayed to show he wasn't armed. With his

4

graying hair and bulging belly, he probably had kids this woman's age.

Wild eyes stared out from an ashen face, heavy with black and red makeup smears. The woman's hair hung in strings over her face. She glanced right and left, then focused on the guard nearest her. "I didn't do anything. Leave me alone."

"We can't do that," Doofus replied, edging closer. "You attacked a man. We need to ask you a few questions."

Stupid assholes. They ought to know better than to say such shit. Tell her whatever lies were necessary to calm her ass down.

Lucky held back, cataloguing symptoms: delusional, paranoid, any number of street drugs produced the same effect. The woman quieted, and the guards held their ground. Fat tears rolled down her cheeks. Torn knuckles oozed blood. Her hand would hurt like hell once she came down. "I didn't mean to, I really didn't mean to."

Crazy lived in her eyes. By day she probably drove a fancy car to a high-rise office complex downtown. Tonight, she lived in a hell created by her own mind. And her demons were more real to her than two security guards trying to talk her down off the proverbial ledge.

The guards exchanged worried glances. Between the two of them, they'd probably never dealt with bad drugs to this degree before. And why the hell were their guns still holstered? Didn't they have a taser? They sure as shit needed one. One hundred and five pounds of unpredictable with superhuman strength, no pain threshold, and no concept of right and wrong made one volatile threat. Little Miss Red Dress might be the most dangerous person they'd ever met.

The guards took a few steps back. Bad move. A split second later, the woman screamed, staring past the first guard's head. "They're back! Oh my God, they're back!" She dove toward Dipshit's sidearm while Doofus grabbed his gun. "Don't let them get me!"

She wrestled with the guard while his partner hesitated a moment too long. Lucky raced across the alley on his uncooperative leg. He slammed into both guard and the attacker, knocking them to the ground. The woman snatched the gun

5

from the guard's holster. Lucky fished his own weapon out from beneath his jacket and took aim.

The tiny assailant gawked at something Lucky couldn't see. "I can't let them get me." She knelt on the pavement, shivering with unknown terrors one minute, and the next she pointed the gun.

Lucky lunged. A shot rang out.

CHAPTER ONE

Lucky shoved a handful of bills at a bored cab driver after yet another trip to the emergency room, followed by the police station. Sometimes the order varied. Sometimes the cops came to him, especially if whatever shit he found himself in proved too deep to swim out of with merely a look-see and a bandage. He flexed his shoulder. Sore, but only a graze. Too bad he'd lost one hell of a fine jacket. He should have kept it, worn the ruined leather to work to freak out his coworkers. Nothing beat bloody cowhide and a bullet hole to say, "I'm a badass motherfucker and stay the fuck away from me."

Home sweet home after one hell of a day—or night. Darkened windows greeted him on his side of his rented duplex. Alone. So much for a home-cooked supper, or rather breakfast, at this hour. Apparently, the only other person besides himself and his landlady to have a key wasn't here. Might be for the best. Lucky needed a hot shower and a few hours of uninterrupted shut-eye. Of course, a hot meal and a blowjob might make both more pleasant.

A red glow and the familiar scent of cherry pipe tobacco from his landlady's side of the duplex gave away her presence. At four fucking a.m. Didn't she ever sleep? Lucky squinted, barely making out Mrs. Griggs' form on her porch. "Evening, ma'am," he said. Even in the darkness, he clearly pictured her bathrobe-wrapped frame surrounded by the usual half-dozen cats piled up on the swing with her.

"Another wild night?" she asked.

Too tired to explain, or risk her knowing too much, Lucky responded, "Something like that."

He turned the key in the lock and pushed the front door open. A dark shape flitted across the porch, dashing into his house before he'd even gotten inside. He flipped on a light, drawing his gun and checking out the room before entering. Nothing like getting shot to make a man jumpy. Besides, he'd rather have a gun in hand and not need the damned thing than need it and not have it.

"Mrrrooow?" asked the black and white cat strolling across his living room like it owned the place.

"What the hell do you think you're doing here?" Lucky asked, though without much heat. He bent and scratched its furry ear. In the kitchen, the refrigerator hummed and a clock ticked off the seconds, adding to the sense of isolation in his obviously empty place. The feline he called "Cat Lucky" added his own gristmill harmony, butting his head against Human Lucky's hand. After a moment of cat spoiling, Lucky traipsed through his house, clicking on lights and checking in closets. He stopped at his bedroom door. Holy shit. Someone had definitely violated his personal space.

The quilt on his bed hung perfectly even. The pillows, dressed in matching cases, sat propped against the headboard. A dragon sculpture, a gift his lover gave him meant to offer protection, perched on his nightstand.

He sucked in a deep breath and exhaled in a steady rush as he catalogued missing items. No coffee cups lined his dresser top, and not a single pair of jeans obstructed his path across the floor. A Harley Davidson brochure kept the dragon company. Damn. He'd been missing that flier for months. A quick duck into the bathroom showed a towel draped from the rack for possibly the first time since he'd moved in. Wasn't that what the shower curtain rod was for? Or the floor? A wicker basket he'd never noticed before held folded washcloths, and a bath mat took up space beside the tub. He didn't recognize the rug either. Nice, though. And might keep him from busting his ass the next time he got out of the shower.

He didn't mind a clean house, but he didn't like the subtle reminder of his slob nature. For years his lack of domestic abilities hadn't mattered. No one darkened his door without a survey clipboard, a case full of Girl Scout cookies, or a trick or treat bag in hand.

Dare he hope his intruder left gifts in the kitchen too?

The cat followed him from room to room, stropping against Lucky's ankles. He'd never figured himself a cat person, since his crazy schedule of being gone for weeks at a time didn't allow much time for pets. Technically, the fur ball belonged to Mrs. Griggs, but he laid claim to Lucky whenever possible. The critter wasn't too much trouble, and it provided company. Lucky might wait a while before shooing the furry intruder back outside.

Superstitions lived in weak minds. That didn't stop a shudder. Even science left mysteries too often unexplained. Every time Lucky set eyes on the cat he recalled a poor little girl he'd met last spring, who'd captured his heart and then broke it by dying from tainted medicine. Either the cat was a pain in the ass stalker who wouldn't take no for an answer, or a message from Stephanie, sent from beyond the grave. Either way, Lucky put the gun away to open a can of tuna. "Don't you dare tell anyone about this," he said, placing the can on the floor and adding an ear scratch for good measure. "Mrs. Griggs probably already fed you, didn't she?"

The cat made "*grwwwwnnnn, grwwwwnnnnn, grwww-wwnnnn*," noises, face buried in the tuna can.

Now to feed the human. A fresh jug of milk sat in the refrigerator, a message in black marker reading: "Use a glass! And yes, I'll know!" A plastic container marked "Spaghetti," sat beside the milk, lettered in the same neat print.

Nothing said, "I got tired of waiting and went home" like a plateful of refrigerated spaghetti and a spotless house. But there'd been no need calling and getting Bo riled up over what didn't even amount to a flesh wound. Two seconds later, he would have charged to the hospital to hover and fuss. And nothing said, "We're more than coworkers" than hovering and fussing when the boss showed up to ask a million questions.

Not quite as good as the freshly created meal of Lucky's dreams, but reheated leftovers beat fending for himself. The microwave turned the contents of the container from a congealed mess to a late supper in five minutes. The scent of tomato sauce and herbs conjured images of a dark-haired man

9

in an apron, flitting between the stove and the sink. Damn the woman in red for taking bad shit. And damn the son-of-a-bitch who'd supplied her. Lucky could be lying in bed right now in a fucked-out stupor instead of eating alone with only a cat for company. And his right hand, later.

He ate in silence, save for the occasional slide of the can over linoleum as the cat pushed the tuna tin around the floor, attempting to get every little nibble. After eating, Lucky gently but firmly showed the cat the way out. The darned thing snored, and there were much better ways to wake up in the morning than to tuna-scented cat kisses.

Shedding his clothes down the hallway to the bathroom, Lucky stopped mid-motion and returned to pick up the offending garments. "I can't even walk through your house without tripping," he muttered in an approximation of his lover's tenor. In his own deeper tones, he added, "And I won't get laid until the lecture's over."

Maybe he should call Bo and explain why he'd been late. Nah, wouldn't do to appear overeager. Especially if the object of his desires happened to be sleeping.

He showered, keeping his bandaged shoulder out of the water, imagining Bo's chestnut locks blackening under the shower's spray, and his mahogany eyes, further darkened by lust, gazing down with wicked intent. He rubbed a soapy hand down his chest, hefting the weight of his cock. Bo knew exactly how to grip him, how hard and fast to stroke. But Bo wasn't here. Lucky would have to make do, working himself to the one-two beat of an imaginary body rutting against him.

"Soon," he promised himself. "Soon."

Wait! Was that a knock? A quick turn of the shower knobs silenced the water's spray, leaving a warm swirl of fog. Silence. Towel wrapped around his waist, Lucky gave up hoping and locked up. *Yowl!* How did Cat Lucky know it was bedtime, even though the clock said six a.m.? Maybe if Lucky were quiet... Halfway down the hall, another yowl stopped him in his tracks. Gone for a few hours, and the moment he got home he's wrapped around a furry paw again.

"All right," Lucky grumbled, stomping back down the hall to the front door. "But just 'cause Bo ain't here. Don't even think you're invited in when my bed's already full."

He pulled the door open and Cat Lucky pranced down the hall, head and tail held high. Kitchen light off, coffee pot set, front door locked. Human Lucky interpreted the meowing from the bedroom to mean, "Come lay down and be my cat bed!"

"Yes, your lordship." Lucky trudged down the hall to his room. Before settling into bed, he punched his way through the office phone tree to the department's uncaring voice mail. "I'm calling in 'shot'. I'll be in sometime after noon."

Let the gossip begin.

CHAPTER TWO

A few sleepless hours, a blur of a commute, an overenthusiastic greeting from a perky blonde receptionist... yup, all the signs of morning, or rather, afternoon. Decaf Starbucks coffee in one hand, a cup of green tea in the other in case he ran into Bo, Lucky turned and nearly slammed into a co-worker.

"Got a drinking problem?" Keith sneered, eyeing the two cups.

"I bring my own so I don't have to drink the stump water you call coffee," Lucky snapped. No need mentioning the other cup wasn't for him. Often enough in the past, he'd toted in a double-shot of Starbucks, albeit the full caffeine kind, before Mr. Healthy Bo switched him to decaf.

Keith's disdainful glare fell on Lucky's scuffed second-best jacket. "Nice jacket. Been shopping in dumpsters again?"

Walter Smith, the giant who ruled the Southeastern Narcotics Bureau's Department of Diversion Prevention and Control, traipsed up the hallway, face lighting up when his bifocaled gaze fell on Lucky. *Saved by the boss, fuckwad.* Five people. Only five people's opinions mattered. Walter Smith used to slide between one and five on a regular basis, but he never dropped completely off the list. Now Bo permanently occupied the number one spot. Walter presently came in at number two. "I'd hoped you'd be here today, Lucky," said the man who'd freed him from prison and given him purpose in life, "although I wouldn't have blamed you for taking the day off."

"Awww, it's only a scratch." Lucky gave Keith his smuggest grin. "But I did lose a perfectly good jacket."

"Still, you were shot," Walter persisted.

Keith raised his brows but kept quiet. *Take that, asshole.*

"After you're settled, I'd like to see you in my office, please."

Once Walter's office door closed behind his broad back, an evil leer twisted Keith's face. "Let me guess, you were cleaning your gun and it went off, right?" He pantomimed jacking his cock, then stalked off, denying Lucky a snappy comeback.

"Don't you have some filing to do?" Lucky snarled at the frozen-in-place receptionist before sauntering down the hall. "No good motherfucking Keith," he mumbled, "no good motherfucking afternoon, no good motherfucking... what day is it anyway?" Damn, but he missed his butter-soft leather jacket, now filling an evidence bag at a precinct. "No good motherfucking jacket, no good motherfucking crackheads." Or whatever the fuck the woman took. Down the corridor, he ambled past the cubes of his fellow agents, past the mailroom, past a bank of filing cabinets to the double cube he shared with the department's newest addition. Both desks stood empty. As Lucky'd made it a point to arrive after lunch, chances were Bo wouldn't be in. If he wasn't at his desk at twelve forty-five, he wasn't going to show.

Lately, Lucky's schedule had him coming while Bo seemed to be going, which meant they hadn't crossed paths much in the last few weeks. Lucky tossed the cup of tea into the trash and covered the peace offering with empty Styrofoam cups off his own desk, left since who knew when. Even housekeeping avoided Lucky's end of the hallway. Bite a few heads off and folks learn to leave you alone. And while Bo might clean up the house, he and Lucky carefully maintained a "we're only coworkers" façade at work. Mr. Neat-Freak Bo Schollenberger didn't dare inflict his cleanliness here.

Lucky took his time assembling his notes and adding the finishing touches to his report before polishing off the dregs of his coffee and preparing for a visit with the boss. After roughly thirty minutes of busy work, he dragged himself down the hall. Keith stood near the copier in the mail room, rolling up his top lip when Lucky passed by.

Ignoring the resident asshole, Lucky tapped on the door to his boss's office.

"Come in," Walter called.

Lucky almost smiled at the friendly greeting but rearranged his mouth to something that probably looked more like the results of a severe gas cramp. No need to let "Uncle Walt" know he wasn't on the shit list.

Pushing the door open, Lucky peeked inside. "You wanted to see me?" He slumped down in the chair Walter pointed to with a hand roughly twice the size of Lucky's. "I gave you my initial report last night at the hospital, but I need to read over my typed version once more before sending it in." Or get Bo to check for typos, if by some miracle he appeared in the cube when Lucky got back.

Walter's chair rasped when he leaned back. Hands folded across an ample belly, the man who'd taught Lucky to be one of the good guys gazed over the top of his glasses. "How's the arm?"

Crap. Idle chitchat usually led to shit Lucky didn't want to hear. "Fine." He flexed his shoulder to prove the point. "Hurts some, but not too bad."

"Good, although I'm afraid the woman who shot you added assault with a deadly weapon to her simple assault and possession charges."

Lucky bit the inside of his mouth and didn't reply. Most people would have pissed him off by aiming a gun his way, but the woman last night wasn't in her right mind. Besides, it wasn't the first time he'd taken a bullet. Only, last time it was a BB fired by his kid brother, Daytona. Little twerp. But his jacket? Did she have to go and shoot his jacket?

"Please do try to take care of yourself, Lucky. While I've nothing against socializing with my team after working hours, I'd prefer to meet in a restaurant, not the emergency room."

Hardy, har, har. Yet the lack of twinkling in Walter's eyes betrayed his true concern. If Lucky bit the big one, Walter would be one of a handful of people who might miss him. He and Walter had enough history to achieve a bass-ackward kind of affection, and the old coot never had pushed Lucky to share little details like aches, pains, or doubts. No, if Lucky were going to rile the boss, it wouldn't be "I got nicked in the arm". He'd make it huge. A fuck-up of colossal proportions.

"Anyway," Walter continued. "I asked you in here to talk about Bo. To be honest, we should have had this conversation weeks ago."

Lucky's heart plunged off a cliff and landed hard in his stomach before bouncing back up to lodge in his throat. "Bo?" The trainee he'd formerly referred to as "Newbie" wasn't someone Lucky wanted to discuss across the paper-strewn surface of the boss's desk. "What about him?"

Piercing eyes dared Lucky to lie, and he swallowed hard. While Bo's crimes hadn't come close to Lucky's, he'd still earned himself a stint of probation to be worked off in service to the Southeastern Narcotics Bureau. Sleeping with a coworker, particularly a convicted felon, might defy the terms of the agreement. "Is there anything you'd like to tell me?" Walter asked.

Oh shit! What now? Drug dealers. Convicted felons. Unscrupulous doctors. Lucky stared them in the face and lied easier than most folks spoke the truth. Walter asking a direct question was another matter entirely. But he didn't actually ask if Lucky and Bo were fucking like bunnies, did he?

"'S far as I know he aced our last assignment," Lucky replied. Where was Bo? If the man's fate hung in the balance, he should be here. "I thought he'd be in today. I'd hoped to tie up some loose ends."

Walter regarded Lucky a minute more. The stiff set of his shoulders relaxed somewhat. "I've been keeping him busy. Which gives us time to chat."

Lucky filled his lungs and forced his fingers to remain still on the chair arms. Walter could read body language with the best of them. "Is something wrong?"

Bushy gray brows knitted together over Walter's eyes. "Wrong? Why would anything be wrong?"

The *pitter-pat* of Lucky's heart shifted into overdrive. "Then what's this about?"

"Lucky. It's nearly November. Since October of last year you've trained Bo and worked with him on several cases. It's standard policy to ask for your input. It's past time for his annual review."

Annual review? Lucky peeled his white-knuckled fingers from padded leather chair arms. Annual review. Walter wanted to talk job performance, not kick Bo out of the department because of a complaint of fraternization against policy. Sure, in Lucky's mind, he and Bo were already involved when Richmond "Lucky" Lucklighter bit the dust and Simon "Lucky" Harrison came on board, meaning an existing relationship loophole. However, he wasn't ready to test the waters of exactly how the top brass viewed two male agents warming the sheets together. They didn't always agree with Lucky's opinions.

"Now, in areas of attendance and on matters of procedure, I've awarded him high ratings, and he turns in immaculate reports." Walter raised a single brow, one side of his mouth crooking upward. *You might learn a thing or two from him* remained unspoken. Lucky heard the jibe in his head anyway, and in Walter's distinct Bostonian accent. Lucky turned in thorough reports, complete but rambling, loaded with opinions and commentary in the footnotes. Furthermore, he always considered spell check wrong because of the few times he'd trusted the program and wound up with embarrassing words for his efforts.

He weighed his response. Walter probably expected cutdowns and criticism, Lucky's trademarks. When he didn't answer quickly enough, Walter huffed out a sigh. "Please don't tell me the two of you have had a falling out."

Brown hair streaked with gold, fanned out against a pillowcase, low moans filling the room, peppered by pleas of "harder," "oh yeah," and "right there." Breathy little whines growing more and more insistent, followed by a guttural "Aaahhhh!" of completion. Nope, no fall outs on the Lucky/Bo front. Not that Lucky planned to share intimate details.

"He's not too much of an asshole," Lucky allowed, chasing back images of a naked Bo stretched out on the bed, the roundness of his bubble butt clearly on display. *He's got a perfect asshole though.*

17

"Oh? That's certainly an improvement over the last review we discussed. Though I must admit you were right. Vinson didn't last."

Vinson? Oh yeah, the gung ho super-cop wanna-be who'd cut and run after a mere thirteen months on the job. One of many trainees who came and left again before anyone got the chance to know them.

If Lucky gave a glowing review, Walter wouldn't buy it. And after only a year on the job, the latest addition to Walter's team hadn't yet passed the learning curve.

Honesty. Not Lucky's strong suit. Too little, and Walter would call him out. Too much, and Walter wouldn't believe. Walter smelled bullshit. Somehow Lucky always managed to make up convincing tales on the fly for drug lords, but not his boss.

"Let me make this easier." Walter dropped his professional demeanor and adopted an air of favorite uncle. Time and again he'd used the ploy to get suspects to fess up. "Where do you see Bo has need of improvement?"

Narrowing down the question helped. "He gets too close to the subject sometimes, can't separate himself from the role he plays, and trusts too easily."

"He'll learn discernment with experience and further training. As for the other…"

"The other?"

"He shows a lot of promise undercover and his ability to fit in, immerse himself, is an asset we hope to further develop."

Lucky considered Bo's forgetting their assignment to play pharmacist on their last shared case a liability. He'd had to keep reminding the man who they worked for. "What do you mean 'develop'?"

"As you're fully aware, the biggest problem with undercover operations is to remain undetected, not give yourself away. One flinch, one nervous blink, could put a man's life at risk."

Yes, Lucky was fully aware. A dedication page on the Southeastern Narcotics Bureau's website memorialized the men and women who'd died while serving. He'd rather die himself than find Bo's name there. "And?"

"Based on what you and others have reported, and what I've seen with my own eyes, I believe Bo has what it takes to go deep undercover and remain unscathed. Which brings me to our next topic. Budget cuts."

"Budget cuts?" Lucky scowled. Surely Walter wouldn't praise Bo with one breath and lay him off with the next.

"Look at it as less of a budget cut and more of bureau restructuring," Walter clarified.

"Can you be more specific?" At one time Lucky'd lived in hopes of being fired. Now, with a job instead of a sentence, he wasn't sure any more about leaving. Not that he'd share that information with Walter.

"We're going to be working more in cooperation with other divisions. Due to this arrangement, entities such as the Northeastern Narcotics Bureau will combine forces with us for greater effect. Policies will change as we adapt best practices and consolidate expertise bases. We'll also occasionally host law enforcement officers and even members of the Drug Enforcement Administration, and assist with cases outside our normal area of expertise.

"There seems to be a desperate need for deep undercover operatives. In fact, as we speak, Bo is in training."

Deep undercover. Weeks and months spent in someone else's life. Should Lucky be thrilled with his trainee's progress or appalled that his lover might soon be in the line of fire? He'd already witnessed firsthand how the lines between agent and alias blurred. And what training did Bo possibly need beside what Lucky provided? "What do you know about the trainer?"

Walter leaned forward, elbows on his desk. "He spent fifteen years with the New York Police Department before beginning work with the DEA, and he's acted as a consultant to the Food and Drug Administrations and the Northeastern Narcotics Bureau. Plus, he has a theater background."

A bunch of guys prancing around in tights quoting dead poets. What did theater have to do with undercover work? "What's he teaching?"

"For this week's sessions, consider him an undercover ops coach."

Wait! What? "Did you say 'coach'?" Lucky forced his slack jaw upward, closing his mouth with a sharp click of teeth.

"Yes, Lucky, a coach. The DEA has had great success with him. Surely you've heard of Jameson O'Donoghue."

"No, can't say that I have." Heard? No. Seen? Only in about a zillion articles, normally entitled something along the lines of "Better Warriors for the War on Drugs." Like the tried and true methods didn't work. Well, since the war hadn't yet been won, maybe the articles made a point, but none of Lucky's battles had ended in defeat. Not yet anyway.

"I had the pleasure of meeting Jameson a few years ago. He's quite impressive. Bo's spending his days in seminars."

Before Walter had given up on trying to teach an old dog new tricks, he'd sent Lucky to seminars. Seminars, places to drink lots of free coffee, eat free donuts, and tune out while some man or woman in a business suit with zero practical experience tried to explain how to do a better job. "To be flat honest, Walter, I never learned much at the seminars you sent me to. All I did was sit in a conference room, listening to some guy drone on and on."

Walter's smile didn't have to appear so indulgent. "This particular seminar is more interactive. At a basic level, I suppose you might call them acting classes."

Bo? An actor? Well, he did seem to rein in anger when Lucky would be livid. "Why him? Why now?" Lucky took in the stiffening set of Walter's shoulders, the steepled fingers. Walter may not have realized it, but he gave things away. Any moment now, he'd suggest something Lucky wouldn't like.

"I predict great things for Bo. In our conversations, he's expressed an interest in continuing with the SNB after his probationary period ends. I must say I'm all for the idea."

Yeah, Bo'd mentioned staying on. Lucky would deal with ducking department rules on a long-term basis when they got there.

Behind glass lenses, Walter's eyes took on a fervent gleam. "From what Jameson's told me, we may have picked ourselves a winner the day Mr. Schollenberger darkened our door."

At least Lucky had, though he still wasn't quite ready to admit his feelings publicly. A memory replayed itself of one of the last afternoons he and Bo'd spent together.

"Can I get you a cup of tea?"

Bo lay on the couch, nursing a headache. His pained grimace eased into a fleeting smile. "That'd be nice."

After delivery of a cup of warm chamomile, a run to CVS for more ibuprofen, a few forehead kisses to "make it better," a backrub, a serving of veggie soup, and a blow job, Bo told Lucky, "I'm feeling much better now."

Lucky'd nearly choked the first time he'd uttered the L word, and *asshole* wasn't much of an endearment, though Bo'd never batted an eye. But Bo had fallen asleep that night despite Lucky checking on him every five minutes. He knew Lucky loved him even without a dozen "I love yous" a day, right?

"Yes," Walter continued, derailing Lucky's side trip into domestic bliss. "Jameson likens Bo to a younger version of himself. And since the man is considered an expert in the field of deep undercover operations, that's high praise indeed."

The buttoned-down pencil pusher probably had never actually been on the inside, never had a drug lord offering good money to make him disappear. Had never watched friends living on the wrong side of the law go down. He'd likely been a desk jockey at NYPD and only a consultant at the DEA.

"Bo's learning a thing or two. That's good." *But what's it got do with me?* Although acting...Hmmm... Bo decked out as a leather-clad biker, spread-eagled against a wall while Lucky did a little frisking. *Oh, yeah, baby, go on... resist arrest.* Unlike some folks he'd met over the years, Lucky wasn't afraid to pat down strategic places. And Bo had some pretty impressive strategic places.

"In fact, tomorrow afternoon you and I are invited to sit in on a class to evaluate for ourselves the possible benefits. Bo's in the pilot program along with a few new hires and agents from other divisions. Based on how much they take away from the specialized training, we may make the classes mandatory."

Oh fuck. He said *mandatory*. Sitting in a conference room while some failed actor demonstrated how to walk while balancing a book on his head. Oh, hell no. "Why me?"

"Because you're my number one undercover agent. Jameson requested someone with real life experience to share their stories."

Standing up in front of a bunch of sneering little college-educated slackers and let them laugh at him wasn't going to happen. No fucking way. "Thanks, boss, but I've got a lot to do this week."

"I merely said I'd bring you. I'd never commit you to address the class without asking you first."

Damn. Walter knew Lucky too well. "I'll go, I'll sit, I'll listen, I'll drink coffee. That's all I'm promising."

"Fair enough. However, there's one more thing."

Prickles gathered on the back of Lucky's neck. "What?"

"In the past when we've staged undercover maneuvers, I've coordinated and chosen someone from my group for the supervisory role. In light of some recent failures..."

Yeah, Lucky'd heard rumors about two agents from the Northwest going over to the other side. It hadn't happened in the South for a while.

Walter grimaced and hastened to add, "In other divisions, mind you." A note of pride tinged his words. At one time, the department betting pool gave ten to one odds of Lucky returning to a life of crime. It was worth staying on the straight and narrow to watch the self-righteous bastards lose money to Walter, who always had Lucky's back.

"We'll also be restructuring our methods of operations," Walter continued. "Each case will have an agent, a supervisor, one or more operators, and monitoring as necessary. It's been suggested that I train additional personnel to act as case agent."

The disappointment spreading across Walter's face effectively cut off any smart-assed answers from Lucky. Whatever the higher powers chose to shove down Lucky's gullet wasn't leaving a pleasant taste in Walter's mouth either.

"Who'll be coordinating, then?"

"For the time being, until we train proper resources, myself or Jameson."

Lucky nearly growled. No matter how much experience the fuckwad may have had up in Northeastern territory, he didn't know his ass from Atlanta down here in the South. "He's been moved here?"

"He's on loan as part of our new cooperative efforts."

Maybe the bastard fucked up at his last job, and they transferred him because he knew too much. In Lucky's experience, the DEA looked down their noses at the SNB, referring to them as "wannabees". "Who have you tagged for supervising?"

"You and Art, for now. It seems other agencies are backlogged and can't spare senior personnel, although they are sending junior agents here for training."

Streets of Atlanta, New York, Tucson. Drugs thrived in them all.

Walter inhaled a long breath and huffed it out. "We're about to embark on the biggest case to land on my desk in years."

"Oh?"

"The woman from last night admitted to using a substance called 'bath salts' on the street. You're familiar with the product." A statement, not a question.

Of course. The recent secretary type losing her mind wasn't Lucky's first encounter with the shit. "Synthetic drug undetectable by drug dogs and most standard drug tests. Causes violent behavior and hallucinations. Makes people see aliens and demons. Most states dealt with the problem by making it a control one substance." On a scale of one to five, control ones were the most dangerous of drugs, illegal, and with no accepted medical use in the US.

The new laws hadn't helped much, though, and the bureau still dealt with a chemical equaling meth in Lucky's eyes, and that at one time filled convenience store shelves, advertised as a legal high. The episode in the club opened the lid on a huge can of worms.

"Government measures curtailed the issue for a time, but the drugs are back. We've uncovered a pipeline from Mexico, traveling across the South and up the East Coast."

Interesting. Lucky used to travel that way back when he'd hauled narcotics for his former lover and boss, Victor Mangiardi. "Source of intel?" While Lucky wasn't above using criminal informants, they weren't often reliable. He'd much prefer shared information from law enforcement.

"Informant."

Figured. "What's he got?"

"A routine traffic stop uncovered two cases of packets later identified as bath salts, similar to the evidence taken from the lady arrested last night. The suspect wants to cut a deal. According to his statement, he wanted out but was afraid what the others in the drug ring might do to him."

Yeah, right. It's all fun and games until someone gets busted. "In other words, he's in bed with dangerous folks, got caught, and now wants us to bail him out."

Walter nodded as he spoke. "He's been cooperative thus far, allowing us time to build our case and position our personnel."

Finally, a job worthy of Lucky's experience. He nodded, itching to get back in the field. "I can be ready to leave in two days."

A flicker of confusion beetled Walter's brows, smoothing out a moment later. "Not you this time, Lucky. You're still recovering from injuries. Besides, you'll have your hands full."

"There's nothing you've got for me here that any other agent can't handle." Albeit not as well.

Walter's jowls eased back, revealing a shit-eating grin. "That's where I believe you're wrong. You'll soon have a few more rookies to train."

Rookies? Oh kill me now. "I'm already training a rookie."

Walter tapped a finger against a file lying on the desk. "As of today, and the completion of his annual review, Bo Schollenberger is no longer a rookie."

Reports filed, news articles about bath salts read, and forty-five e-mail inquiries to illegal internet pharmacies later, and Lucky was ready to call it a night. But first, time for more research. He keyed "Jameson O'Donoghue" into the web browser, clicking on the first link to appear in a long list.

"Jameson O'Donoghue, highly decorated officer of NYPD, consultant for the Drug Enforcement and Food and Drug Administrations, author of three books on the subject of undercover investigations," a web page declared.

Lucky expected a wizened grandpa of a man or a suited businessman type. Instead, judging by the picture posted online, O'Donoghue preferred jeans to dress slacks and T-shirts to button-downs much as Lucky did. The man also inspired, or more than likely paid for, pages upon pages of officer testimonials to his teaching techniques. Apparently, the man fooled some of the people most of the time. No way could anyone learn in a classroom the lessons the street taught, yet Jameson laughed all the way to the bank.

Based on this jerkoff's opinion, Walter might shove Bo out into a big ugly world he wasn't ready for, where a single botched move meant the difference between life and death. Should Lucky have lied for the review? Told Walter Bo never learned a thing or challenged authority? Wait. Walter would have simply pointed out Lucky's own authority-defying ways. And look where being a hard nose got him.

More pages covered news articles of Jameson's field work with the DEA. Okay, so maybe he did have some street smarts after all. But not here in the South and definitely not on both sides of the coin, like Lucky.

A click of a finger left Jameson behind and brought up the SNB home page, where an icon beckoned on the far right of the screen. A glance right and left ensured no one approached. Lucky clicked on the innocuous looking *Memorial* button.

A twenty-seven-year-old father of two smiled from the page, wearing a 1970s era SNB uniform. Agent Martinez, the first casualty of the then newly-formed Southeastern Narcotics Bureau, shot at close range during a raid. He'd be retired by now if he'd lived and stayed with the department; his kids were grown with kids of their own, more than likely, with no grandpa to bounce them on his knee.

Scrolling down the page revealed poofed 80s blonde hair, bright green eyes, and an eternal grin, immortalizing the accountant who'd been hit by a drunk driver on her way to pick her kids up from school. Poor buggers never saw their mom alive again. She may not have been an agent on a drug bust, but she'd been a member of the SNB nonetheless.

Several more former SNB agents' and employees' biographies filled the page: some succumbed to natural causes, many more died in performance of their duties. Most were younger than Lucky at the time of their deaths. Narcotics enforcement and longevity didn't run hand in hand.

At the bottom of the page, a pictureless obituary stated, "Agent Richmond Eugene Lucklighter, killed on assignment." The image of an SNB shield further marked the man's status of having died in the line of duty, along with a gold ribbon proclaiming that he'd saved the life of a fellow agent. Was something wrong with the sudden surge of pride? Although Lucky now bore the name Simon Harrison and continued in the land of the living, to have left the world fighting for the good guys choked him up every time.

What did his parents think of their son dying to save another man's life? Or did they remember Lucky at all? Did Mom and Dad visit this memorial page, regretting having turned their backs on their oldest child?

Lucky scrolled back through the listing, stopping whenever the shield symbol popped up. Each of the men and women who'd died on the job had gotten up for work one morning and hadn't come home, firmly believing they'd learned everything they needed to about the job and how to stay alive for another day. Hell, even Lucky's fake death could've been real. A few lofty words from some overpaid hotshot in a classroom didn't mean jack shit either. Walter, typically rational, wasted his time by even putting stock into such nonsense. However, if O'Donoghue lived up to his hype, the department could save a bundle of turnover-related training costs and worker's compensation claims.

Footsteps sounded in the hallway outside the cube, heralding the evening mass exit for the elevators. Five o'clock. And

Lucky had a date to keep, though his target didn't yet know it. He powered down his laptop, waiting until the last of the stampede passed to make his way to the nearly deserted parking garage.

CHAPTER THREE

Creatures of habit made easy prey, and if Lucky couldn't run his man to ground with a badly healed ankle, he'd rely on the element of surprise. The normal crowd of skateboarding or loitering teens deserted the park, heading for home or warmer places to plot how to piss off their parents.

Huff, huff, huff, a lone runner panted, tennis shoes pounding an even beat on the park's worn jogging trail. Muscles bunched, Lucky waited. Ah, the thrill of the hunt. When the guy slowed around a curve, Lucky jumped.

"Yah!" the man screamed. Lucky knocked into him. The "Yah!" changed to a yip. They crashed to the ground together, their fall broken by a cushion of fallen leaves. The impact still jarred Lucky's shoulder. He bit back a yelp of his own, pinning his quarry.

Months of observation and learning his opponent taught him what to expect, though he barely dodged a right hook. A left jab caught him in the good shoulder. *Nice one!* The world spun and Lucky found himself staring up at furious brown eyes and a fist drawn back to punch again. "Hey, darlin'. Miss me?"

Those eyes narrowed, brown-black brows nearly touching. The anger gave way to recognition. "Damn it, Lucky. How many times do I have to tell you? Don't sneak up on me. You nearly gave me a fucking heart attack." Bo braced on his arms, taking some of the weight off of Lucky.

"Pretty good lick you got in there." Lucky rubbed his shoulder. "Aren't you glad to see me?" Damn, how he'd missed the man the last few days. Their schedules and determination to keep their personal relationship on the down low separated them far too often. Unbidden, a low moan escaped. He thrust his hardening cock at his partner, and was met by an answering hardness.

"I've been saving up since Walter told me about your close call last night. You should have called me! Don't you ever..."

"A little more than a close call. A lady shot me."

Bo changed his tune. "Shot? Oh my God! Are you okay? I didn't hurt you, did I?" He ran his fingers over the shoulder he'd hit.

Lucky shrugged, planning to play up his injury for sympathy points later. Maybe a blowjob after a tasty dinner, cooked while the invalid lay sprawled out on the couch. "Other arm, and she only grazed me. I'll show you later. Did you miss me?"

"Did I miss you not telling me shit?" Bo poked a finger into Lucky's side. "No. Giving me heart attacks?" He poked again. "No. Miss you knocking me over?" *Poke, poke.* "No. Miss you greeting me with a training exercise instead of a kiss?" *Poke, poke, poke.* "No." Lucky's extra squirming brought his cock closer against Bo's. Neither body part seemed to mind the contact, judging by how they stood to say "Howdy."

Despite his squirming, Lucky couldn't quite evade the poking finger, especially after Bo captured both of his arms in one hand, robbing Lucky of enough leverage to wriggle free. Bo probably didn't even realize what he'd done. A year ago, due to a traumatic childhood, even the thought of restraining someone or being restrained would have freaked him out.

"You're an insufferable asshole who lives to give me grief. Why should I miss you?" Bo continued, holding up the poking finger for another attack. He cupped the back of Lucky's head instead, his voice dropping to a murmur. "Yeah, maybe I did." Then he took the brief kiss he'd complained about not getting.

"What did you miss the most? Having someone around to eat all the food you keep cooking? Or to appreciate what nature gave you?" Lucky took advantage of Bo's distraction to roll them again, breaking the grip on his wrists. He tunneled a hand beneath Bo to grope a handful of ass cheek. He whispered, sending his breath skating along the exposed skin of his lover's neck. "Did you miss having me in you? Sucking you off? Shoving hard into you..."

Bo scrunched his brow in an exaggerated thoughtful expression. "Now that you mention it, I haven't been fucked senseless in a while."

Lucky's cock lurched at the thought of sinking into Bo's heated depths. "Glad to be of service."

Bracing his weight on the short arms that'd earned him the nickname "T-Rex" from Bo, Lucky stared down at a disheveled mass of gold-streaked brown hair and a slight smattering of freckles across a ski-slope nose. His chest tightened.

"Lucky?"

"Yes?"

"Will you let me up so we can quit talking and get to doing?" Bo waggled his brows. "That is, if I forgive you for scaring the crap out of me."

"You'll forgive me."

"I will? Why?"

"'Cause I'm adorable and hung like a moose?"

"A moose with arms like a T-Rex!"

"There's an advantage to short arms." Lucky harrumphed. "Look." He nodded down at the small space between their bodies. "They put me closer."

"Yes, now will you please move?"

"But I'm comfortable." To prove his point, Lucky rammed his erection against Bo's again.

"And risking obscenity charges. We're in a public park, not some back alley."

Back alley? Oh, reeeeallly? Lucky filed away the suggestion for later use and writhed to make more room for his suddenly much harder cock.

"Come on, let's go to your place," Bo said.

Was this a trick? Often enough they'd argued over whether to go to Lucky's duplex or Bo's apartment. While Lucky preferred his own home, he'd learned better than to demand his way all the time. Besides, like a dog getting a treat for good behavior, he was always rewarded for staying at Bo's: breakfast in bed, including bacon (turkey bacon, but still) or some added bit of kink to their play. Being on his own turf seemed to free Bo to explore his wilder side.

The advantages of Lucky's home included more square footage and a real, honest to goodness coffee pot instead of Bo's wimpy little K-cup dispenser that spat out a too-weak brew and only half of Lucky's favorite cup's worth at a time. Then came the matter of a certain demanding feline who'd cat-erwaul Lucky into submission for daring to be away unneces-sarily. Somehow the damn cat knew the difference between Lucky's being gone for assignment and spending the night at Bo's, and gave Lucky hell when he came home after a night of wild sex. *Bossed around by a freaking fur ball. What's the world coming to?*

Lucky tested the waters. "Are you sure you wouldn't rather go to your apartment?"

"Are you kidding? And have to deal with His Supreme Highness's baleful eyes the next time I come over? Mark my words, Lucky. One day you'll piss that cat off once too often, and they'll never find your body." Bo laughed at his own joke. Lucky wasn't sure it was a joke.

However, the four-legged counselor always sensed when Human Lucky hurt deep inside. The day Lucky'd found out about a young friend's death, the cat climbed up in his lap and helped him ride out the storm. On his sister's birthday, when Lucky would've given anything to be in Spokane taking Char-lotte and the kids to dinner, the black and white tyrant hadn't let him out of his green-eyed gaze. And the day Charlotte broke the unspoken rule of not talking about Mom and Dad and re-vealed Dad's place on a liver transplant list, reproachful feline eyes ensured Lucky didn't hurl anything breakable.

While technically the cat belonged to the landlady, by all appearances, Human Lucky belonged to Cat Lucky. And Cat Lucky apparently viewed caring for his human as a serious responsibility.

"I can't believe we let fifteen pounds of cat boss us around." Lucky rose and extended his uninjured arm toward Bo.

"Closer to twenty, and speak for yourself. Unlike some people, I don't require a cat chaperone to keep me out of trouble." Bo grasped Lucky's hand and hoisted himself to his feet. "And he wasn't nearly as big when you first got him. Have you been bribing him with tuna not to smother you in your sleep? I mean, at the rate he's going, he'll be bigger than you by next week."

"I'm big where it counts."

Bo opened his mouth; Lucky slapped a hand over his lips. "All ya gotta do is nod, 'cause you know it's true."

Lucky had once met an agent who spoke six languages, and yet that man couldn't come close to how well Bo communicated with a lifted brow, a lowered chin, and upturned eyes that said better than words ever could, *Oh, please, give it a rest. And if you don't take your hand off of my mouth, I will hurt you.*

With descending darkness and declining temperatures chasing away any possible witnesses, Bo and Lucky strolled hand in hand to their vehicles, although Lucky did keep their joined digits low and close to his body to minimize undue attention. Wasn't anybody's business if a fine man like Bo took leave of his senses enough to want to hold hands with Lucky. No fire, no brimstone, no falling sky resulted from the public display of affection, and no coworker popped out from behind a tree, pointing and yelling, "Aha! I knew it! Wait until I tell Walter!"

Bo's heartwarming smile and a quick squeeze of his fingers conveyed his approval, though Lucky kept a watchful eye on the trees and shrubs.

They made their way to Bo's truck and climbed inside. "Are you cold? Want me to turn on the heat?" Bo asked.

"Fuck the cold," Lucky replied. Their eyes met, and they moved as one, mouths meshing over the console. Bo's insistent tongue forced its way into Lucky's mouth at the same instant Lucky aimed for Bo's. Lucky wrestled Bo into the backseat amidst groping hands scrabbling for purchase, and his lover's mouth latched onto his neck on *that* precise spot.

Bo sprawled on his back, one leg on the backseat, one on the floor. Lucky knelt on the seat between Bo's spread legs, bracing his weight on his knees and one arm.

"Oh, God!" Bo exclaimed, plunging his hand into Lucky's pants and wrapping chilly fingers around his full erection. He threw his head back against the side window, arching his neck and giving Lucky room to explore. Bo's skin tasted of salt and man, with the slightest bitter nip of cologne. Lucky rolled Bo's T-shirt up and off to pay homage to smooth skin and hard muscles with his fingertips. He mapped out Bo's chest, the smattering of hair on well-defined pecs, rigid nipple nubs, the flat planes of belly. Bo's muscles were lean like a runner's or swimmer's, as opposed to Lucky's more pronounced bulges, acquired from a punishing workout bordering on penance.

Lucky put his muscles to good use. He crawled off the seat and onto the floorboard, lifting enough to tug Bo's shorts down and slip the long length of the man's uncut cock between his lips. Again the saltiness and musk of man exploded on his tongue, along with the tang of pre-come. Lucky moaned, taking Bo's ass cheeks in his hands and pushing, forcing Bo's flesh deeper into his throat.

Bo threaded his fingers through Lucky's hair. "That feels so fucking amazing," he slurred.

Lucky stilled Bo's hips, bobbing straight up and down to minimize the truck's rocking. Darkly-tinted windows and nightfall obscured the vision of passers-by, but please Lord, let no curious cops wander by with Maglites. Because Bo would wrest the light from the cop's hands to smack Lucky upside the head with, even if public sex wasn't exactly Lucky's idea. Well, not totally. But then again, Bo didn't seem to mind. Oh, kinky... Lucky liked.

Worries about cops or anything else soon vanished. Lucky bucked against the backseat, rutting through his pants in a desperate battle for friction. The pressure built. With fumbling hands, he unbuckled his belt and unzipped his pants, then pulled them down enough to free himself. Crawling on top of his partner, no longer caring who passed by, he melded his cock with Bo's, catching them both in a saliva-slickened fist.

"I want you to fuck me," Bo groaned.

"Have to wait for later," Lucky responded. He hadn't planned ahead for supplies, and wasn't going to last long at any rate. He increased his speed, thrusting against Bo and locking their mouths together. Their combined moans echoed in the truck's cab. Rhythm faltering, Lucky chased ecstasy, hell bent and determined to take his lover with him. He pulled back, watching a range of emotion flitting across Bo's features in the pale light. Bo froze beneath him, veins standing out in stark relief against the straining tendons of his neck.

"I'm coming," Bo cried.

Lucky opened his mouth to speak, but unintelligible sounds emerged, his own orgasm racing through him. His grip grew slick, the scent of come filling the cramped space. Every muscle in his body seized, and his cock pulsed out thick droplets on Bo's belly.

When the torrent of his climax subsided, he collapsed onto his lover.

"I love you," Bo said, fingers petting the back of Lucky's head. "And yes, I missed you."

In response, Lucky scattered kisses up Bo's chest, then plundered his mouth again. They lay in the semi-dark until Lucky feared Bo might get cold. He began to rise when Bo asked, "Lucky?"

"Yes?"

"We've been together now for about a year."

Lucky curbed his usual tendency to do the math, subtracting time they'd spent apart, for he'd no idea where the conversation might be leading. Oh fuck. Surely the man didn't want some kind of soppy anniversary thing, did he? "Yes?" Lucky repeated.

"We're both tested on a regular basis during our physicals, and we haven't seen other people." He framed Lucky's cheeks with both hands, pulling Lucky's head up until their eyes met. "We haven't, have we?"

Lucky didn't turn away. "No."

"You don't have to answer right now, but I've been thinking."

While thinking often came before good decisions, like serving Lucky turkey bacon in bed, the same thought processes sometimes heralded shit storms too. "And?" Lucky held his breath.

"Personally, I think we're to the point where we no longer need protection between us." When Lucky didn't answer, Bo added, "That is, if you're comfortable with the idea."

No condoms? Sweat broke out on Lucky's brow. He could count on one hand the times he'd barebacked, years ago in his young and foolish days. He'd even taken precautions with Victor, with whom he'd lived. A bevy of lovely young men had filled Victor's bed whenever they were apart, but Victor also didn't deny Lucky the right to find his own amusement while away from home.

For better or worse, Lucky had thereafter managed to keep men at arm's length through that infinitesimal barrier of latex. Going without now, with Bo, suggested permanence.

"Just think about it, okay?" Bo asked.

"I will." *A lot.*

"Will my being in your bed tonight help?"

Despite the sudden shock to Lucky's system induced by talk of commitment, he found himself smiling, though a glimpse of what might have been hurt flickered for a moment in Bo's eyes. "I believe it might."

Those eyes turned away. "C'mon then. Let's get dressed." Bo lowered his arm and fished in the floorboard, coming up with a pair of boxer shorts. "Sponge Bob? Really?" He snickered.

Lucky snatched away his plain blue boxers. As if he'd ever wear cartoon characters. It wasn't even a snicker-worthy joke. In fact, if Lucky didn't know better, he'd say Bo made a dud of a pun in a half-hearted attempt to change the subject. They dressed in silence, Bo not meeting Lucky's eyes.

Twenty minutes later found Lucky sitting shirtless in a kitchen chair and Bo in a better frame of mind. "Hey, it's been nearly twenty-four hours since I left here and the house is still clean," Bo remarked while opening a tube of doctor-prescribed salve.

Lucky moved his foot to hide a stray sock beneath his shoe. "Hey, I'm not a total slob."

Bo opened the dishwasher to reveal the previous night's unrinsed spaghetti bowl. "Uh-huh."

An empty tuna tin sat partially hidden by the trashcan. Maybe Bo wouldn't notice.

"Oh, darn. You got gauze?" Bo asked.

"Medicine cabinet. Or maybe top drawer in the vanity." Where had Lucky seen the roll last? "You might try under the sink."

Bo blew out a breath. "I'll find it." He stalked off to the bathroom.

Lucky snatched up the tuna tin and dropped it into the trash.

"Cans are recyclable. You should rinse it out and keep it," Bo called from down the hall.

Damn. Just damn.

Bo came back, clutching a roll of gauze. "Now hold still."

"Ow," Lucky exclaimed.

"But I haven't touched you."

"It still hurts."

"But I haven't touched you."

"You will. And it'll hurt."

"Wuss."

"Hey! I got shot." Lucky added extra whine to his voice for good measure, recalling the pampering he'd received for a broken foot and ankle.

Bo let out a low whistle when he peeled the gauze back. "Holy fucking shit. No wonder it hurts. This is gross. The doctor sent you home like this?"

"What?" Lucky craned his neck, trying to get a better look.

Bo blocked the view with his hand. "Trust me, you don't want to see this. I'm thinking we better get you back to the hospital. This looks infected. You might wind up losing the arm."

"What the hell? The doctor said it was just a scratch." Lucky rolled his eyes upward to Bo's pursed-lip scowl.

"It is. Now stop acting like a four-year-old and let me clean and re-bandage."

"Jerk," Lucky muttered under his breath. "You don't play fair."

"Aww... poor little thing has a scratch on his arm." Bo's mocking tone fell and one brow raised as he stared intently into Lucky's eyes. "I'm glad you're not hurt, but if you ever get shot again and don't call me, I'll finish what they started, understand? And don't forget, if you don't take care of yourself, and the wound gets infected, I'm licensed for injections. I have absolutely no qualms about jabbing a gram of cefazolin into your ass cheek every six hours." He smacked his hand against the back of Lucky's head. "Now, how's your ankle?"

Lucky's not answering immediately gave him away.

"It's still sore, isn't it?"

"Some," Lucky confessed.

"Yeah, well if you'd gone to physical therapy like you were supposed to..."

Lucky bit down on the *Yeah, yeah, yadda, yadda* that nearly escaped his mouth.

Bo let the topic die. "How about you go out into the living room and rest your boo-boos while I fix dinner. If you behave yourself, I'll give you a blow job later."

Ah, but Lucky loved the way the man's mind worked. Most of the time.

CHAPTER FOUR

"Humor me, please." Walter held the conference room door open for Lucky to pass through.

Lucky's sigh could have blown papers out of a closed briefcase.

A rough semi-circle three rows deep and ten chairs wide left the front of the room open except for the space occupied by a guy barely out of his teens sitting at a table. Fifteen fairly young men and women sat alone, in pairs, or in one case, a trio. Lucky recognized Bo and a few others, but the rest were new to him. Some, like Bo, seemed intent on their tasks, other radiated boredom, *I don't care* painted over their too-young faces. Out in the big bad world of crime fighting, *I don't care* equaled *dead*.

A wiry little guy in jeans and a faded button-down stood lecturing at the head of the room, maybe twenty years older than Lucky, but fit, and with an accent straight from a New York cop movie. *Well, whadda ya know? The great man himself.*

Bo glanced behind him, gave a brief nod of acknowledgement and turned back toward the front of the room.

Wow! A tight-fitting, sleeveless T-shirt and jeans? At work? That was a first, even if casual clothes looked good on the man. Then again, he pretty much looked good in anything...or nothing.

"Ah, right on time, gentlemen," said the man whose picture Lucky'd seen on the Internet. He shifted his gaze to the students gathered near the front. "Class, today we're being joined by two undercover ops veterans, Mr. Walter Smith and Mr. Simon Harrison of Southeastern. Feel free to ask them questions, and I hope they'll contribute to today's lesson."

If looks could kill, Lucky wondered if they'd ever get the smirk off of Walter's corpse. "Questions?" Lucky whispered, pouring a truckload of disapproval into the one word. Boss better explain, and fast.

"Like it or not, you are an expert in your field, Lucky, and can teach these junior agents a thing or two," Walter murmured, taking a seat at the back of the room. Lucky chose a chair nearby. His boss bore watching, the sneaky bugger. As if providing practical experience for rookies while on assignments wasn't bad enough. Walter had promised no public speaking.

"If you don't trust the man," Walter added, "and I'm sure you don't, wouldn't it be best to find out what he's saying? Keep him from telling the kiddies something that'll get them killed?"

Yeah, there was that. If the overpriced little peacock let his mouth override his brain, Lucky would be first in line to slap him down. Sure the man's profile claimed time on the streets, but how long ago? Undercover work changed a lot even in the nine years of Lucky's experience. New technology, new fact-finding methods, new laws. Out-of-date information meant a blown case.

"Let's do a recap, shall we, to catch our visitors up?" O'Donoghue scanned the room, his attention falling on each student in turn. He folded his hands behind his back and puffed out his chest. Reminded Lucky of a barnyard rooster. Anybody who referred to Lucky as a cocky little bantam found out pretty soon that Lucky could back up his strut, and this guy was probably the roostah who used ta, or he wouldn't be teaching. "What is rule number one of undercover operations?"

Don't get made.

A young woman on the front row offered a different answer. "Be the part."

"Right you are, ma'am. Be the part." The teacher gestured to Bo on the second row. "Care to elaborate, Mr. Schollenberger?"

Bo sat up straighter, answering in textbook mode, "If you're passing yourself off as a carpenter, you need callused hands, and you'd better know something about woodworking. Don't say you're a chef if you can't even boil water."

"Very good. It's not enough to have it up here," the guy tapped a finger against his forehead, "but you have to feel it in here." He placed a hand over his heart. "Today we'll be studying real life scenarios often encountered on the job, which is why I asked you to dress casually. No bank tellers, just drug dealers and hookers, and together we'll learn the art of the deal. Ms. Vickery? Would you mind joining Phillip at the table?"

A fashionably dressed woman made her way to the table and stopped, glancing at the teacher for direction. With her idea of casualwear, Lucky would hate to see her Sunday-go-to-meeting clothes. She'd stick out like a sore thumb at most of the drug buys Lucky'd been to. Her cashmere sweater screamed, "Mug me!"

"Can anyone tell me what Ms. Vickery did wrong?" the teacher asked.

Getting out of bed this morning and coming here where she doesn't belong?

Even from the back of the room, Lucky heard the disapproving snort. Ah, a lady used to getting her way, and who didn't like being corrected. Lucky cringed. She'd better not be one of the rookies who'd wind up under his care.

A stockily-built woman in the third row spoke up. "They'll eat her alive if she's waiting to be asked to sit down. You gotta show some attitude, honey. Park your ass like you own the chair."

A bit of lip-pursing betrayed the woman's annoyance. She grabbed the vacant chair and nearly flung it down in her hurry to sit.

With a practiced hand, Phillip poured white powder onto the table, forming two even lines. The guy appeared too at ease divvying up the goods. The rolled-up dollar clasped in his fingers might as well have been a cobra the way the woman stared without making a move. Ah, the ubiquitous dollar bill. *And that, boys and girls, is why ninety percent of US currency is laced with cocaine residue.*

"He who hesitates is lost," O'Donoghue retorted. "Next!"

Ms. I-Need-To-Update-My-Resume slunk away, replaced by a gung-ho officer candidate school dropout who also failed the savvy test, as did the next student, and the one after that.

Lucky's vision began to blur, his eyelids becoming heavier, and he no longer muttered, "No, you idiot..." for each attempt.

"Schollenberger!" O'Donoghue barked.

Given Bo's years of military training, Lucky expected a sudden snap to attention. Bo didn't. He took his time in standing, the picture of nonchalance. What a saunter! The man needed to strut his stuff more often. Lucky's cock took notice. If Bo swayed like that while wearing chaps and nothing else...

In no apparent hurry, Bo moseyed to the table, grabbed the chair, flipped it around backwards, and sprawled, arms folded across the back. Yeah, he totally fucking *owned* the chair.

Phillip held out the dollar. Bo barked a laugh. "I may lead the lemmings to the sea, but I don't follow them in." Possums chewing briars didn't grin so widely as Bo.

Was this Bo? Mr. Meek-and-Mild? Champion of treed kittens everywhere? Bo strolled back to his seat, having fucking owned Phillip as surely as he'd owned the chair. Damn. Just damn.

Lucky squirmed in his seat, imagining Bo bringing that confidence to the bedroom, tying Lucky's hands to the headboard and having his wicked way. Oh hell. *Gotta stop thinking about sex with so many people around.*

"Good, Mr. Schollenberger. You didn't flinch, and you controlled the situation. The arrogance at the end, looking down on the shmucks who buy this shit... brilliant. Next!"

The woman with attitude enough for half the room stood, and stood, and stood. Damn. She topped six feet, easy. Black Celtic designs added contrast to her dark skin, and her nose ring glittered in the light. Wait until Keith got a face full of her. Lucky might even have to violate his policy of not going in on one of the office's betting pools. His money said she'd stomp Keith's ass. She clomped up to the table, jerked the chair out, snatched the dollar bill, and sucked up every bit of the white powder from one line. Head held back, eyes closed, she uttered, "That's the best you got? Man, you're shitting me, right? This crap wouldn't get a fly high."

Phillip better have used a placebo. Lucky watched the woman. If she went down, it wouldn't be pretty.

"Ms. Johnson, while it might be necessary to partake in dire circumstances to avoid blowing your cover, attempt to talk your way out of the situation first, if possible, okay?" The teacher rolled his eyes toward the heavens but didn't attempt to hide the beginnings of a smile.

Bo whipped his head around, wide eyes seeking out Lucky. The color drained from his face. Oh shit. If circumstances boiled down to either him using or getting made, would his sensibilities allow him to hold a dollar bill to his nose and snort drugs off a tabletop? Lucky sealed his gaze to Bo's, wishing he had his partner's ability to communicate with a glance and an expression. He willed the man to hear *You'll be fine. You'll manage. You always do.*

Johnson grinned and opened her fist, releasing a powdery stream. Damn. What a show. Without a doubt, she'd been around the block a few times. On the other side of the room, someone muttered, "Showoff."

The teacher's eyes stopped rolling and fell on Lucky. "Mr. Harrison. As a seasoned veteran, would you mind sharing your technique for handling this situation?"

Lucky glowered, emitting a growl when Walter gave him a nudge.

Oh, somebody's gonna pay for this shit. While Lucky specialized in pharmaceuticals, not street drugs, this didn't even come close to being his first rodeo. He swaggered up to the table, eyes riveted to Phillip's, daring the man to look away. He sank into the chair. Phillip handed him the dollar. Lucky peeled back his top lip in his best sneer. "Do you honestly think I'm stupid enough to fall for amateur shit?" He leaned forward, pouring evil into his leer. "After you," he rumbled.

"Excellent!" O'Donoghue clapped his hands together. "Class, paranoia is expected on both sides, but however you choose to react, never, ever let the suspect call the shots. You must maintain control at all times. Now tell me, Mr. Harrison, what would you do if he accepted your challenge?"

"I'd laugh at him, call him a fucking idiot, and walk away."

"Thus securing the upper hand. Outstanding. Next!"

A skinny guy with a short layer of copper-red hair took his place at the table. Word for word he mimicked Lucky's bravado, but without enough heat to lead credence to the claim.

"Close, but no cigar, Mr. Brunelli. It's not enough to say the words, you have to feel them. There's no pat answer for any given scenario. What works for him," the teacher nodded at Lucky, "may not work for everyone. When in doubt, claim a medical condition or an upcoming drug test as part of your parole restrictions. But if you use your parole officer as an excuse, be prepared with a backstory of your arrests and where you did time."

One by one the students sat at the table and attempted to intimidate Phillip.

"That's all the time we have for today, folks." O'Donoghue actually said *folks*. Lucky wasn't quite sure what he was hearing. Since when was there an L in "fowks"? Oh, a Yankee. Right.

"Bright and early again tomorrow."

Lucky glanced at this watch. They'd been play-acting for three hours. Didn't seem nearly that long.

"You're welcome to attend tomorrow's class if you'd like," Walter said. "You might learn something or impart some wisdom to the youngsters."

"Youngsters?" Thirty-six wasn't old, damn it. Merely... seasoned.

"I lead the lemmings to the sea, I don't follow them in." Bo sniffed, mouth twisted in annoyance.

"Nah, not quite right. Like you did today in class." Lucky sat at the kitchen table, two lines of stevia drawn out on the surface, and a rolled up dollar bill clutched in his fingers.

"Lucky, do we have to do this? I mean, I've spent all day..."

"Humor me. When the chips are down, you gotta get this right." Not that he hadn't done one hell of a job, but practice made perfect. Besides, Bo's earlier confidence in class had turned Lucky on, no end. His cock swelled at the memory of

Bo's swagger. The soundtrack in his brain offered up Bob Seger's "Her Strut". *Oh yeah, Bo's strut.*

Bo lowered his eyelids, emitted a snort, and when he opened his eyes again he became... someone else. No gentleness shone in his narrowed gaze, and lines formed around his scowling mouth, erased a moment later when he laughed. "I only lead the lemmings to the sea, I don't follow them in." His smoky gaze and come-hither smile froze Lucky on the spot.

Oh shit. There it was, the irresistible something that set Bo apart from any others in the classroom. A larger than life presence guaranteed to draw all eyes in a room. Shivers raced up Lucky's spine. Something lived inside of Bo, something brash, fearless, and utterly appealing. Something that would never back down to Lucky in full asshole mode, or to a thug with a gun. Something that had made him a good Marine. Something...

"Bo?" Lucky managed to get out with a too-thick tongue.

"Yes, Lucky?" Bo tilted his head to the side ever so slightly, and based on the teasing upturn of lips, no doubt he knew full well the effect of his actions.

"Meet me in the bedroom?"

"What's wrong with here?"

Oh hell, yeah! Lucky grabbed Bo by both shoulders and yanked him out of the chair. He attacked in a frenzy of lips and tongues and grasping hands. The kitchen clock ticked off the beat, mingling with the *thump* of shoes hitting the floor. He wrestled his partner to the linoleum. Somehow in the melee, they both lost their shirts, and Lucky flipped Bo onto his back to mouth the man's cock through a layer of denim. He tuned out the vague stinging in his shoulder; he had too much else to take his mind off his pains.

Bo's fingers scrabbled at his zipper, making short work of freeing his cock for more direct attention. Lucky attacked, opening wide and then humming around Bo's length. His brain fizzed out, primal instinct taking over. Throwing finesse out the window, he sucked Bo down, breathing in Bo's natural muskiness. He worked his own jeans open and thrust in a hand, stroking his flesh in time with his sucking.

"Oh God, yes," Bo hissed, back bowing up off the floor. He curled his fingers through Lucky's hair, urging the rhythm faster.

"Uhmmmph," Lucky replied around his mouthful. Bo tensed further and Lucky plunged down, taking the man deep. He held his position as Bo sent pulse after pulse down his throat.

The moment Bo pushed his head away, declaring, "Too much," Lucky sank back onto his thighs, running his hand faster over his flesh. He shot, a gob of pearly fluid landing on Bo's stomach, to be joined by another and another. At last the trembling stopped and Lucky joined Bo on the floor.

"Lucky?" Bo asked.

"Hmm?"

"Is this going to happen every time we study together?"

"God, I hope so."

"Yes, Lucky. What can I do for you?" Walter glanced up from his computer screen.

"About the class thing?"

"Now, Lucky, I know you're old school and rely on first-hand experience, but I truly believe we can learn from Jameson's methods. Don't dismiss his techniques out of hand."

"Umm..." There was no easy way to say this. Lucky braced for snickers. "Actually, I've been giving the matter some thought."

"And?"

"Anditmightbeworthfurtherstudy," Lucky whooshed out. Especially if a few days spent in a classroom turned Bo from a mild-mannered pharmacist into a force to be reckoned with.

"Oh?" Walter peered at Lucky over the tops of his glasses, the familiar gesture sending a silent message of victory. "Are you telling me you'd like to attend a few more sessions?"

Lord, Lucky hated proving the man right. "Yeah, well, I mean, someone with practical experience needs to sit in and make sure this O'Donoghue guy isn't making shit up, right?"

Walter snorted, his disbelief written plainly in every fiber of his oversized body. "You're selflessly volunteering?"

Lucky faked a grin. "You know I'm always willing to take one for the team, boss." Walter didn't have to snort.

"Actually, Lucky, I've already agreed to your participation." He quietly regarded Lucky for a moment. "I also boasted of your skills to Jameson. You wouldn't want to make a liar of me, would you?"

Lucky swallowed all the ripe insults rushing his head, not wanting to give Walter the satisfaction of getting him riled. Instead he smiled and said, "Thanks, boss."

After a catered lunch, O'Donoghue sought Lucky out while the other students mingled, drank coffee, and munched cookies. "I know who you are."

Lucky forced "Simon Harrison, SNB agent" to the forefront of his mind. One quick wallet search would confirm the claim. Plus nine months on a lease, the registration to his car... "Yeah, since you've been calling me by name, I assumed you knew I'm Simon Harrison." Lucky faked a yawn. *Simon Harrison. I'm Simon Harrison of the Southeastern Narcotics Bureau's Department of Diversion Prevention and Control. I've never even heard of Richmond Eugene Lucklighter.*

"Sure you are." In the crystal depths of the blue-eyed gaze locked with Lucky's pulsed the soul of a predator.

Warning signals flared and seldom used calming techniques kicked into gear, spurred on by a man radiating danger. Lucky mentally catalogued five visual cues: a bristly growth of five o'clock shadow on a deeply cleft chin, a dusting of white in a head full of straight, dishwater blond hair, a scar that lifted O'Donoghue's mouth on one side, a Saint Christopher medallion, and flecks of green in the man's eyes.

"Says so on my driver's license." Lucky summoned his best good-ole-boy grin. Walter hid Lucky's tracks well, but if one searched hard enough and spoke with the right loose-lipped people, there's no telling what they might find. O'Donoghue had to sign a non-disclosure agreement to work with the SNB. No matter what he uncovered, he couldn't share his knowledge with the outside world.

"You've got ex-con written all over you."

Don't let him see you sweat. Lucky barely stopped an angry comeback, toning his reply down to, "If you don't like what you see, nobody's paying you to look."

"Actually, they are." The bastard raised his Styrofoam coffee cup and gestured toward Walter, chatting with Bo on the far side of the room. O'Donoghue placed his mouth near Lucky's ear. Every bit of the Bronx accent disappeared from his voice. "These guys," he motioned with the cup again, this time encompassing the entire room and nearly sloshing the contents onto Lucky's shirt, "can learn in a classroom, and out of a dozen people, a couple might be passable, another might make the grade to good. You, on the other hand, have advantages they don't have."

Okay, time to play along with the crazy man. "Like what?"

"While they memorize lines and can answer as long as the right questions are asked, their college degrees mean dick when stacked against knowing what's on the menu at the Durham Correctional Center every Thursday night. They're sheep in wolves' clothing. No matter how well they wear the disguise, they're still sheep. You, my friend, *are* the wolf. And I mean that as a compliment, providing you stay on our side."

Was that a warning? The arrogant little asshole strolled off, calling out to the members of the class in his fake, late-night cop show accent.

Meatloaf. On Thursday nights the Durham Correctional Center served meatloaf, with mashed potatoes, corn, and baked apples.

"Next scenario," O'Donoghue began. "Most of you deal exclusively with narcotics, but bear with me. The ability to function while undercover takes on many forms, and you never know what role you might be called upon to play. We're doing a vice sting, and you're the bait. Ms. Johnson?"

"Man, please!" the woman exclaimed. "Ain't nobody gonna pay for this!" She waved a hand to indicate a body built to bench press Mazdas. Chances were she'd give Lucky a run for his money in the boxing ring.

A half-smile chipped away at the teacher's serious demeanor. "Humor me."

The woman rose and positioned herself in an exaggerated pose laced with blatant innuendo. "Come hither, darlin'," she taunted Phillip, pooching out bright red lips to blow him a kiss. A couple of titters escaped the other agents.

Phillip, so soon out of college that the scent of day old pizza and beer still followed him around, approached her, a folded bill in his hand. "What'll twenty dollars get me?"

"Twenty dollars? For twenty dollars I'll give you directions to the nearest ATM and you can take your cheap ass on down there and get more money." Johnson glared down at Phillip with all the affection typically reserved for palmetto bugs.

What style!

"Very convincing, Ms. Johnson. Next?" The teacher gestured to a student who'd bombed out on the previous day's exercise. "Now remember, the point of the operation is to get the client to name an act and a price, which equals solicitation. Intent to commit a crime has to be established. And while entrapment charges rarely make it to court, they're inconvenient, costly, embarrassing to the department, and should be avoided. This isn't like a drug deal. Here, the perpetrator has to call the shots."

The young man, with computer geek practically stamped on his forehead and a *Who, me?* vibe, stepped up. He took his place, far too rigid to play a convincing hustler. Phillip approached with a leer. Even from the back row, Lucky didn't miss the bait's flinch when Phillip touched him.

"That'll never do, Mr. Bernacky. You're supposed to be a hustler. You make your living selling your body." O'Donoghue folded his arms over his chest, his bottom lip caught between his teeth. "But if you slip up and you do flinch, how would you play it off?" A blank stare answered him. "Mr. Schollenberger?"

"Yes, sir?"

"Care to show us how to play off an involuntary flinch?"

After a quick glance Lucky's way, instead of sauntering like he'd done before, Bo sashayed across the room, hips swaying, right up into Phillip's personal space. Once more Phillip reached out a hand and Bo faked a flinch, neatly spinning the recoil into a haughty hands-off maneuver. "Baby, even a touch ain't free," he said, in a voice dredged in innuendo and deep fried in pure sex.

The teacher clapped, letting out a wolf whistle. "Bravo! Now, Mr. Harrison, if you'd indulge us, please?" A nudge from Walter got Lucky moving toward the front of the classroom.

Walter owes me a grande from Starbucks for this. Possibly two. Lucky leaned against the wall, toning down his "come near me and die" telepathic messages.

Phillip approached, a twenty folded between his fingers. "Twenty bucks for a blowjob?"

"Twenty won't even get your zipper down," Lucky smoothly replied.

"Thirty?"

"Guess again."

"Fifty?"

Lucky grabbed Phillip by both arms, snugging him up close. "It'll get you a whole lot more than you bargained for." Phillip's audible gulp made sweet music for Lucky's ears.

"Folks, it's all in the attitude. And while Mr. Harrison is implying a lot, he hasn't really offered anything." The teacher's droning faded into background noise the moment Lucky locked gazes with Bo from across the classroom. Fire danced between them. Bo glanced away first, promises for later staining his cheeks crimson.

"What'll this get me?" Lucky dragged a twenty along Bo's cheek, lips close enough to waft a breath onto the pretend-hooker's ear. Bo shivered. Lucky grinned.

"I believe you have to name the terms of the agreement. Otherwise, it's entrapment," Bo replied.

"Not necessarily. Willingness to commit a crime is established. Besides, you heard O'Donoghue. Few entrapment claims hold up in court." Oh shit. Now Lucky sounded like a textbook. Maybe some of Bo's geekiness rubbed off. Not that Lucky wouldn't like to return the favor and rub off on Bo.

"We're in drug enforcement, not vice. Why are we even rehearsing this?" Bo let out a weary sounding huff and crossed his arms across his chest, making his biceps bulge. Oh yeah, in the real world, Lucky would definitely add a few more twenties.

"Work with me here. Our homework is to write a script to work on actual cases."

A hum from the refrigerator provided a distraction. "Lucky?"

"Yeah?"

"I don't think I'll ever be propositioned in your kitchen by anyone I want to arrest."

"You got a better idea?"

It started slowly, a twitch at the corner of Bo's mouth that grew and blossomed into a full-fledged grin. "Oh, yeah. And a few surprises up my sleeve too. Give me an hour, then meet me in the alley behind Spencer's bar."

Darkness and shadows, the perfect concealment for mischief in the making. A group of teens huddled together on a street corner, plotting how to get into juvenile detention, no doubt. "Don't you kids have a curfew?" Lucky growled in passing, tuning out their clumsy comebacks. No matter what they said, he'd heard it before. He turned up the collar of his jacket and rammed his hands into the pockets. If things didn't turn out quite like he hoped tonight, he might be calling his boss to get him out of jail. Would Walter buy the excuse of homework?

The teens' laughter and taunting faded with each footstep, replaced by the thrum of a bass guitar and the rat-tat-tat of drums from the bar, slightly off-tempo. Amateur night, by the sounds of it. Extremely amateur. Lucky rounded the next corner into a concealed alleyway, the neon of the Spencer's Bar sign casting a rainbow glow. A dead end. Not good. And two doors opening on either side. A perfect ambush spot. Or a good place to hide.

Shuffling footsteps and a quiet "Uh-hmm" brought him back to the here and now. Oh yeah. The reason he braved a cold night without a proper jacket waited ahead. A shadowy figure leaned against a wall at the back of the alley, eyes glittering in the low light. A streetlight illuminated the fog of breath the man exhaled.

Fuck me! Lucky froze. Damn but he'd dreamed something like this before. Tousled hair, a come-out-and-play-I-know-you-want-to smile. A pair of tight jeans emphasized a bulging crotch, and the man turned to allow Lucky a peek at a perfectly shaped ass. A denim jacket gaped open in front to reveal a bare chest, sparsely covered in a dusting of dark hair. The glimmer of a wallet chain led from belt to hip pocket. *I'm hot and I know it* radiated from the tip of the man's gelled-up hair to the soles of his boots. *Holy fuck!* Lucky's cock began to fill.

Unable to resist, he ran his fingers through the enticing wisps of chest hair. The man flinched back, biting down on a laugh. "Cold!" he complained.

"I'll keep you warm," Lucky replied, stepping close enough to share some body heat. Oh, yeah, he'd light a fire to warm them both for days.

"It'll cost you." Bo reclined back against a brick wall, grin gleaming in the semi-darkness. Oh fuck, yeah.

Lucky reached down to rearrange his highly interested cock. "How much?"

"Depends on what you want." Bo ran a hand under his open jacket and slid it slowly down his body.

"What're you offering?"

"Everything." The barest tips of Bo's fingers dipped under his waistband.

"What's everything?" And did it involve getting naked in a filthy alley?

"You know. Ev-er-y-thiiing." Bo plunged his hand into jeans so tight it was a wonder anything besides the man's ample package fit.

Two could play that game. Lucky leaned in and wafted a breath across Bo's jaw. "No, I don't know. Why don't you tell me?" A tongue flick elicited a gasp. Lucky grabbed Bo's wrist and forcibly removed the hand from his jeans, then palmed the fascinating, denim-covered firmness he found there. Oh yeah, the little hellcat enjoyed this too. *Undercover Cop and the Rent Boy* became Lucky's new favorite fantasy.

"Tell me what you want," Bo murmured.

"Tell me what you're offering." Lucky latched his mouth onto Bo's exposed throat. Bo tilted his head back in encouragement, pulse throbbing against Lucky's tongue.

Bo's inhibitions vanished with a moan, and he thrust up against Lucky's hand. Their mouths met in a clash of teeth and a whirl of tongues. Bo stumbled and would have fallen if not for Lucky holding on tight.

A recessed doorway offered the perfect concealment and, knowing what kind of clientele Spencer's catered to, they probably weren't the first to make use of the privacy.

Lucky shoved Bo into the depression face first, plastering himself to a denim-covered back. "I want to be buried to the balls inside you, feel your heat around my dick." Lucky pressed tighter, giving Bo a feel of hardness. "I want to hear you moan, want you to buck against me, to be as desperate for me as I am for you." He rose on his toes, ramming himself more firmly against Bo's amazing rounded ass, and snaked a hand around front to run up and down the solid length trapped inside skin-tight jeans. "I want to take you in my hand, stroke you, feel your muscles straining. I want to pound into you so hard you beg me for release. And when I'm good and damned ready, I'll give you what you need." A quick nip and sucking Bo's earlobe into his mouth earned a whimper. Sweet. "What do you say?"

In answer, Bo rubbed back against Lucky's erection, teasing and then pulling away. The jeans cradled his ass perfectly, accentuating the rounded mounds. Oh, damn. To have him naked. Here in an alley.

"I say, 'that'll cost you two hundred bucks,'" Bo's cheeky comment earned him a swat on the butt.

He glanced back over his shoulder, catching Lucky's gaze. They both froze, the game ending and the *real* beginning.

The cold no longer mattered. Lucky fumbled with the zipper on Bo's jeans.

Bo's hands joined Lucky's in sliding denim down his legs. Lucky groaned, clutching the sweet flesh of Bo's ass in his hands. His heart pounded from an odd mixture of excitement and fear of discovery. He dropped to his knees on the filthy ground and pressed his tongue against Bo's hole, adding a wetted finger. They both moaned when the digit breeched defenses far more easily than anticipated, gliding into an already stretched and lubed passage. Oh fucking hell. The little minx came ready. Lucky visualized Bo's preparations, the dildo he kept in his nightstand, imagined him slicking up and thrusting the plastic phallus inside. *Nope. Gotta stop thinking like that or I'll never last.*

"Do you like it like this? Out here where anyone can find us?" Lucky asked, resting his face against the swell of Bo's glutes, more to distract himself from impending climax than to role-play at this point. One touch. Just one touch from Bo's hand and he'd blow like a horny teen. *I'm going to fuck him, right here in this alley, where anyone could step out of the bar and find us.* Damn, how Lucky's cock throbbed. He worked a finger in and out of Bo, thrusting in to massage his gland.

A breathy "Yes" answered. The pounding beat from the bar nearly drowned the word.

Lucky ran his free hand under Bo jacket to tweak a nipple. "Right now you're exposed to me, open. I can take whatever I want. Do you like being totally at my mercy?" He lightly bit one of Bo's full cheeks.

Again a garbled "Yes" reached his ears.

"That's right, I'm paying, and you're mine to do whatever the hell I wanna do." Lucky rose and punctuated the words with some hip-thrust action.

"Yesssssss." Bo arched his back a little deeper, his ass offered up like a gift.

"Do you know—"

"Lucky?"

"Yes?"

"Shut up and fuck me."

One finger became two. "Only if I want to. Remember, the customer's gotta call the shots." Damn but this role-playing sent bolts of lust straight through Lucky.

"Oh hell, Lucky. Just fuck me already." Bo contracted his muscles around Lucky's finger. Lightning zinged straight down to the uncomfortable tightness in Lucky's jeans.

He freed his cock and slid into the cleft of Bo's exposed ass, gliding on a slick of pre-come and a generous application of lubricant. He patted his back pocket for his wallet and froze. Oh shit. Since Bo, he'd stopped carrying condoms in his wallet when venturing out at night. Everything he wanted he got at home or Bo's.

He groaned, dropping his head between Bo's shoulder blades.

"What wrong?" Bo asked, his muscles tensed, and for the first time tonight he sounded unsure.

"No condom."

Bo thrust back again. "We talked about this, remember? Don't you want to?"

"Yes, I mean... yeah but..."

"But what? There's been no one else... at least for me." A hot stab of suspicion punctuated the words.

"No! It's just been you since...well, since the Ryerson case." He nudged Bo's opening. Oh, how tempting. One more shove and he'd be in, no barriers, nothing but the two of them, melded into one. Icy panic seized his heart. One plunge, no turning back.

"Lucky, please. Don't overthink this. This is me and you and, oh, God, I want you." Bo writhed, pushing back for all he was worth.

Hot man. No, hot Bo. Pleading. Wanting. Lucky should take a deep breath, turn off his brain and slide into tight heat, feel Bo wrap around him. *No. Can't, it's too soon!* Instead, Lucky wedged his cock in the cleft of Bo's ass cheeks, gliding on the slipperiness there. Bo squeezed, giving Lucky more firmness to plunge against.

Lucky reached around, stroking Bo as he prodded as far as he dared. *Do it, do it, do it!* his libido screamed. He rose on his toes and latched his teeth onto Bo's neck, panted breaths mingling with Bo's needy whines. Bo braced his shoulder against the doorframe and reached back, spreading his cheeks, oh so tempting.

Finally Bo shuddered, reaching up to grab the doorway in front of him. Lucky plunged one more time and stilled, pulse after pulse firing to coat Bo's backside while the rhythmic throbbing of Bo's cock in Lucky's hand told its own story of release. Lucky molded himself to Bo's back, skating his lips across Bo's cheek and trying to find the words he needed to say. His heart hammered from more than exertion.

Why balk now? The hottest man to ever notice him, a man who'd give him the moon and stars, wanted desperately to feel Lucky deep inside with nothing in between. *What the fuck is wrong with me?*

In the end he said nothing while pulling up Bo's clothes, redressing him with cold-numb fingers.

"Bo, I..." he began when the silence between them grew oppressive.

"Don't..." Bo replied, placing a silencing finger over Lucky's lips. "You're not ready. It's okay. I understand."

You do? Good, 'cause I sure don't.

CHAPTER FIVE

Stupid, stupid, stupid! Why the hell hadn't Lucky simply taken what Bo offered? It wasn't like he'd never told the man he loved him, words he'd never said to a lover before. *I love you* implied some sort of permanence, right? Maybe Bo needed to hear those words last night.

Lucky stared at coffee made by his own hand, not Bo's. Bitter dregs. Saturday morning should have found the two of them nestled together in bed, not him brooding alone in his kitchen. Bo hadn't followed him home from the alley last night and Lucky, assuming he would, didn't ask him to. A quick glance at his phone showed no missed calls and no text messages. Not that Lucky blamed the guy for wanting distance right now. Hell, Lucky didn't want to be around himself either, but he didn't have much of a choice in the matter.

His muscles ached from the punishing two a.m. workout he'd put himself through when he found himself awake and staring at the ceiling, straining his ears for the jangle of keys and his front door opening.

He eyed the clock. Ten a.m. Surely Bo would be up by now. Hell, he'd probably been for a run already. Cat Lucky slunk into the room from wherever he'd disappeared to during the night. He blinked disapproving eyes and roamed out to the living room without even pausing to beg for food. Even the cat sensed how badly Lucky'd screwed up.

He'd choked down his coffee and started on his second cup, a twisty ball of worry in his belly growing rapidly. With shaking hands he texted, "R u ok?"

No immediate answer. He paced. He dampened a cloth and scrubbed down the kitchen counters. Still no answer. He

57

swept the floor, even vacuumed, and yet no response came from Bo. In less than an hour, he stared at a spotless house, or as spotless as he ever managed.

He flopped down on the couch with his Harley brochure, fantasizing about the machine he'd one day own. Every time he pictured himself astride one of those sleek bikes, however, a phantom Bo always perched behind him. Oh yeah, to be cruising down the road with his man wrapped around him... Only, Bo might not be his man anymore. Was Bo insulted by Lucky's unwillingness to give him what he asked for? He'd said Lucky's reluctance was okay, but did he mean "okay it doesn't matter" or "okay, that's it, we're done"?

Talk about a wood-wilting moment. With pent-up energy and no outlet, Lucky changed into sweats, secured his iPod, and went for a walk.

Clop, clop, clop. His shoes hit the pavement. Neither he nor Bo took others to bed. Ever since the first time they'd slung each other against a bathroom wall, Lucky hadn't looked back. Where was the problem?

With his one other long term relationship, he'd used protection. There'd been no question of commitment. Now, though, with Bo, taking the final step seemed... well, *final*.

Next they'd be looking at property together and picking out china.

Yeah, and what's bad about that? If they did settle in together, the whole issue of what the bureau would have to say came into play. And even if the job turned a blind eye to their relationship, what then? Would he and Bo start to fight like his sister Charlotte and her husband had? Would love turn to hate? Would Bo one day have enough of Lucky's ass and walk away? Of course, to his credit, Bo wasn't a crazy-assed, alcoholic redneck who only wanted someone to take care of him so he could go out carousing every night.

Lucky stopped, selected Pachelbel's Canon on his iPod, and turned up the volume. Pushing aside all conscious thought except for the pounding cadence of his tennis shoes on asphalt and the steady in/out of his breathing, he ran as much as his defective leg allowed.

***

One half-run/half-limp later, his cell phone still yielded no messages from Bo. Lucky's heart leapt when he found an e-mail on his laptop entitled, "What are you doing tomorrow?"

A quick check showed the e-mail had arrived on Friday at 5:15 p.m., shortly before Bo's arrival last night. Funny, he hadn't mentioned the message, at least not that Lucky remembered. Lucky read, "I have an appointment with a realtor at two tomorrow, and would like you to come with me, if you don't mind." The e-mail included a link. Lucky clicked and a house appeared, complete with two car garage, three bedrooms, ensuite master bath and walk-in closet. The square footage easily made three of Bo's cramped apartment. He'd complained often enough about needing more room, but one man didn't need nineteen hundred square feet.

His and hers sinks and closets. Oh shit. One man didn't need so much room, but two might. Oh shit, oh shit, oh shit. Was Bo suggesting they live together? Lucky flipped back to the picture of the master bedroom, mentally inserting a combination of his and Bo's furniture. He pictured the two of them, curled up in bed. Somehow the darned cat wound up in the image, tucked into the space between Bo's bent knees and backside.

Lucky wasn't ready to embark on a live-in arrangement. He continued scrutinizing the house listing. The fenced yard would be a good place for a dog, and the garage even had a doggie door already installed.

No! Lucky closed the e-mail. Bo shouldn't even think about living together, knowing Lucky's temper and foul moods. No way should they confine themselves to the same space until they'd figured out how to deal with each other's baggage. Or their own.

The squirming in Lucky's gut turned to gnawing. He snatched up his jacket and headed out the door.

A steady stream of folks entered and exited Bo's apartment building. A smile and a blurted, "Forgot my key" gained him entrance from a woman he'd met before who probably thought he lived there. His ratty-ass jacket earned him a few stares. Let 'em look. He smoothed his hand along a tear in the plastic-whatever-the-hell-you-called-leather-that-wasn't-real-leather, missing the honest-to-goodness real stuff he'd worn a few days ago.

Adrenaline coursed through his body, and he paced the elevator, chanting, "Hurry it up!" Finally the doors opened. He trotted to Bo's apartment, listening for noises from within before knocking.

Bo opened the door, eyes wide. "Hey. I'd almost given up on you coming. You about ready to go? I can't tell you how glad I am that you're going to help me house hunt." No "About last night" or "insensitive prick" or "loser", just "glad you're here." Lucky didn't deserve Bo's gratitude.

"Why?"

"Why does anyone look at houses, Lucky? I've talked things over with Walter, and when my probation ends I intend to stay with the SNB. That means permanence. I've always wanted my own home." He paced to the couch for his jacket.

Lucky often entertained notions of buying his own place, too, but preferred a cabin in the mountains, far from people. Damn the whole having to work for a living thing.

Excitement tempered by a touch of wariness lurked in Bo's eyes. "Why didn't you answer my text?" Lucky ventured.

Bo patted his pockets. His eyes went wide again. "Oh, shit! I must have left my phone in the truck. Why didn't you e-mail or use the land line?"

"Bo, I—" A knock sounded on the door. They both jumped and Lucky snapped his jaw shut on whatever lame words might have escaped his mouth. He'd fucked up. He'd well and truly fucked up, and now couldn't find the necessary words to apologize.

Bo opened the door. A young woman stood in the doorframe, hand raised to knock again. "Oh hi, Allison. You're right on time. Are you ready?"

"Umm..." she darted a troubled gaze at Lucky and back to Bo. "Did I come at a bad time?"

"No ma'am," Bo assured her. "My friend was..." he cocked his head to the side, a question in his eyes.

"Um, on my way out the door," Lucky said.

Bo sighed, staring down at the floor. The two steps he took back might as well have been miles. "Okay, if you're sure. See you at work on Monday." One moment Lucky gazed at his lover's forlorn face, the next at a closed door. First he recoiled at commitment in one way, then let Bo down when all the man wanted was Lucky's company while finding a place to live. It wasn't too much to ask. "What the fuck is wrong with me?" The image of Bo's face the moment before the door slammed burned itself into Lucky's brain. A haunted soul stared out of Bo's eyes that Lucky hadn't seen in nearly a year—the one who'd explained how someone so good could get tangled up in drugs, or why a grown man dreaded sleeping alone in a bed at night.

And I did that to him. I should kick my own ass.

Dear Charlotte,

I screwed up. I mean really screwed up, as in "I wouldn't blame him for not speaking to me" screwed up. What can I do?"

Being a man of many names, Lucky never signed his messages anymore. He sent the e-mail and spent a lonely Sunday. Even the cat wasn't speaking to him.

Toward evening, he received a reply:

Richie,

Roses and chocolates are the usual payment for fuckups, but I know you don't do things the normal way. (Don't worry, brother dear, it's part of your charm.) You have to make right whatever you did in such a way that he knows you mean it. Words won't get you out of this one. You need to act. Fast. And, Rich? If you let Bo get away I'll hunt you down and hurt you. We only met once, but any man who would come all the

61

way to Spokane and beg to know where you were and not back down even when I pulled a gun on him is worth keeping around.

Love and kisses,
Char

Damn. He'd been afraid of that. She was going to make him figure out how to apologize on his own.

Lucky lay in bed, a diesel engine disguised as a cat rumbling into his ear. Bo. His heart clenched. Bo spread out against a wall, begging, not merely for sex, but for proof that what they had meant as much to Lucky as it did to him. Bo offered everything, held nothing back. Lucky had pretty much spit in his face.

Bo wanted a house, wanted to include Lucky in one of the most important decisions of his life, and Lucky heard "commitment." Bo hadn't mentioned living together; he simply felt cramped in his tiny apartment. And they were committed already, or as committed as Lucky allowed.

What should have been mind-boggling alley sex for the record books had fizzled and died. Because of Lucky. No way in hell could he figure out how to right his wrong. Good thing Cat Lucky slept soundly, for Lucky the Dumbass didn't sleep a wink.

CHAPTER SIX

"Lucky, got a minute?" Bo waited by the elevator in the parking garage at the Southeastern Narcotics Bureau on Monday morning, a Starbucks cup in each hand. He passed one to Lucky.

"Sure, what's up?" Lucky's heart leapt, and he made sure to skim his fingers over Bo's while taking the cup.

Bo gave him a sheepish smile. A man could read a lot into a smile like that, from *I couldn't help myself* to *it's not you, it's me.* "Look, I've been thinking..."

Oh shit. Thinking sometimes led to good things, sometimes bad. Spin the wheel and take a chance.

"You've had a lot on your mind lately, and so have I, what with these classes and assignments coming up." Assignments possibly leading to long separations. "Anyway, until the classes are over, and we figure out what's what, maybe we should focus on work, you know?" Bo dropped his gaze to the cup in his hand.

No, Lucky didn't know. He sipped his coffee, mulling over the words. As letdowns went, this one wasn't brutal, no name calling and no blaming. Still, a knife started at his heart and plunged down to his innards. "Only another few weeks," he said. "Yeah, I can live with that."

A relieved smile replaced the uncertainty on Bo's face. "Good. I need to concentrate right now, put myself into the job. I've even cancelled the rest of my house appointments. Once things settle back to normal, maybe we can get away somewhere for the weekend, talk things over."

"Talk things over," not fuck each other's brains out. Lucky gave a noncommittal grunt. "That'd work."

63

Bo kissed him while riding up the elevator. A consolation prize? Or goodbye?

When they reached their shared cube, Lucky waited until Bo left for the men's room to pull the box of chocolates out of his backpack and toss them into the trash. He buried twenty bucks worth of truffles beneath the half-dozen empty Starbucks cups strewn across his desk. No way could he offer a bribe when Bo had already made up his mind.

At a gesture from the teacher, a rookie from the Southwestern division stepped forward. Phillip snarled, "I bet you're a fucking cop!"

The newbie shrank back. "I am not!"

"Next!" O'Donoghue called.

A woman took his place. "No, I'm not!" she replied with more venom than the last denier, her performance still falling short of sincere.

"Next!"

This time no words were necessary. The guy who'd sat way too close to Bo simply froze. "Way to go, asshole," Lucky groused. "On the streets you'd have earned yourself a ride in a body bag."

"Next!" Apparently O'Donoghue either hadn't heard Lucky's jibe or chose to ignore it.

Bo stepped up. The chance to see his protégé in action piqued Lucky's interest.

"Motherfucking cop!" Phillip screeched.

Bo paused, then threw back his head, howls of laughter pouring from his throat. "Man, you need to lay off whatever shit you're smoking." He grabbed Phillip in a headlock, much like an indulgent older sibling, and rubbed a noogie on the kid's head. "Cut it out, man. Don't go insulting me like that. And you call yourself my friend." Bo's eyes met Lucky's, a question clear. Lucky nodded.

"Excellent!" O'Donoghue crowed. "Mr. Harrison, would you mind showing us your technique?"

Goody. Lucky needed stress relief. Phillip needed hazard pay. Phillip shouted, "Fucking cop!"

Lucky whirled, grabbed the guy by the throat, and slammed him against the wall. A woman shrieked, and Bo might have shouted, "Don't!" Lucky rose up enough to put his nose three inches from Phillip's. "If you ever call me a cop again, you'll be getting half price discounts from your dentist. Got it?"

"Bravo!" The teacher approached, giving a slow clap. "Remember, folks, whenever strong emotion overtakes you, twist the negative into something positive. The best way to confirm suspicion is denial. Humor or anger are the ways to convince your target you're who you say you are. To a criminal, the idea of being mistaken for a cop is either funny as hell or a huge insult. Harrison? Let Phillip go now. He's turning blue."

"Now, when constructing a viable alias, you need to consider a few things." O'Donoghue paced before a long table that held books and other resources. Bo's eyes never left the teacher except to glance down at the notepad he scrawled on. Newbie's eyes stayed on Bo. Maybe a fist to the mouth might change his preferred view.

Wait. Constructing an alias? O'Donoghue won out over Newbie Asshole for Lucky's attention. "What if you're given a role to play?" Lucky wouldn't dare be openly disrespectful about the bureau's policies, but he'd always been handed a new identity packet, usually containing some ludicrous name.

"Who knows you better than you do, Mr. Harrison? For instance, if you're in a crowded room and someone shouts your name, you'd be expected to react instinctively without thinking. If you choose a name close to your own, it's easier to identify with. Also, if you're undercover in a place you frequent in your daily life, would answering to your actual name blow your cover? I want you each to give me a name, first and last, that you believe would be a suitable alias for you."

65

Silence descended but for the scratching of pens on paper. Agents should make up their own names. Cool. Too bad Walter wasn't sitting in on this morning's session.

What name could Lucky put? He still didn't automatically react to Simon. His sister called him Richie, which might get a reaction, but a version of his own name might blow the lid off his deeper cover. Ricky? Close enough. Now for a last name. His grandparents were Getsingers, so he'd heard the name all his life. He wrote down Ricky Getsinger.

O'Donoghue stopped walking a circuit around the room to peer over Bo's shoulder. "Why Joe Swartzentruber?" He held Bo's paper up close to his nose.

A flush crept up Bo's cheeks. "Joe rhymes with Bo, and Swartzentruber has the same first and last letter and a similar rhythm to Schollenberger."

"Very good reasoning. The key to remaining in character is not to stand out or draw attention to yourself. Don't act any differently undercover than you would in real life. If you'd order a beer at a bar on your own time, order a beer. No one says you've got to drink it. Remember, the majority of the folks there drink. Ordering a club soda is an anomaly and makes you stand out in the bartender's mind, even if no one else recognizes the difference."

O'Donoghue made his way through the other class members, stopping by Lucky last. He didn't read Lucky's alias aloud, merely winked and murmured, "Well done."

To the rest of the class he said, "Tomorrow we'll further flesh out your background. As Mr. Schollenberger once said, 'If you say you're a carpenter, you'd better have calluses and know about woodworking.' Mr. Harrison, would you mind staying for a moment, please? Phillip, you go on. I'll catch up later."

Bo gave Lucky a backward glance while leaving the room with the newbie. Some might find the new rookie attractive, with his shock of thick blond hair and sky blue eyes. That is, if they like chiseled jaws and cleft chins. And tall men. Bo didn't like tall men, or he wouldn't be with Lucky. He laughed at something the asshole said. Ice formed in Lucky's veins.

"Mr. Harrison?" O'Donoghue called Lucky's attention away from Bo.

"Yes?" The man better get this over with. Lucky needed to chase down his partner. He didn't like the gleam in the new suitor's eyes.

"Why are you here?"

"What?"

"You heard me. Why are you here?" O'Donoghue plunked down in the chair next to Lucky, putting them eye to eye. Walter would have done the same. "The bureau pays a lot of money for my time and for good reason. Agents take my classes and live to work a new case. I'm not sure why you're still here, but you barely pay attention, and as part of class preparation, I've viewed films of your operations. You may have it up here..." he poked two fingers against Lucky's forehead.

"Hey!"

"...but you don't have it here." O'Donoghue stroked his fingers lightly over Lucky's breastbone.

What the fuck? "I'll have you know I've never blown an assignment, and I've never been burnt."

"And that's how you measure success, Mr. Harrison? Can you return to a character you used two years ago and seamlessly pick up where you left off? Can you? Can you get so deep in the mind of an alias that you nearly forget who you are?"

"Wait a minute—" The cocky little peacock went too far.

"No, Mr. Harrison, *you* wait a minute. You think you're invincible, that you know it all, but you don't know shit. You have it in you to be great, but before you can reach your potential, you have to accept that someone else might, just might, have something to teach you." All traces of the Bronx cop left the man's voice. He could easily have passed himself off as a college professor. Subtle rearrangement of his shoulders, stiffer posture, and something different in the eyes totally changed the man. Lucky blinked hard. O'Donoghue no longer resembled the former cop he'd been dealing with.

"I'll make you a deal, Mr. Harrison. If you want my respect, you'll respect me in return. With my help, you could very well be the second best undercover operative in this room."

Oh, now he *really* pushed too far. "And I suppose first place goes to you?" Arrogant little bastard. But what Lucky wouldn't give to be able to so easily don another persona.

"No. Mr. Schollenberger takes those honors. That is, he would if you'd get the hell out of his way and let him. You're a distraction."

I am?

"He's always glancing your way for approval, doubting himself until he wins it. On the job, distractions and doubts get you killed. Either you toe the line and put in some effort, or stay out and let me do my job. Schollenberger listens and wants to learn. Learning will keep him alive. Can you promise him that?" He paused just long enough to recognize Lucky had nothing to say. "No? Then put up or shut up. And by the way, most of the class is meeting later for some practical application. You're welcome to join us, providing you apply yourself."

The man rose and stalked off. Who the hell did he think he was?

Lucky's TV dinner and soap opera reruns that night made a poor substitute for taking down bad guys, but he wouldn't give O'Donoghue the satisfaction of attending a classroom field trip.

"Everyone listen up." O'Donoghue clapped his hands. "Last night Mr. Schollenberger, together with his Atlanta PD escort, took down a major drug dealer."

The most Lucky'd accomplished the night before had been reorganizing his CD collection. Atlanta PD escort. Major drug dealer. Didn't the group simply run more practice drills with Phillip during the off hours?

"Well done," Walter's voice boomed. Lucky glanced to the back of the room to find his boss filling the doorway. "Bo, would you mind sharing your triumph?" Walter's eyes twinkled when he winked at Lucky.

Bo flushed and ducked his head. "It was nothing. Right

place, right time. I'd been following a suspect, and he led us straight to a warehouse."

O'Donoghue added details. "He's being too modest. Last night's bust yielded oxycodone and other narcotics with an estimated street value of $400,000 dollars, $20,000 dollars in cash, stolen guns and jewelry, and eight suspects, one wanted for questioning in a murder case in Ohio."

Damn. Lucky wouldn't let himself regret not hanging with the class last night. Nope. Not happening.

Walter slapped his palms together, leading the class in a round of applause. Bo hazarded a glance at Lucky. Lucky raised his hands and joined the clapping.

If Lucky'd known Bo intended to place himself in harm's way, he'd have tagged along. *And done what, exactly?* Good point.

So Bo did good without Lucky's help. If Newbie high-fived the man again, or didn't get his hand off of Bo's shoulder, he'd soon be turning in a worker's compensation claim for a broken arm. Lucky mentally tripped the man and sent him sprawling with a groin punch. Would serve the asshole right.

Lucky waited after class, even staying behind, expecting a scolding from the teacher that never came. Just as well. O'Donoghue couldn't possibly beat up on Lucky any worse than he beat himself. Especially since it wasn't Lucky's approval Bo sought today. It was the newbie's.

That night Bo didn't answer his phone. Walter's voice-mail message said he'd be in meetings until late. Cat Lucky was out doing whatever tomcats did on their own time. A frozen dinner held no appeal. O'Donoghue's words still ringing in his ears, Lucky drove back to the office and parked his car in a nearly empty parking lot. Art's car near the elevator didn't surprise him. The man had no life. A couple other vehicles might belong to employees up in the gym.

Bo's truck sat in its usual place. Bo, best in the class. Took down a drug dealer. Well, what did you know? And asshole O'Donoghue thought Lucky was in his way? *I'll show him!*

Yet when Lucky stepped off the elevator, he ambled down the hallway to his cubicle instead of turning toward the gym. He accessed the bureau's server and punched up training video number one-seventeen on his laptop, from a few months prior when Lucky busted a trio of dock workers pilfering bottles of product from pharmaceutical shipments. Leaning back in his chair, he watched the footage of himself at the takedown, running from the cops, resisting arrest, and being forcibly shoved into a car. A textbook training exercise, ending in the arrest of three felons.

And yet, no matter how thrilling he found removing scum from the streets, his heart hadn't been in the job. Compassion rarely overcame him as it did Bo, roping him totally and completely into a case. Hell, he hadn't even bothered to learn his assumed name on the warehouse assignment. No matter how good he pretended to be, if he were in the field dealing with big fish instead of relatively harmless guppies, he'd be fish food.

An icy chill settled over him. O'Donoghue had a point, further confirmed by three more training videos. Lucky took stupid chances. Look how easily he'd been taken out of commission the summer before for not watching his back. He reached down and scratched an itchy scar, the embarrassing reminder of his previous poor judgment.

What if he wasn't as good as he boasted? He didn't suck. Walter wouldn't allow him to remain on the team if he did, and certainly wouldn't have handed out praise for jobs well done. But only giving half of yourself, being more worried about reputation than actual performance classified as sucking too, in Lucky's book.

Shuffling in the hallway startled Lucky, and he glanced upward. A sweaty vision from his fondest wet dream stood in the doorway of his cubicle, dressed in a T-shirt and nylon shorts that clung damply to strategic areas, with a towel wrapped round his neck. "Lucky? What are you doing here?" Bo's welcoming smile warmed Lucky's heart, and he rose to meet his lover halfway for a kiss until Bo's smile fell. "Sorry, I've been to the gym and remembered that I hadn't watered the plant lately. I forgot to ask anyone to do it while I've been busy with classes." He crossed the cube in three longs strides and stuck a finger in the dirt of the Christmas cactus they'd used in lieu of a Christmas tree a year ago. "Huh. Looks like someone's taken care of it. You didn't water it, did you?"

"No," Lucky admitted. As much as he'd like to take credit for doing something right, he couldn't. Just his luck a coworker would pop out of the woodwork, pointing a condemning finger and screaming, "Liar!"

"Oh," Bo replied. Not *of course you didn't*, but the accusation rang in Lucky's head anyway.

"How have you been?" *Have you been lying awake nights, wishing you were with me?*

"Okay, I guess. Staying busy. You?" Bo toyed with the shoots of the cactus, keeping his back to Lucky.

"I've been better."

"Lucky, I don't suppose I ever told you about my grandpa, William Patrick Schollenberger the first, did I?" He regarded Lucky over his shoulder.

"Not that I recollect." Of course, when they found time to talk lately, it usually revolved around kink and cases, not family matters.

"He worked as a weaver in the cotton mill for most of his life."

Lucky nodded. His own grandpa took a turn or two in the cotton mills during bad farming years, and he suffered brown lung to prove it. "Yeah, so did mine."

"He used to tell me a story from when he first started, about a sweeper named Andy who'd been with the company for years and knew the factory inside and out."

A sweeper occupied the absolute lowest rung on the mill ladder. Most folks worked their way up to better paying jobs. To stay a sweeper implied either a lack of education or ambition. Probably both.

"Now this man only finished the sixth grade and, in hindsight, probably had a learning disability."

In other words, back in Grandpa's time, he'd have been labeled "slow," or worse.

"One day, Grandpa said this man sat outside the manager's office most of the morning, insisting he speak to the boss. When the boss finally showed up, he pushed old Andy out of the way, thinking there was nothing a *retard* could teach him." A shudder proved the word's impact on Bo's political correctness. "Anyway, Andy wouldn't take no for an answer, and every day he waited for the boss. Every day the boss turned him away."

"I have a feeling this story ends badly," Lucky said.

Bo answered with a grimace. "Yup. One day the accountant came in, yelling about an audit, and the boss sent a secretary down into the basement for a box of records." Bo shuddered again. "They had one of those open elevators, like a cage. Grandpa said she started screaming before the elevator touched down." He closed his eyes as if reliving whatever horror befell the secretary.

"And?" Lucky urged.

"And by the time they got her out of there, she'd been bitten four times by copperheads."

Copperheads. Brrr... Wasn't a country kid in the South who hadn't learned from a young age to give the critters wide berth.

"Anyway, the boss called Andy into the office and you could hear the man screaming clear out into the weaving room. Guess what Andy said."

"What?"

"'I been trying to ask you for six weeks what you wanted me to do 'bout the snakes in the basement.'"

"As amusing as this is, why are you telling me?" Lucky forced a chuckle. "Are you saying I got snakes in my non-existent basement?" *Is that another way of saying, "You've got your head up your ass"?*

Bo turned and every trace of emotion fled his face. How'd he do that? He'd never been able to form a poker face before.

"No, the moral of the story is that no matter how dumb or inconsequential you think a person is, he might be trying to tell you something important. Jameson O'Donoghue gave me a wake-up call. I've learned from you, and you're good, but you can't teach me everything. I want what's in the man's head, because at the end of the day, I don't want to be bitten by any copperheads—the two-legged or the no-legged kind. I have plans for my life that don't involve dying young on the job because I went into an assignment unprepared."

One minute Bo stood by the filing cabinet, the next he kneeled at Lucky's feet, taking Lucky's face between his hands. "I'm at the point in my life where I'd like to settle down, have the house and the dog and maybe even kids."

Lucky flinched.

Bo lowered his eyes and took a deep breath. Did he even know how tightly he now squeezed Lucky's face? He murmured, "Yes, Lucky, I'd like kids. Not today, but someday."

He didn't have to sound apologetic, like wanting a life somehow betrayed Lucky. It didn't, did it?

Bo continued after a moment. "Judging from your reaction, you don't plan on being the one I walk that road with."

Huh? "Wait a minute! I never said..."

Bo's mahogany eyes rose. Lucky noticed tiny flecks of gold concealed in the brown of his irises, but the sadness on his face wasn't hidden at all. "You didn't have to. At least not with words. Every time I try to get closer, take us to the next level, you run. You're obviously not ready for whatever comes next, and you may never be. I love you. Nothing's going to change that. But sometimes loving someone isn't enough." Dark eyes bored into Lucky's, sorrow peeking out of their depths. "I'm willing to wait for a while, but not forever. I have dreams. I'd like them to include you, but if we don't share the same vision of the future, I won't try to convince you that you don't know what's right for you."

He placed a far too chaste kiss on Lucky's brow.

Easier to latch onto the *I love you* by discarding the *but*. "I might not have the right, but can I ask you something?" Lucky asked.

"Sure, though I can't promise to answer if you ask me something smart-assed."

Shit. Once Lucky'd been proud of his asshole reputation. Now a sudden burn of shame heated his cheeks. "The guy you've been hanging out with from class..."

"Owen Landry?"

"Is that his name?"

"Yes, Lucky, that's his name. Though I'm sure you refer to him as Rookie Boy or something equally unflattering. Don't think I haven't noticed how you refuse to learn people's names if you don't consider them important. My counselor calls that a defense mechanism to keep folks from getting too close."

"You've asked your counselor about me?"

A flash of a half-smile made an appearance. "I might have mentioned you a time or two."

Interesting. "You didn't answer my question."

"What question?"

"About you and what's-his-name."

Bo's scowl told him that wasn't good enough. Crap. There'd be no moving the man once Bo dug in his heels on a matter.

"Landry, okay? Are you and Landry seeing each other outside of class?"

Bo never batted an eyelash while replying, "Yes."

Lucky's heartbeat scudded to a halt. It began again in double time when Bo added, "Do you think so little of me? That I'd ask for... well...what I asked for one minute, then hop into bed with someone else the next because I didn't get what I wanted? Huh? Do you honestly believe I take myself and my commitments lightly?"

"You mean..." God, but the passion flaring in his eyes only made the man more beautiful.

"Lucky, someone once told me they were the best. Well, I want to be the best, too, and sometimes to be the best you have to shove everything else to the side and keep your eyes on the prize. Right now my goal is to learn everything I can from Jameson O'Donoghue. After that, who knows? Now..." Bo tried to pull away. Lucky captured his wrists lightly, one in each hand. Bo stiffened and Lucky let go. "Lucky, I need go back to my apartment and try to get a good night's sleep. We have a full day of class tomorrow."

"What now?" *Is it over?*

"Now, we pretend good isn't good enough, and we kick ass and take names. Who knows if one day our lives will depend on it? Look at you." Bo nodded toward Lucky's recently shot shoulder. "With the skills and reflexes I have now, would I have survived in your place? With more training, could you have kept the situation from escalating to violence?"

Another far too innocent kiss landed on Lucky's brow. Blowjobs, wild monkey sex in public bathrooms, countless hours spent in every manageable position. Lucky held his breath. One more kiss and another *I love you*. Just one more. Bo left without another word.

Lucky huddled in his chair. After a while, he gave up waiting for Bo's return and called up another training video, this one of Bo. After the first ended, he selected a second and a third. Holy shit. O'Donoghue was on to something. Familiarity blinded Lucky to what a video revealed. Something special lived in Bo, something that inspired a shudder in Lucky's inner felon. Like a sharpshooter in an old western, in each training video Bo carried himself like someone to be reckoned with—if Lucky wasn't there. Did he really stand in Bo's way?

But damned how well the man played his roles. He made one hell of an actor; now if he could only learn to lie.

CHAPTER SEVEN

Lucky entered the conference room where he'd spent the past few weeks and took his normal spot as far away from everyone else as possible. Bo nodded and offered a fleeting glimpse of smile, a crumb tossed to a starving dog, but nothing compared to the full meal a night spent in Lucky's arms would be. Rookie boy... Something-or-Other Landry, took a seat next to Bo. A TV stood in front of the room, but Phillip hadn't yet arrived.

O'Donoghue strode in, heading straight for the front. "Good morning, people," he said in the accent he donned when in *I blend in* mode. He clutched a Starbucks cup in a tight grip. Lucky took a sip from his own cup. The man had good taste in coffee, if nothing else.

"Today's class is Lying 101." O'Donoghue turned to face the group, now whittled down to Lucky, Bo, Whateverhis-namewas, Johnston, and three others who'd matured one hell of a lot in a few short weeks. "The average person lies about ten times per day. Those may be great big, 'No, officer I didn't do it,' blood on the hands kind of lies, to ones of the 'Sure, Honey, I love when your mother visits' variety. They might be an innocent, 'I don't mind' when you actually do, to lies meant to save your life. As much as we lie though, without mechanical assistance we can statistically only detect lies about half the time." He approached the white board in the corner and scrawled "sweating and fidgeting" on the surface. "Who can name more giveaways?"

"Incomplete details," Johnston offered. Her suggestion joined the others on the board.

"Yes," O'Donoghue replied, "but also bear in mind, giving too many details means a rehearsed story. Anyone else?"

77

"Open hostility," someone called.

"While I agree," O'Donoghue answered, "when dealing with suspects, defensiveness is par for the course. Anyone else?"

Lucky ventured, "Failure to make eye contact."

"Points for Mr. Harrison! Any more?"

Bo added, "Dilated pupils and fluctuations in vocal pitch." Trust him to recite from a textbook.

"Yes, though those might not be apparent without equipment. C'mon, I know you can think up a few more examples."

Rook— Landry spoke up. "The suspect keeps stopping to make the next part of his story up."

O'Donoghue added to the growing list, the felt-tipped marker screeching against the board.

Inconsistencies, words like "basically" or "honestly", elevated heart rate and blood pressure, and nervous twitches joined the others.

O'Donoghue put down his marker. "Now," he said, "the average person can control maybe five of these." He pointed toward the board. "A good interrogator can detect many, but not all. Review your notes. Use aliases and other information you've already come up with. Your classmates will ask questions and Phillip will film your responses. We'll play back the recordings, looking for red flags."

Phillip staggered in under the weight of two heavy bags slung over his shoulder and began setting up camera equipment.

"Johnson. Would you mind going first?"

"Not at all." She blew a kiss to Phillip and took the designated chair, which had wheels to reveal self-conscious fidgeting. Phillip busied himself with setup, a deeper shade of pink in his cheeks.

O'Donoghue threw back the last of his coffee and tossed the cup in the trash. "Now, don't give out any information you don't want disclosed to your teammates. Each of us will ask one question. Remember, while agents need to learn how to detect lies, we also need to tell them effectively. For my question, what is your full legal name?"

"Annie Mae Johnson," Johnson replied.

Lucky darted a glance from Johnson's stoic profile to Phillip, who gave a little lip-twitch. Ah, she lied, did she? Better file the info away for later use.

"What's your favorite food?" Peckerhead asked. Oops. Better make that *Landry*.

Some questions bordered on ridiculous, others tried to be witty, some serious. Lucky asked, "What kind of car do you drive?" when his turn came. He damn sure didn't want to pry into the woman's personal life.

Johnson returned to her seat, and O'Donoghue replayed the video.

"Lie!" chorused the class when Johnson slid the chair back two inches while answering the question about her favorite food. Lucky kept quiet, checking off his suspicions on his list of clues picked up from Johnson and others who apparently knew her outside of class.

Twice more the accusation of "lie!" rang out. He never said a word, but Lucky pegged the correct response each time.

O'Donoghue pointed his way. "Mr. Harrison? Would you mind taking a turn in the chair of doom?"

Oh, fuck. Lucky'd been afraid he'd be called on sooner or later. Later got his vote. Much later. As in never. He took a moment to mentally prepare before taking his place front and center.

O'Donoghue started off the interrogation. "What is your name?"

"Simon Harrison," Lucky replied without hesitation.

"What's your favorite beer?" someone asked.

"Coors Light."

"What's your favorite TV show?"

"*Cops*," Lucky replied. *Cops* still came on, right? No way in hell would he admit to an addiction to the soap opera *South Bend Springs*.

"Are you in a relationship?" Johnson asked.

"No," Lucky replied, trying not to flick his gaze to Bo.

Bo took a turn at questioning next. "What's your favorite food?"

"Broccoli," Lucky lied. Green stuff. *Brrr*.

When at last came time for him to step down, he carefully controlled his footsteps back to his seat. Torture. A tongue-lashing from Walter. Ten minutes trapped in a car with Keith. He'd take any of those horrors over the ordeal he'd just endured. It'd been a long time since his last interrogation. Except for his name, he'd lied to every question except the relationship thing, which he didn't have an answer to at this point. And his name boiled down to perspective.

The class chorused "Truth!" for each one.

Bo's questioning gaze met Lucky's during the relationship question. The corner of his mouth twitched.

Next came Bo's turn. For a time, Lucky feared the woman wouldn't ask again, leaving him to broach the relationship issue. In the end she asked, and Lucky offered, "How do you like your steak?" to which Bo answered, "Extremely rare."

Not a single class member detected a lie in Bo's answers, though he'd never once told the truth. Lucky studied the man hard, feeling let down when Bo offered a "No" about a relationship without fidgeting. Heaviness gathered in Lucky's heart until he witnessed the same reaction to the question about steak.

Lucky stopped Bo in the hallway after class. "How the hell did you pull that off in there?" He hiked a thumb toward the classroom door. "You lied through your teeth."

"Easy," Bo replied, adding a sheepish grin. "Before we started I told myself that for the next ten minutes my name was Dennis Michael Schollenberger, my cousin, and I did something similar with each of the other questions. It helped that the class asked the same things every time. Gave me time to prepare."

Lucky wasn't going to ask about the relationship thing. He really wasn't. Instead he tried, "What's this about liking your steaks rare?"

Bo snickered. "My exact words were 'extremely rare' as in 'still on the cow'."

They shared a moment of eye contact. As Lucky turned to leave, Bo called, "Simon?"

Lucky stopped in the middle of hallway.

"When asked about a relationship, I mentally added 'with a woman' to the end of the question."

Bo winked and hurried down the corridor. Lucky remained in place, mouth hanging open. "Oh, he's good, very good."

O'Donoghue entered the room for the last class, his steps somewhat hesitant. Only six people remained besides the teacher and Walter, who'd stopped by for a visit: Lucky, Bo, Johnson, a computer geek from SNB, Landry, earmarked for the DEA, and an Atlanta PD lieutenant who reminded Lucky of a younger version of his landlady.

"And now the moment you've been waiting for," O'Donoghue quipped, "for me to shut up, get the hell out of here, and let you folks get back to work.

"I'm happy to say that you've all passed, and certificates have been forwarded to your regional bureaus for inclusion in your personnel files. In a few days you'll get an e-mail survey of the course, and I want you to be honest with your answers. While I'd love nothing but glowing reports, flattery won't help us improve the curriculum. Any final questions?"

A few students took the time to complement O'Donoghue or chitchat. Walter inclined his head to speak to Lucky. "I need to see you in my office."

While the others milled around munching a cake Walter had brought in, Lucky made his way to his boss's office. Walter didn't snag a slice of confection to go. Oh shit. Walter passing up sweets? Not good.

"I'd hoped to put this off, but we simply can't wait any longer," he said the moment he'd closed his office door.

Lucky took his usual chair in front of Walter's desk. "What's up?" Walter wasn't one to rush anything.

"The case I mentioned, the bath salts? Art is already in place but can't get close to our target. We need someone else in play as soon as possible."

"You've already said I'm grounded," Lucky groused, "so what's this got to do with me?"

Walter considered Lucky for a moment, in a thoughtful way that creeped Lucky out and convinced him the boss read minds. "We're working in cooperation with the DEA, FDA, and the local authorities in six other states. We've been given jurisdiction in Georgia. And though fairly local, this assignment could keep an agent on location six months or longer. I'm recommending Bo, if he meets the criteria."

Six months. Bo gone for six months. And Lucky not sure where they stood right now.

"I do apologize," Walter added. "Especially in light of the holidays. I'm afraid he'll be leaving right after Thanksgiving."

Shit! Another Christmas alone. The whole Lucky dying thing kept them apart last year, and now an assignment would separate them. They couldn't fucking get a break.

"I'm sorry. Really I am." Puppy dog eyes backed up Walter's words. Not a good look for him.

Lucky bit off a "for what?" His hackles rose at Walter's sympathy-laced regard. *What do you know, and why aren't you coming out and saying it?* Oh, hell. A confession wouldn't change a damn thing. If Walter had something to say, he needed to spit it out.

No spit.

Heart heavy, Lucky plodded toward the door.

CHAPTER EIGHT

"Here's what we got." O'Donoghue remained uncharacteristically quiet, allowing Walter to run the show. Now there were two alpha males Lucky'd love to watch duke it out. For a moment, he wondered at O'Donoghue's presence before remembering the man's newly formed ties to the SNB. DEA or not, he still bore watching.

The usual venue of Walter's office wouldn't work due to the number of people present. A conference room served instead. Landry (the weasel) sat entirely too close to Bo, Keith (the asshole) occupied a seat in prime suck-up position to the boss, and O'Donoghue (the wild card) occupied neutral territory midway down the rectangular table. Rounding out the group were Bo, Lucky, Walter, a few faces Lucky'd seen but didn't have names for, and Johnson. "Our informant is a suspect in our smuggling operation, working for us in exchange for a reduced sentence." In full professor mode, Walter asked, "What does that mean for us?"

"He's a two-bit lowlife who can't be trusted?" Keith offered with a narrow-eyed scowl at Lucky.

"He can help us get a man on the inside," O'Donoghue countered.

"Right on both parts," Walter replied, "though I wouldn't put it past him to disappear if given the opportunity." While the rest of the group sat at the conference table, Walter marched back and forth in front of the windows. Lucky stared past him at Stone Mountain. Not too long ago he'd stood in that very spot, holding Bo while making peace with a few inner demons. Seemed a lifetime ago now.

He glanced down the table. The side of Bo's mouth lifted into a half smile.

"According to him, a man arrived in Athens two years ago and took over leadership of a local motorcycle gang. He offered members jobs making deliveries. Our guy turned him down. The man came back with force, flashing a lot of cash, and he gave in."

"As if we haven't heard that sob story before," Keith cracked.

Lucky bit his tongue. The whole scenario brought to mind Victor Mangiardi's methods of operation, except he'd thought bigger and distributed pharmaceuticals, not illicit drugs. Victor wouldn't have soiled either his hands or his reputation with something as low class as bath salts. Back in his and Lucky's day, Victor scoped out a new area and found a reputable drug distributor. Next, he moved in some contraband to travel side by side with the legitimate supply. Against the owner's wishes, if needed. If a bust occurred, Victor quietly bowed out, leaving his unwitting and usually unwilling business partner to face the brunt of the trafficking charges alone. Many lives had been ruined before the Feds finally tracked the narcotics to Victor's door.

"Our lead suspect's name is Mateo Reyes, and he's president of a motorcycle gang known as the 441 Cruisers, so named for the highway leading from I-85 to Athens." Walter paused long enough to toss a picture onto the table. Lucky stared at the eight by ten glossy of the back of a leather jacket, adorned with the patches that made up a gang's distinctive "colors." "441 Cruisers," the letters "MC," and "Athens, Georgia" surrounded a central image of a stylized *441* in flames.

"He's an illegal?" Keith asked.

"No. A naturalized citizen from Abilene, Texas. Arthur is living in Reyes' apartment building. Unfortunately, Reyes resisted any efforts for Art to get closer. Our informant met the man in a bar catering to motorcycle enthusiasts."

Leave it to Walter to make a biker bar sound classy.

Walter stopped his pacing and turned to face the table. "Here's what we've learned thus far. It's believed that

84

the product originated in Mexico. Cargo arrives in retrofitted trucks from Texas, to be added to Reyes' inventory." He paused and grabbed the back of a chair, leaning against the padded leather as he swept his gaze up and down the table. "Couriers deliver the product to buyers in the Southeastern area. Most ride motorcycles and are between the ages of nineteen and fifty. Many have felony convictions. The informant is already laying the groundwork, dropping comments about a friend who's moving into the area, a drifter in his late twenties with a few petty crimes, nothing major."

"Is this a real person?" Lucky asked.

"Until about two weeks ago when he overdosed in a Dallas hotel room."

Shit. Lucky'd played plenty of characters over the years, but he'd never impersonated the recently departed. Not that'd he'd be allowed to impersonate this one.

"For this assignment, we need a male agent in his twenties."

What the hell? Discrimination! Lucky could play the role of a twenty-something. A *seasoned* twenty-something, but a twenty-something nonetheless. *Give someone else the rookies to look after, I wanna see some action!*

"Schollenberger?" O'Donoghue finally spoke up, eyeing Bo up and down.

"Thirty-two as of September, sir."

O'Donoghue studied Bo some more. "Don't look a day over twenty-four to me." He perused the rest of the room, squint-eyed scrutiny sliding right past Lucky.

Walter had the good graces to soften the slight. "Simon is still recovering from injuries, and I have other plans for him. We'll let him sit this one out." Okay, two points to the guy for recognizing Lucky's ability to portray twenty-ish. Walter lost the points by nodding to Keith and adding, "And we need your expertise on surveillance."

He resumed his pacing. "Now, experienced motorcycle riders, raise your hands. Bo, age limitation aside, this includes you."

Hah! Lucky would still have been in the group if allowed to raise his hand in the first place. Bo'd raised a hand. Bo?

Bo rode a bike? He'd never mentioned riding during Lucky's fantasies about buying a Harley. Yet he'd ridden to Lucky's rescue last spring on a four-wheeler he'd handled like he'd been grafted on. A man of hidden talents. Lucky liked. A lot.

Bo, Landry, and one other guy held their hands in the air. "Reyes runs a garage," O'Donoghue said. "Any of you a work on cars and bikes, by any chance?" Bo and Landry kept their hands up. Fuckwad Landry rode a bike. Probably one of those foreign crotch rockets, not a real bike like the Harley Davidson of Lucky's dreams.

"You can put your hands down, gentlemen. Mr. Schollen-berger, I believe you're the more experienced of the two of you, and you also favor the real Cyrus Cooper."

"Cy," Bo replied, adding gravel to his normally soft tones. "I go by Cy." Bo's perfect posture melted. He slouched down in his chair, turned away from the table, and stretched his long legs out before him. As O'Donoghue had done on several occasions, with posture, a bored expression, and a hardness around the eyes, Bo morphed from a straight-laced, by-the-book pharmacist to a man with "Born to Raise Hell" tattooed somewhere the general public didn't get to see. "Based on what you taught us in class, Cy will be easier for me to work with. I've... I've used the name before."

Walter quirked a brow, but when Bo didn't offer more, he merely smiled. "Cy, it is. We'll meet in my office later for the particulars. The rest of you, some of the product has made its way here to Atlanta, as Simon found out a few weeks ago. Jameson, if you want to take it from here?"

O'Donoghue reached under the table and pulled out a cardboard box. He handed the carton to Johnson. "Take one and pass them on. We're dealing with a synthetic drug that's no stranger to most of you, I'm sure. Methylenedioxypyrovalerone."

Heh. Try saying that three times fast.

"Known on the streets primarily as bath salts, it's also called 'plant fertilizer' and a host of other misleading names. Until classified as a control one substance, it was sold commercially with names such as Vanilla Sky, Ivory Wave, and

Bliss. Our guys are bolder and apparently don't feel the need to hide behind flowery advertising."

Walter picked up the story. "These synthetic cathinones produce hallucinogenic effects, delusions, and paranoia, and have been cited in both violent crimes and suicides. The particular product we're dealing with comes in crystal powder form and is often sold in packets, as seen here. This..." he held up a tiny cellophane square, scarcely larger than his thumb, "is accurately named, for it can corrupt normally law-abiding citizens with one dose. For some, the substance produces a euphoric high. Others hallucinate. A young man stabbed his friend to death after seeing him sprout horns and a tail. Up until a few months ago, this..." he shook the packet. "... was obtainable legally in convenience stores and head shops. It's popular as a club drug and is often sold illicitly in bars or at concerts."

Lucky lifted one of the packets, though fully aware of the product in all its forms. The crystalline powder resembled Epsom salts, from which the drug took its name. The packet bore a black skull and the name "Corruption." Victor could have made a fortune off this stuff if he hadn't found such substances beneath him. Now, Stephan, Victor's pitiful excuse for a nephew? He'd deal in any shit he got his hands on, which was why Victor'd kept the little snake away from his business dealings. What ever became of the bastard? Probably hiding under a rock somewhere. Good riddance.

Walter said, "Since June, six deaths in Atlanta alone have been attributed to bath salts, sold to a group of young men at a local club. When new legislation outlawed the compounds used in manufacturing, distribution moved underground."

"If we have the source, why not stop it now?" Johnson asked.

"Actually, we don't have the source. We merely have a portion of the pipeline, and a relatively small portion at that. And as much as I agree with you that stopping the poison from going anywhere should happen posthaste, we need to discover where it's coming from, and possibly allow our counterparts in Mexico to find the source. We also need to identify as many players as we can involved in the smuggling ring, which will require agents to enter clubs and make buys."

A collective groan sounded from around the table. Club buys meant late hours and expecting spouses to accept coming home in the early a.m. reeking of tobacco and other kinds of smoke. Not to mention the occasional drink spilled on clothing.

"When do we go bang heads together?" Johnson asked, cracking her knuckles for effect. Newbies. All eager and ready to go. She'd learn.

But hell, Lucky might have to find out her first name. Damn, what an agent she'd make some day.

Lucky waited for Bo to emerge from Walter's office. Two hours? What the hell kind of briefing lasted two hours?

At last Bo slumped out, grim faced. He plunked down at his desk. A sigh wafted from his slightly parted lips.

Don't ask. Let him make the first move. Oh, what the hell... "How'd it go?"

"Okay, I guess. But I have to admit, I'm nervous as hell." Bo swiveled his chair to face Lucky, full lower lip tucked between his teeth. "I've been studying in a classroom, and I've been on assignments before, but never anything this big. What if I screw up? What if I fail? Even that night a few weeks ago, I wore a wire and had police backup. I'll be on my own much of the time this go round."

Lucky summoned what he hoped passed for his normally arrogant smirk, while the bottom dropped out of his stomach. "How can you fail? You learned from me, didn't you?" Holy shit. Deep undercover. Months spent building an entirely new guise. While maintaining a constant, though fake, identity for months on end wasn't quite as grueling as being someone new every day, keeping up the act took a toll on a man. A toll some agents never recovered from.

Two years into Lucky's time with the SNB, a man had crossed the line. One of their best, Walter had called him. Yet driving a fancy car and flashing a lot of cash while posing as a shady supplier proved too great a temptation. He'd never returned from assignment, never arrested the suspects, never even made a report. For three years the department had mourned him, thinking him dead. Then they'd busted a smuggling operation in Birmingham and found him running the show. The guy now sat behind bars, serving out a twenty-year sentence.

Discovery. Getting caught in the crossfire. The lure of easy money. Yes, many enticements waited outside the door, ready to sink their talons into Bo. And this time, Lucky wouldn't be there to protect him. Screwing up and failing were merely the tip of the iceberg when it came to the worries involved in undercover work.

"I spoke with O'Donoghue about you," Lucky confessed. Poor Bo could use the ego boost.

"Really? What'd he say?"

Never in a million years would Lucky disclose the full nature of the conversation. However, creative use of the truth couldn't hurt. "He called you one of the best in class. He wouldn't say that, and Walter wouldn't have assigned you, if they didn't believe you were up to the job." No, Walter's experience had only failed him once, with the guy from Birmingham, and he'd never put a member on his team that he didn't think was competent. The Department of Diversion Prevention and Control suffered a high turnover rate, both from Walter's demand for perfection and the pressures of the job. Only one in ten agents lasted five years with the department. Bo'd just completed his first.

Bo closed his eyes, slowly sucked in a breath, and exhaled with a sharp *whoosh.*

Lucky peeked down the hallway. Good. Not a soul in sight. He spun his chair and placed a hand on each of Bo's shoulders. "Listen. You're smart. You've got good instincts, you've got the training. You're in top physical form, and Art's already inside. You're gonna do fine."

"Do you actually believe that?" Bo's deep brown eyes snapped open, staring into Lucky's. A man could get lost in those eyes and never want to be found.

"Have you ever known me to lie?" Wait. Yes, he had. "Don't answer that," Lucky growled. They both chuckled.

A quick lunge planted Bo's lips to Lucky's for a fleeting kiss. "You've never lied to me when it counted."

The day drew to a close and Lucky deliberately stuck around after hours, hoping Bo would issue an invitation. None came.

"What ya doing tonight?" Lucky swallowed enough pride to ask.

"Oh. I'm meeting with O'Donoghue to go over more about Cyrus Cooper. You?"

Damn and double damn. "Nothing much. Maybe watch a few back episodes of *South Bend Springs*."

Bo stopped, disappointment rolling off his stoop-shoul-dered frame. "Damn. I'd love to watch too. I'm behind about two weeks, and I hear Lila's on the prowl again." The moment stretched. Bo appeared to be waiting, but for what? Finally, he said, "We haven't seen much of each other lately..."

Crap. Lucky had a really good mad worked up over be-ing pushed to one side, and now Bo was gonna say something sweet and Bo-like and kill the righteous indignation. "When do you leave?"

Silence, followed by, "In two weeks. I'll spend those learn-ing what I need to in order to pull off being Cyrus."

"About that. What did you mean in the conference room about having used the name 'Cy' before?"

A wry grin chased away the shadows on Bo's face. "Re-member how I told you I danced while in college? Cy used to be my stripper name, 'cause someone said I looked like a cer-tain celebrity with 'Cy' in his name." Bo winked.

Lucky waited until Bo wandered off before adjusting the tenting in his jeans enough to stroll down the hall without at-tracting too much attention.

CHAPTER NINE

"You wanted to see me?" Lucky stepped into Walter's office, scanning the room before closing the door. Bo wasn't there, darn the luck, though he shouldn't expect the man to be in on a meeting when they weren't sharing a case.

"Sit down, Lucky." The tight-lipped smile didn't bode well and wasn't in character for Lucky's outgoing, outspoken boss. Lately more and more job pressures seemed to zap Walter's jovial moods.

"I'm not gonna like this, am I?" Lucky dropped down into his usual chair.

Walter stared at his fingers, gripped tightly together on the gleaming wood surface of his desk. "Maybe so, maybe not."

Oh shit. Though no longer in danger of being thrust back into prison, for some odd reason Lucky hadn't quite worked out, disappointing Walter as a man and not as his boss might be worse. Walter was the only one in the department besides Bo who knew the full story of Lucky's dark past, including his guilt over Victor's death, and didn't hold past mistakes against him.

"Spit it out."

Walter slowly lifted his head. "I've spoken with you about the restructuring taking place within the bureau."

"Yes."

"While you've probably noticed a few changes, you've not seen everything yet."

Holy shit. "I'm being fired?"

"No, no!" Walter raised a staying palm. "Nothing so drastic. But you've been one of my best agents for close to nine years."

Lucky sat up straighter. "Damn right, I'm the best. But you didn't call me in here to tell me what I already know." *Take that, O'Donoghue.*

"No. I didn't. Lately I've been questioned about you, particularly in light of your last review."

It'd been one hell of a good review too. "Don't those asshole higher-ups get tired of finding fault with your hiring me? It's not like we haven't proven them wrong a million times."

Smug satisfaction rearranged Walter's facial wrinkles, making him resemble a self-satisfied walrus. "Actually, some have tried to take credit for my decision to bring you on board, but that's neither here nor there. Their latest concern, I have to admit, is well-deserved."

Walter made a mistake? Oh hell no, he didn't. Not Walter Smith. "What are you talking about, boss?"

"It seems I've allowed a highly prized member of my team to go unrecognized. After the earlier push-back over your hiring, I felt it best to keep you under the radar." He grinned. "Or as much under the radar as you fly, Lucky."

Yeah, well, Lucky couldn't help if his cases occasionally ended up making headlines when a drug kingpin fell. But he wouldn't call himself unrecognized. Walter wasn't into grand gestures, but neither was Lucky. Still, the boss never failed to heap praise where it was due. "I'm afraid you've lost me."

"A promotion, Lucky. In all the years you've worked for me, you've never been given a single promotion."

Promotion? A desk job? Fuck, no. "If this is about my leg, the doctor says I'll be back to normal in another few weeks." *Please, dear God, not a desk job.*

"No, it's not about your job-related injuries. It's about building a better team that doesn't replace members every six months."

Lucky settled back into the chair, ignoring the squeak of leather that sounded too much like a fart. "Go on."

"Instead of allowing the separate divisions to hone their own methods, creating diversity in how each is run, we've consolidated." Walter heaved out a body-crumpling sigh, tapping an ink pen against his desktop. "The Southeastern division

92

will serve as a training center. The classes you attended were part of a pilot program."

Training center. A bunch of whining newbies underfoot all the time. Say it ain't so.

"Jameson will conduct classes and head up the efforts to mix classroom with practical application, while instilling inter-agency cooperation among various drug enforcement agencies. That's where you come in."

"Me? What do I have to do with this?" Give Lucky the streets and a couple of two-bit drug dealers, or doctors cranking out illegal prescriptions. Oh, hell, give him a truckload of stolen narcotics, but keep him the hell out of a classroom.

"Congratulations, Lucky. You're now supervisor of the training division. You'll be working in close cooperation with Jameson until you're ready to handle the task on your own, but will still report directly to me."

Promotion? Good thing. Reporting to Walter? Another check in the plus column. Working with O'Donoghue? Yet to be seen. "Raise?"

"Eight percent."

Eight percent would add a nice cushion to Lucky's motorcycle fund. "What do I have to do?"

"Funny you should ask."

I'm a babysitter. A motherfucking babysitter. Lucky scowled at the toddlers under his care and attempted to hear over the pounding tempo of some gawd-awful squawking that reminded him of Cat Lucky's screeching to get into the house. Give him some classic rock or even country music over this teeth-jarring shit.

A few feet behind him in line, Johnson and Landry chatted up a trio of mini-skirted young women who couldn't be far from their teens. Not that Johnson and Landry didn't fit right in. *Black eyeliner, Landry? Really?*

Lucky almost didn't recognize Johnson in a form-fitting white dress with a low-cut back, seemingly designed to show off her muscle definition. For the first time in their acquaintance, she wore makeup, and her dangly earrings flashed in the pulsing neon lights outside Armageddon, or Armadillo, or whatever the hell the club's name was.

"I've always wanted to come to Amarillo," a woman in front of Lucky said. Amarillo. Yeah, Amarillo. Close enough to Armageddon.

One of the girls placed a hand on the newbie's butt. Landry didn't even flinch. *You're not here to get laid, hot shot.* Of course, if Landry got into females, maybe he wasn't interested in Bo. *Go for it, big boy. Take a walk on the other side of the street. Yeah, take her up on her offer and keep your mitts off of Bo.*

Johnson wriggled to the music filtering out of the club, crowding the predatory woman back a few steps. Another of the women gestured with her hands, and the third? Paydirt! Neon green fingernails dipped into a purse and returned with a tiny packet similar to the ones presented in the conference room.

The women smiled. Landry and Johnson completed the ritual with their own display of teeth. Any more gleaming brightness might blind a man. *Jeez, people, put those things away.*

At last Lucky stood before the bouncer, who had the audacity to wink. "Back again, I see." He took Lucky's money and allowed him through the door. The man didn't even glance at the bulge in Lucky's jacket. *What does it take to get frisked these days?* At least this muscle-bound gym rat might actually stand a chance against a drugged-out secretary.

Lucky strode up to the bar and ordered a beer, the better to blend in. He didn't have to drink the hoity-toity imported shit with a name he couldn't pronounce. Damn O'Donoghue for being right.

Johnson and Landry showed up a few seconds later, still in the company of their new friends. He hoped the women hadn't talked the rookies into paying their cover charges. Accounting would have a fit. *Oh crap, now I'm thinking like a supervisor.* What came next? Defending Landry's honor against the touchy-feely woman?

From the corner of his eye, Lucky watched the group order drinks and then drift toward the back door. Wow. Fast work. "They're all yours," he said, hoping his mic picked up over the blaring music. Asshole Keith better do his job.

Lucky waited a few minutes, set his beer down on a table, and sauntered outside. Flashing lights pulsed from the alley leading to the back. Oh, yeah. Mission accomplished. Three young women, most likely out for a night of fun, with barely enough goods on them to get them arrested and probably no leads to any key players. Damn it. While the extra promotion money helped ease the pain, enough with this picking off fleas shit. Time to bring down a top dog or two.

Lucky waited, yet no Bo. He gave up and turned the porch light off at ten o'clock. His phone rang a few minutes later. He stared at Bo's name on the screen, heart pounding, and let the gizmo ring. No point in seeming overanxious. On the third ring, he picked up. "Harrison."

"Lucky?"

"Yeah." He kept his tone neutral. No way in hell would he let on how much he'd missed the man. *Ignore me, why don't 'cha?*

"Listen, I'll be leaving soon."

The desperation in Bo's voice softened Lucky's anger. "And?"

"We didn't get to spend Christmas together last year, and this year's not looking too good either."

Oh. That. What did Bo want him to say? *It's okay, there'll be other times?* At the rate they were going, there wouldn't be. And it wasn't okay. For the past ten years, Lucky'd spent Christmas alone, unless staring at his sister through plexiglass while talking on a phone counted. After listening to her sob about injustice when he'd deserved his place behind bars, he'd warned her away, not wanting his nephews' memories of the holidays forever tainted by a no-account uncle. No way in hell would he take Walter up on the offer of dinner at the Smiths' either. He wasn't that much of a loser to accept a pity invite. Truth was, though, Lucky'd gotten fucking tired of playing martyr, especially after going to Walter (Walter!) to get special permission for Bo's gift. And Bo *had* to call and remind him that once again he'd eat a frozen dinner instead of celebrating the holidays with someone else.

"We're big boys," Lucky ground out. "We'll live."

Bo's "What are you doing Thursday" caught Lucky off guard. "Come again?"

"Thursday. What are you doing for Thanksgiving? Christmas is a few weeks away, but I was thinking, if you wanted to..."

"Okay." No brainer there.

"But you haven't even heard me out."

"Does it involve you being here?"

"Yes."

Hallelujah! "Then the answer is yes." Tension slowly melted. Bo was coming over. Maybe he'd not written Lucky off yet.

"Do you want turkey or ham? My grandmother used to fix both."

Turkey and ham? A die-hard vegetarian offered to cook poultry or meat. All Lucky wanted was Bo in his bed. Best not say that right now and ruin the mood. Ahh... a chance to win some points, maybe. "The Tofurky you cooked for Thanksgiving last year wasn't too gawdawful. I could deal with having wish-it-was-turkey again. But why?"

"We're going to have our own combination of Thanksgiving and Christmas. I'll be there around six. See you then." Bo hung up, sounding much happier than at the start of the conversation. Lucky scowled at his duplex, which definitely suffered from inattention. The stove hadn't been used since the last time Bo cooked.

Lucky stared at the mound of black and white fur on the couch. "Get up, Lucky. Time to make a plan."

The tree listed to one side. Fishing line and a few nails pinned the eyesore against the wall. As long as Bo didn't peek behind the monstrosity, he'd never notice. Hmmm... Too many candy canes on the right side. Lucky rearranged the ornaments and fluffed the branches. The cheap dollar store baubles made the tree appear pathetic rather than festive. Cat Lucky swatted a stray glittery star. It landed on the floor. So much for impressing Bo with a home-style Christmas.

A lone package sat beneath the branches, its paper crinkled under far more tape than was necessary. Lucky sucked at wrapping gifts. He'd had limited practice. Victor had simply paid professionals to gift shop, expertly wrap Lucky's gifts, and decorate whatever house they spent the holidays in.

Of course, there was the whole Victor's brother and sister pretending Lucky was merely a family friend thing, and evasive maneuvers around Victor's overly ambitious nephew Stephan. After the first few years, Lucky gave up trying to fit in and went home to his folks at Christmas. Now, even that choice wasn't open. What fucking wrong turn had he taken in life to end up unwanted? Oh, yeah. Ex-con. And whether or not Bo wanted anything more to do with him remained to be seen.

Stop being so fucking gloomy. It's Christmas, damn it. Sorta. Lucky stared at what he'd hoped would be a masterpiece of spruce and tinsel. Fucking pathetic. A shower of tinsel fell and splattered. The more Lucky stared, the uglier the tree grew. *Fuck it.* He tossed the damned thing, ornaments and all, out the back door and drove to the office for the Christmas cactus Bo kept on the filing cabinet. Hell, it'd worked last year. If it wasn't broke, why fix it?

A knock sounded on the door a few minutes after he'd set the plant on a brick and arranged its flowery tendrils. Bo had his own key. Why knock? Lucky answered the door. Bo raised his leg to knock with his foot again, his arms filled with a huge cardboard box. "Let me in, this is heavy!"

Lucky stepped back and Bo waddled into the kitchen to set the box on the table. The scent of Tofurky and dressing trailed in his wake. Lucky slammed the door on the cool snap they'd gotten earlier that day. Snow rarely fell in Atlanta, but there'd been some talk on the radio earlier about falling temperatures.

A whirling dervish spun around the kitchen, opening and closing cabinet doors, setting plates on the table, and popping a pie into the oven. The absence of a hello kiss didn't go unnoticed.

"What can I do to help?" Lucky asked.

Bo dashed back to the box and extracted a bottle of wine. "Would you pop my cork, big boy?" he purred in his best decoy rent-boy voice.

Lucky's mouth went dry. Fuck dinner. Bring on dessert.

CHAPTER TEN

"That was damned good." Lucky let out a belch and shot a wary glance to Bo, expecting a few harsh words. Hell, a few harsh words would beat the casual small talk of the last hour. Even the day they'd met, they'd been more relaxed around each other. Bo sat stiffly on the edge of his chair and barely ate, while Lucky spent his time adding hidden meaning to each sparse word.

Bo's smile didn't quite meet his eyes. "I've missed you," he said, finally spearing and eating the tiny piece of pumpkin pie he'd been pushing around his plate for the last five minutes.

Lucky nodded. Words weren't his friends at times. If he opened his mouth now, sure as shit he'd wind up cramming his foot right in.

Bo carefully folded the paper towel serving as his napkin into a fan shape. "Can we go out into the living room?"

They'd fucked on every last flat surface in the house, and many that weren't, and now the man *asked permission* to go to the living room? Bo topped off their wine glasses for the long, twenty-foot trip.

Once they'd left the kitchen, the odd stress seemed to pass. Bo let out a laugh. "What's this?" Oh, hell. The cactus. "Lucky! You remembered. For me?"

"It's Christmas, or rather Christgiving. It's a Christmas cactus." The unspoken *well duh!* didn't quite come across the way Lucky intended.

Bo set the wine glasses down on the coffee table and whirled, catching Lucky by surprise. "You can deny it all you want to, but I know good and damned well you didn't put the cactus there for you and the cat."

Cat Lucky sprawled on the couch, head tucked beneath his paws.

Get my back, buddy! "I...well..."

Words lost their meaning. The press of Bo's lips erased weeks of loneliness, the gentle insistence of his tongue seeking entrance chased back every fear. Strong arms drove away the darkness, enfolding Lucky in security. He answered Bo's silent request with his own arms, his own lips, his own tongue.

Bo retreated first and gazed down at the floor. "I love you, Lucky. Sometimes I don't understand you. Sometimes I don't believe I ever will and, to be honest, I've questioned if constantly fighting your insecurities is worth the effort."

Oh. Not a kiss hello, but a kiss goodbye. Lucky stepped away, swallowing hard against the boulder lodged in his throat. He deserved this.

Once more the sweet bliss of Bo's body molded against his, and hot breath washed over his ear. "Damn it, Lucky. You're worth every exasperating moment, even if you don't agree with me. As much as I'd like to push you off a cliff sometimes, I can't stop loving you, and believe me, I've tried. Well, not the pushing off the cliff, maybe, but the loving you thing. Every single time you've nearly convinced me that you're an unredeemable asshole, the clouds lift and I get to peek at the good man you try hard not to be.

"But I'm going away, and while I'm gone, I'd like to think I have someone to come back to. Yeah, we need to sit down one day and have a long talk about where we're going, but for now, I think I need things to stay the way they've been." He withdrew and gave Lucky a tremulous smile. "I have you, you have me, and we'll cross whatever bridges we meet when we get there."

Thank you, dear sweet Lord in Heaven. Lucky rose on his toes, pouring weeks' worth of heartache into devouring his lover's mouth. They might be fucked up and never come close to normal, but at least they still had each other. Lucky fumbled with the buttons on Bo's shirt, kissing a pathway down each newly exposed inch of skin.

He trailed his lips over the pulse point in Bo's neck. *Please don't leave me.* A soul-searing kiss declared *I love you.* Lucky's gentle grip on the back of Bo's head said, *I won't let you fall.*

He took a nipple into his mouth, rolling the hardening nub against his tongue while tweaking the other with his fingertips.

Down and down he traveled, re-familiarizing himself with a man he'd worried he might never hold again. A throaty half-moan, half-sigh urged him on, and he eased Bo's zipper down to reach inside and free the gift underneath the wrapping. He dropped to his knees. With flattened tongue he lapped a swath up the underside of Bo's cock, tracing a bulging vein.

The scent of soap, man, and cologne made an intoxicating mix, and Bo's pre-come carried a slightly herbal taste, as though flavored by the green tea he drank. Lucky wrapped his lips around the head and slowly worked his way down.

Months of practice had taught him the right pressure and speed to play Bo's arousal, how to work the uncircumcised flesh to full advantage. Casual fucks offered release without strings attached, yet nothing beat knowing exactly how to please a man and having the man return the favor. And beyond the bedroom, they'd learned so much about each other: favorite foods, music... *No, not going there. Not thinking about commitment now. Like Bo said, we simply need something to cling to in the coming weeks. No need thinking about the future.*

He wriggled his fingertips between Bo's thighs, stroking behind Bo's balls while he sucked and bobbed. Bo fingers alternately stroked or applied pressure to Lucky's scalp, offering instruction on when to take things up a notch.

Bo wriggled his jeans down his hips, backing away long enough to kick off his shoes and step out of the pile of denim. Hands beneath Lucky's arms, he tugged, bringing Lucky to his feet. In short order, Bo stripped Lucky of his T-shirt, shoes, and jeans. Without quite knowing how he got there, Lucky found himself on his back on the floor with Bo's cock in his mouth. Bo hovered above him, lips counterpointing Lucky's own suction.

How in the hell had he existed without this man in his arms? With a bit of maneuvering, he turned, rolled Bo over, and climbed on top. Bo grabbed a leg of his jeans and dragged his pants across the floor to plunder the pockets. They locked eyes. Not a word was spoken, and they didn't break eye contact as Bo opened a packet and rolled latex down Lucky's shaft. No challenge, no hurt, no questions in his eyes, though he'd proven his lying skills in O'Donoghue's class. Lucky's erection wavered, quickly recovering when Bo took matters in hand. Bo passed Lucky a tube, and Lucky made short work of opening Bo up.

Lucky gradually sank in on a series of little thrusts, Bo rocking upward while he rocked down. Firm hands on his ass urged him on, along with the warmth of Bo's body. Weight braced on his arms, Lucky plunged in and out of sweet heaven, Bo's erection rubbing against his abs. Nearly perfect, yet...

Lucky pulled out and Bo gasped. "What?"

"Sh..." Lucky straddled Bo's body and leaned down to kiss him. "You can't be comfortable on the floor. Come to bed."

They rose and took a few shuffling steps. Lucky halted mid-hallway to pull Bo down for another kiss and a few quick humps against a muscular thigh. They made their way to the bedroom and collapsed onto the bed. Spreading out in the center of the mattress on his back, Lucky said, "Come here."

Bo smiled and took his place over Lucky, guiding Lucky's still-hard cock back inside of him. Oh, yeah. Heaven. From this angle, Lucky could stroke both hands up Bo's torso, pull him down for a kiss, and stroke his stiff cock in time with his up and down pace.

Heart either too full of Bo being here or too empty from him leaving, Lucky almost wished it were him being fucked, Bo's cock breaching him and forcing out all thoughts but the present.

Lucky lost himself in the slide of body against body, reaching out his free hand to brush Bo's arm or leg, skate fingers across his full lips and touch Bo everywhere, simply because he could.

He watched the intensity on Bo's face gradually change into rapture. Eyes closed, sooty lashes swept his cheeks. The cords in his neck stood out. "Oh God, oh God," he chanted, splashing warmth on Lucky's belly. His fingers dug into Lucky's biceps and he panted, uttering "uhs" and "ohs" and "Oh my God, Lucky".

The rhythmic squeezing of Bo's internal muscles hurried Lucky along. Bo's pleas from the alley penetrated his lust-filled fog. What would it be like to fill the man's body with nothing in between? Oh hell. Nothing between. His come filling Bo's body in the most intimate way. Shockwaves raced through Lucky, and he plunged over the edge with Bo's name on his tongue.

"Here." Bo handed Lucky a square silver box neatly tied with glittering ribbon, then dropped his hand to Cat Lucky's head for a quick scratch. The foil wrapping paper wasn't torn or taped over. "It's not much, but I hope you like it."

A present. Bo'd gotten Lucky a present. Shaking didn't produce a rattle. Not big enough to be another dragon statue, though the last one Bo'd presented had kind of grown on Lucky. It made one hell of a paperweight.

Taking care to preserve the paper like his mother, the ultimate re-user, would have, Lucky peeled up the tape and slid a box out of the wrapping. The lid snapped open to reveal a watch far nicer than any Lucky'd owned since the Feds took the Rolex he'd gotten from Victor. "Wow! Thanks," he said, allowing Bo to help him put it on.

"It's an Eco-drive," Bo explained while tightening the band. "It's powered by light and never needs a battery." Bo's fingers lingered on Lucky's wrist a moment, tracing the pattern of an old scar.

Lucky raised his arm toward his nose for a better look. Sweet. No scratched crystal, and the timepiece looked like something worth owning, unlike the shoddy ten-dollar model he'd left lying on a rock somewhere in North Carolina during an unplanned, one-legged hiking trip. He wrapped his arms around Bo, both in thanks and memory of being without him last spring in the mountains, thinking he'd soon bite the big one. *Don't go there. You're here now. He's here now. Stop thinking so damned much.*

"Now for my gift," Lucky said, rising from the couch to retrieve the poorly wrapped package from beneath the Christmas cactus. He took a deep breath. "I hope you like it."

Unlike Lucky, Bo ripped open his gift with reckless abandon. His mouth fell open. "I... um... Am I allowed to have this?" He stared at the box holding a .38.

Oh wait. Was he anti-handgun? "I talked it over with boss man. Your circumstances are different from mine. You only got probation, you weren't convicted. Given your assignment, we both thought it best if you took your own piece with you." He'd never forget the day he'd found a package containing a .38 on his desk, undoubtedly from Walter. Right now his sidearm occupied an evidence bag somewhere in Canada, while he used a department loaner. Damn, but he missed his gun.

The cold metal shimmered when Bo lifted the weapon from the box. It'd taken weeks of Internet research to select the right one; Lucky'd even turned a blind eye to price. Bo deserved the best. "I've no idea what to say."

Not good. Not good at all. "Don't you like it?"

"Like it? I love it. You got me the perfect gift. Thank you." He wrapped Lucky in a one-armed hug while hefting the gun with his free hand.

"Know how to shoot?"

Bo gave Lucky an "Oh, please!" scowl. "I'm an Arkansas country boy. Of course I know how to shoot. My aunt taught me."

Lucky wondered if the aunt who'd gotten custody of Bo after the courts took him from his daddy taught him to shoot in case her brother came back. Providing Bo with the means to take care of himself earned her points in Lucky's book.

Their gazes met, and for a moment neither spoke. Bo broke the silence. "I'm scared, Lucky. I've never done anything like this before, and you won't be there to catch me when I fall."

"You won't fall. Besides, you'll have Art." While Lucky would rather have the honor of watching Bo's back, if Lucky had to choose anyone besides himself, Walter or Art topped the list.

"What happens if I'm made?"

Don't think about that. A vision sprung to his mind of Bo surrounded by pistol-wielding desperados. "You won't be."

'Cause you can't let that happen. "Get a good cover story, stick to it, and if questioned, get mad." *Be safe. Watch your back. Come back to me.*

"Works for you, doesn't it?" Bo offered up a tired smile.

Lucky'd seen more sincere smiles on the faces of used car salesmen. "Yeah, it does. Be the meanest motherfucker around and no one will dare mess with you."

Lucky placed the paper, boxes, and gun aside to distract Bo the best way he knew how. No way in hell did he want to dwell on what might happen without him around to watch out for his partner. He might not be ready to settle down in the house with the picket fence, but damn it, Bo was his, and nobody messed with Lucky's man.

He lifted a nearly empty wine glass, dribbled burgundy droplets across Bo's lap, and collected the sweet moisture with his tongue. They finished off both glasses from each other's skin.

The next morning over breakfast Bo asked, "Lucky? Did you know there's a tree lying in your backyard?"

CHAPTER ELEVEN

"Cyrus!" Lucky shouted from across the living room.

Bo spun around without the least hesitation, nearly dislodging the cat on his lap. "Yes?"

"Good." First test passed. "Now tell me, when were you born?"

"September twenty-third."

Lucky raised his brows.

"Jameson says we're to stick to the truth as much as possible. Easier to remember. Cyrus Cooper and I have the same birthday, even if he's four years younger than me."

Made sense. "What's your background?"

"I grew up in Arkansas, got locked in juvie for six months my senior year for vandalism."

Oh, now Bo being in juvenile lockup skated the edges of credibility. "Can you give details of the detention center?" Lucky would have liked to say more, hiding his fears behind his usual snark. But Bo's life depended on him being a believable Cyrus Cooper.

A rueful laugh answered him. "Sure can. My roommate's name was Archie. Can you believe it? He'd gotten in trouble for shoplifting." Bo's placed a finger on his chin, giving him a thoughtful expression. "I took auto mechanics there under a teacher named Lewis, who owned a 1977 Harley Davidson Super Glide. He used to bring the bike into the classroom, which is how I got interested in working on motorcycles."

Lucky observed closely, but Bo didn't show any of the telltale signs of lying. No stumbling over his story, no accidental body language. "Where'd you get the information?" Whatever lies he told, he'd have to be able to back up.

Bo's smile fell. "Firsthand. My dad waited outside of the school and talked shit to my brother one day after we'd moved in with my aunt. I found out where the asshole stayed and took a baseball bat with me to have a chat." He shrugged. "You know how it is to be young and pissed off. Consequences are the last thing on your mind."

"What did you do?" Mild-mannered Bo played vigilante?

"I busted the windshield out of his car." Bo stared at his fingers, slowly tracing the black and white pattern on Cat Lucky's head. Without the cat, no doubt those fingers would be twisted together in his lap.

"Why on earth did you bust up his car?"

Raising his head, Bo issued a full on challenge with nothing more than a scorching glare. "I aimed for *him* and missed. Still, it's easy to stretch the truth, say I got locked up for gang activity if it'll win Reyes over."

Oh. The death glare said *we ain't talking about this now.* Time to move on to the next question. "You ride a bike. How'd you learn?"

"I picked up the basics from my teacher. Then my aunt's boyfriend had an old Sportster that didn't run. When I got out of juvie, he told me it was mine if I got it running, so I got it running." Pride chased back the storm clouds on Bo's face.

"What happened to it?"

"I gave the bike to my brother when I left for boot camp."

They grew quiet, Bo petting the cat, Lucky staring unseeing at the notes they'd created to quiz Bo, and Cat Lucky churning out contented feline noises. Lucky posed a question not on the list, hoping to lighten the mood. "I've been meaning to ask you something."

"Fire away."

"You're vegetarian, yet you wear leather chaps. Won't they throw you out of the vegetarian guild for wearing animal skin?"

"If I go down while riding, nothing's gonna save my sorry hide better than leather. If given a choice between my skin and—"

"Good choice."

"Besides," Bo's half smile grew into a grin, "someone gave me this cool set of chaps and totally gets off on me wearing them."

Oh yeah. Now's he's talking. "Have you ever turned too fast and knocked something over with that bubble butt of yours?" Lucky added a leer for good measure.

"Yeah, actually I have. But I haven't heard you complain."

"And you never will." Lucky waggled his brows. "I have an idea. Why don't we strip down and play questions and answers in the nude."

"If we do that, we'll never get anything done."

"Yes, we will."

"No, we won't."

"Prove me wrong."

Bo stripped. They resumed their question and answer session two hours later, somewhat worse for the wear.

"Got your gun?" *Be careful out there.*

"Yes, Lucky," Bo huffed, giving his luggage a final inspection. No fancy Pullman case this time, just a ratty old duffle.

"Leaving behind all traces of your real identity?" *I know it's against policy, but if you need me, call. I'll be right there.* Lucky peered into the bag. Sure was a lot of black in there. Of course, Bo's black Harley shirt and scuffed boots matched the color scheme. The man made one fine biker.

"Yes, Lucky." Bo opened his wallet to display Cyrus Cooper's driver's license.

What could he have possibly forgotten? "Got plenty of trackers?"

"Yes, Lucky."

"Got the address?"

"Lucky?"

"Yes?"

"I'm a big boy. I can take care of myself." Bo took the sting out of the words with a kiss. "I have to go now. I'll call you if and when I can."

Lucky stood his ground for a long moment. Long enough to earn another pulse-pounding kiss.

"I'll miss you, Lucky. Take care of the cat while I'm gone,

and the cactus, okay?" Bo grazed his lips against Lucky's ear. "And take care of yourself."

Though they'd both said the words before, they didn't yet trip easily from Lucky's tongue. "You too," would have to do. Bo didn't push for more

When Lucky didn't move, Bo stepped around him to get out the door. His footsteps stomped across the porch and down the stairs. "Bye, Mrs. Griggs," he heard Bo call to the landlady, doubtlessly sitting on her front porch.

Bo's truck's engine rumbled to life, the growl growing fainter while Lucky's heartbeat thudded faster. *Oh shit! I know what he forgot. He forgot to take me!*

Lucky sat on the couch, staring at the reminder of the night he'd celebrated Christmas early with Bo. Fallen blooms littered the floor under the cactus. Maybe watering might help, if Lucky could summon the energy for a trip to the kitchen sink. Too bad he couldn't teach the damned cat to do chores, but the critter barely answered when called.

A turkey club sat uneaten on the coffee table, and Lucky raised his wine bottle in a toast. "Here's to you, William Patrick Schollenberger the third. Merry Christmas, wherever the fuck you are."

He wrapped Charlotte's homemade afghan tighter around himself to ward off a chill. *Must be coming down with something.* She'd done a better job this year, for none of the stitches had come unraveled yet. Who'd a thunk it? The woman he used to call Suzy Lumberjack for her lack of domestic skills had taken up knitting at the advice of her therapist for stress relief. With two teenaged boys and a job at a hospital, he imagined she built up a lot of stress to work off.

His phone sat next to his uneaten dinner. How he'd love to call, wish her and the boys a merry Christmas, but no telling where she was right now, and the boys believed him dead. He sighed and swilled another mouthful of wine. Bo would have a fit if he saw Lucky now, chugging from a bottle and fast approaching the "one too many" point. Christmas Eve and all alone. Rain pounded a steady beat against the windows, adding to his gloomy mood. He could turn on the TV. Or maybe call up a favorite playlist on his iPod. Both required motion, and the bundle of black and white fur on his lap didn't seem to want to move.

Back on the farm, Mama probably had a ham in the oven, slow-cooking through the night, and she'd be up early to candy sweet potatoes, bake pies, and make green bean casserole. His mouth watered, and he glared at the poor substitute for a feast sitting on the coffee table. Maybe he'd feed the turkey to Cat Lucky later.

Tomorrow the family, except Lucky, who was presumed dead, and Charlotte, still hiding out from her ex's family in Spokane, would gather around the table in the old farmhouse Lucky'd grown up in. Mama and Daddy, Grandma and Grandpa Lucklighter, Dover, his wife and daughter, Bristol and whoever he decided to date this week, and Daytona. Had Daytona ever gotten over his drug habit, and if so, had he finished college and found a girlfriend? Of all the family, Daytona came closest to joining Lucky in black sheep-hood.

The next swallow of wine tried to go down the wrong way. No sense dwelling on his folks. Even before he'd been reported dead, they'd had enough of his lawless ways and disowned him.

Cat Lucky hopped down and strolled to the front door. "Merrroow?"

"Hell, I'm such bad company even you can't stand me tonight." Lucky opened the door and the cat streaked out into the chilly night, his tail high.

Lucky's phone buzzed, and he hurried across the floor the grab up the device. A text message from an unknown number said, "Merry Xmas. Love you. C."

C? Who the hell was C? Ah, shit. Cyrus Cooper. Cy. Bo. Lucky smiled and typed back, "U 2."

He polished off the rest of the bottle of Boone's Farm, let the cat in, and shuffled off to bed. Staring at the ceiling, he recalled a Christmas from long ago. He'd kept his sister's kids on Christmas Eve while she finished up last minute shopping.

Dressed in footie pajamas, his nephews had climbed into his lap while Lucky told them all he remembered of *'Twas the Night Before Christmas*. Normally boisterous, they remained wide-eyed and fascinated by Lucky's clumsy efforts, while Charlotte's perfectly decorated tree glittered in the corner. Fat snowflakes drifted by the window, and Lucky'd pulled one of his mother's homemade quilts tighter around him and the boys.

In his mind's eye, the tree and all the trimmings crammed themselves into Lucky's living room. Lucky held a small child whose face remained vague, while Bo held the spitting image of Stephanie, the girl who'd entered Lucky's life only to leave it a few days later. Bo read from a story book, while the kids "oh'd" and "ah'd."

Lucky'd never really considered having a family of his own before. At least he'd never entertained such thoughts during his time with Victor. And he'd only recently finished paying his debt to society. Having a child of his own wasn't happening, and Bo wanted children. Could they adopt with Lucky's criminal record, or had Walter's magic wand truly erased all traces of Lucky's past?

The kids in his daydream stared at Bo with adoring eyes as he pulled presents from under the tree. Bo deserved kids. He'd make a wonderful father, as he'd proved earlier in the year when he'd gone over and above the call of duty to help young cancer victims he didn't even know.

Not only did Bo want a family, he hoped one day to have that with Lucky. With all he'd done in his life, Lucky didn't deserve the unfailing love Bo sent his way, and he certainly didn't deserve kids. What kind of father would he make?

"You're so good with the boys," Charlotte had told Lucky upon arriving home that long ago Christmas Eve to find her sons tucked into bed.

Charlotte and Bo obviously saw something in Lucky that Lucky himself didn't recognize. What if they were right?

***

112

"Happy fucking New Year," Lucky groused, glaring down at the packed dance floor. He raked his eyes over the writhing masses. Landry and Johnson worked the crowd along with a newbie in from Texas for training. They'd managed to make a few small busts, mostly users or small-time dealers, no one with quantities for sale or with more access to the supply chain than *friend of a friend*. Fuckers. Why waste time locking up casual users? Why not send the team out into the real action? And if the jerkoff standing next to Lucky with the noise maker tooted the thing one more time...

Thus far, Lucky's new job hadn't pissed him off too badly, and he'd not gotten called into Walter's office all week. Of course, with Walter and Mrs. Smith gone visiting for the holidays, he'd caught a break. His phone buzzed, and once more an unknown number showed. While Lucky appreciated the gesture, and the "Love you, happy NY, C," the man took chances.

Was Bo spending time in a club for different reasons, or was he sitting at whatever counted as home, alone? Back in Arkansas, he had a brother and an aunt. Did he miss them, think of them as often as Lucky did his own family?

Movement down below drew Lucky's attention. Johnson reached up and tugged on her earring, the sign for *I'm gonna go out back and make a buy*. She, Landry, and Newbie worked their way toward the door, a half-dozen young men with shifty eyes following. Ah, hell. Show time. Lucky sat his full beer bottle on a nearby table and went to work. A few twenty-somethings were going to get a hellacious start to the new year.

Lucky's saunter carried a bit more spring in the step as he followed his team out the door. They might be aggravating wet-behind-the-ears rookies, but they were Lucky's rookies. That made them the best.

CHAPTER TWELVE

Three months. Three months without Bo, without even a phone call. Chill temperatures gave way to sunny days, and Bradford pear trees spewing pollen on Lucky's Camaro. If Bo didn't come back soon, Lucky'd be at the doctors for treatment of carpal-tunnel syndrome. He'd been giving his right wrist one hell of a workout lately.

He grumbled all the way to work, glaring at the cars whizzing by in the *Peach Pass* lane. Lucky paid taxes for road use. Asking a man to buy a pass to use the express lane didn't sit well with him. How could they guarantee that their little electronic whatchamajiggies would only charge for his own tolls and not someone else's? So he glared, and he growled, and he seriously considered crashing the privileged assholes' party. And he would, too, if it wouldn't have meant another call to Walter. Last time Lucky'd given in to temptation, a trooper had pulled him over and called the boss, questioning what work emergency led Lucky to break the law. Sometimes flashing a badge hurt more than helped.

He'd no sooner gotten to work when his desk phone rang. "Lucky? Could I see you in my office, please?" Walter didn't bother waiting for an answer.

Lucky stepped into Walter's domain, surprised to find O'Donoghue parked in a chair before the desk, but not the one Lucky'd claimed long ago for his. "You wanted to see me?"

"Come in, sit down," Walter invited with a wave of his hand toward the chair.

O'Donoghue's slit-lidded gaze followed Lucky across the room. Though he reclined in the chair, his ankle crossed over his knee and arm flung over the padded leather back, he held himself stiffly. A muscle twitched in his jaw. "Mr. Harrison, we have a problem." Nothing new. Narcotics bureaus and problems seemed to travel hand-in-hand.

Walter sat forward in his chair, lips clamped into a thin line and hands folded into a white-knuckled clench upon his desk. Must be a problem of shit-hit-the-fan proportions.

Lucky sank down into the chair. "What's up?"

A cocked brow and shift of Walter's eyes toward O'Donoghue fielded the question.

"Arthur Patterson's in the hospital," O'Donoghue drawled in the Brooklyn accent he switched on and off at will.

Holy shit. Not Art. "Someone tried to take him out?" Lucky might have to find the son-of-a-bitch responsible and settle the score.

"No, thank God. Freak accident. A young woman hauling a bunch of balloons to a birthday party T-boned Patterson's vehicle when the balloons impaired her vision." O'Donoghue bounced his foot on his knee, tapping out a cadence with his fingers on his patent leather shoe.

Art. Call him Art. Lucky darted a questioning glance to Walter. He forced his fingers to loosen on the chair arms. *Don't make me ask.*

Walter didn't. "He's been admitted to Athens Regional Health in guarded condition. Once his condition stabilizes, he'll be transferred to a hospital here in Atlanta."

Good. Half of Lucky's unvoiced questions were answered. Now for the rest. Before he could ask about Bo, O'Donoghue added, "And we lost our informant. The lady slammed into the passenger side of the vehicle, where our man sat. The impact killed him instantly."

"What now?" Lucky might not have known the guy, but he wouldn't wish death on anybody.

"Now we get out the word about a motorcycle accident to stop any questions as to why he was in a car with his leader's neighbor. Art never got in close with anyone but our guy. A heart attack is his cover story."

Fuck. With Art and the informant both gone, where did Bo stand? Lucky chose his words carefully. "What about his assignment?" *What about Bo?*

"He's out of the game," O'Donoghue replied. Lucky swiveled his chair to the right.

"You mean, B... a rookie's in there alone?" An hour. Lucky could be in Athens in an hour. Less if forgot his promise to be a law-abiding citizen and crashed the Peach Pass lane. Lord help any slow shoppers at the Tanger Outlet park where he'd exit I-85 for Athens.

"For the moment." O'Donoghue met and held Lucky's glare, his eyes probing down to Lucky's soul. "Reyes' gang is always on the lookout for drivers. They tend to favor ex-cons, and I understand you have an active commercial driver's license and experience driving larger rigs."

"I do." *And I meet the ex-con requirement. Thank you for not bringing that up.*

"You're also familiar with routes from Texas to Georgia, among others."

No telling how many trips between those two states Lucky'd made in his time with Victor. Pick up a load near the border, drive to one of Victor's warehouses, and cash in on his share of the take. "I know my way around."

"Good. Now we need to establish your cover."

Lucky's heart skipped a beat. *Going in. I'm going in.*

Pivoting squeaked the chair and let Lucky give Walter the hairy eyeball. "What stupid-assed name do I get this time?"

"We're changing our methods," Walter said. A muscle at the corner of his mouth jumped. "While I know you eagerly await your next bizarre moniker, it's come to our attention that perhaps it's best to let our agents decide for themselves." He shifted the focus back to O'Donoghue with a nod of his head.

O'Donoghue accepted the tag and stepped back into the ring. "What name did you choose in my class as your ideal alias?"

"Ricky Getsinger."

"We'll draw up ID as Richard. What's your occupation?"

Talk about a no brainer. "I finished my sentence in December a year ago. Now I'm unemployed, mostly doing freelance local deliveries. Which explains my commercial driver's license."

"You'll need a vehicle."

One deep breath, one slow exhale. Finally, finally, some-one asked his opinion. "It needs to be a car I'm familiar with, right?" Another fact learned in class. Several textbook exam-ples showed cases blown when an agent didn't know how to work features on their assigned vehicles.

"That's always best."

"Boss? Do we still have that butt-ugly green Malibu?" Ve-hicles seized during drug busts found their way into a holding pen while awaiting police auction, but were available to the SNB for use in undercover operations until they sold. *It's ugly, it's old, I hate the shit out of it. I also know where to hit to get the glove compartment to open, and how to unlatch the trunk with a busted lock.*

"I'll call and find out. In the meantime, I believe you're go-ing to need this." Walter slid a padded manila mailer across the desk.

Lucky's heart thudded hard. He opened the package and reached inside, wrapping his hand around a familiar grip. His gun. They'd gotten back the gun the felons had stolen from him last year. He fought back a smile. No telling what strings the boss had had to pull to reclaim this piece of evi-dence. "Thanks, boss."

Two hours later, Lucky left Walter's office, a manila enve-lope filled with facts tucked under one arm. He stopped by the reception desk long enough to scoop a set of car keys off the counter. Apparently, the Malibu of Lucky's nightmares had gone up for auction three times with no bidders. He checked out the contents of a plain white envelope. New license, an ad-dress, and a receipt for a month's rent in the name of Richard Getsinger. Dang, but somebody worked fast.

The receptionist glanced up when Lucky cleared his throat. "You're a friend of Bo's right?"

She nodded and took a step back. Smart lady. Lucky had no right asking on his own, since he'd not exactly been kind to the woman, but maybe Bo's name might soften her up for a favor. "You know where he sits, right?"

Again she nodded. For a normally chatty type, she sure stayed tight-lipped around Lucky, not that he blamed her.

"There's a plant sitting on the file cabinet behind his desk. Would you water it while I'm away?"

He barely caught her whispered, "Sure."

Lucky gave what he hoped passed for a grateful smile. Her eyebrows shot up to her hairline. He added a "Thank you," and braced to catch her if she suddenly fainted. Heh. This being nice crap might have its uses after all. And the best part? If she told anyone, they wouldn't believe her.

In the parking garage, he stopped by his own vehicle, taking out his iPod and the device that channeled his favorite tunes through the Camaro's speakers. If allowed, he'd simply take his own car. He ran a hand across the hood. "Don't worry, old girl. I'll be back."

He locked the door and strolled across the asphalt to the ugliest chicken-shit green Malibu on the planet.

Later in the evening, Cat Lucky curled up next to him on the couch, Lucky studied pictures and profiles, familiarizing himself with the enemy.

The next morning, he dropped the cat and a two month's supply of tuna off with his landlady and headed down I-85.

Buford's Bar and Grill sat on the farthest outskirts of Athens, yet still managed to attract a decent-sized crowd for a Wednesday afternoon.

Today he'd make his presence known. Nothing flashy, simply a "Hey y'all, I'm your new neighbor" and get the hell out. Too bad Walter wouldn't let him play a biker, but Bo'd snagged the only motorcycle currently at their disposal while awaiting auction, and O'Donoghue claimed, "A biker with a big rig license at the very moment they need one? Too convenient. They'd get suspicious."

Lucky wandered into the dimly lit bar shortly after noon, keeping his head down and heading for an empty table. A sign over the bar announced the day's specials, though the scent of burgers and fries in the air did a better job of advertising. A grease-splattered menu offered more choices, few of which would meet with health-conscious Bo's approval. Oh well. Bo wasn't here, Lucky was hungry, and when in Rome, or rather, Athens...

A thin young man in a "At Buford's We Do It Southern Style" T-shirt approached, pencil and pad in hand. Who the hell used a pencil these days? A Clemson Tigers' hat sat backwards on his head, the brilliant orange clashing horribly with the lime green shirt. *Let me get my sunglasses out before you blind me, boy.*

"Welcome to Buford's," the server said. "What can I get 'cha?"

"I'll have a Buford's burger, all the way, a large fry and a Coke." A squirmy sensation took root in the pit of Lucky's stomach. Pre-indigestion or guilt? *Too much fat, too much salt, not enough vitamin A or C*, his conscience chided. Sounded like Bo.

"Sure, I'll be right back with your drink." The kid pronounced "right" as "riiiiiiiigth", in true Georgia style. He moseyed across the plank flooring, disappeared behind a door, and returned a few seconds later with Lucky's drink.

Lucky sipped his Coke and surveyed the room. Four men played pool in the back, swilling beer and sniping obscene comments at each other. Each wore a black leather vest with *441 Cruisers* emblazoned on the back. Lucky recognized two of them from the material Walter supplied.

To the left, a guy sat with his back to Lucky, intent on a game of pinball, or whatever the hell the machine was. The pings and whirls could have been anything. He also wore a leather vest, devoid of gang colors, and kept casting wistful glances at the bikers. A wannabe, then? A group of men in construction garb got up from the next table, tossing dollar bills among the wreckage of their lunch.

The waiter brought his meal, setting down a ton of artery clogging fat before quietly turning away.

Forcing back his better judgment, Lucky munched his hamburger, pausing intermittently chew on a few greasy fries or wash down his mouthful with a swig of Coke from a twice-refilled glass. Keeping his eyes on his meal for the most part, he snuck peeks at the man who'd abandoned the video games to hang out with the pool players.

Sandy blond hair, dark eyes, scrawny build, and maybe a few inches taller than Lucky's five-six. Ninteen-ish, maybe twenty, tops. Bingo. He'd found Jeremy Wilkerson, also known as Jerry. Not part of the gang, but a hanger-on, and a possible way to gain admission into the inner circle, or at least until hooking up with Bo.

The bikers laughed at something the kid said, and one slapped him on the back in an indulgent fashion, while another rolled his eyes behind the boy's back. Not an equal, then. More like a pet. Interesting.

Lucky moseyed over to the bar to pay his bill rather than wait for his server, ensuring the pool players got an eyeful. *Look at me, I've got nothing to hide.* Never glancing behind, he strolled out to the parking lot and climbed into the Malibu. First contact, over and done. Now to find a drug store before indigestion burned a hole through his chest.

After days of self-induced digestive torture, Lucky lunched at Buford's yet again, now set as a daily pattern. Saturday found the place packed. Both pool tables had games going, and a wall of bodies obscured the video machines, many wearing the flaming 441 of the Cruisers colors. Damn, they'd better not put any of those men on recruitment posters. Brrrr... Where was "Queer Eye for the Might-Be-Straight Biker" when you needed them? Sheesh. When was the last time any of them had gotten a haircut from someone qualified to wield scissors?

No tables stood vacant. Lucky grabbed a seat at the bar and perused the menu, a pack of Tums secure in his front pocket. Maybe something less greasy this time, like a grilled chicken breast with a side of coleslaw. Hell, breathing the air in here alone probably raised a man's cholesterol levels.

He ignored the jostling next to him as someone pulled up a stool and sat down. Stale beer and cigarette smoke from the guy's clothes momentarily overpowered the burnt grease stench.

Somebody's watching me. A sidelong peep to the right revealed deep brown eyes staring back over a slightly crooked smile. Contact. Already. Yippee. "I seen you in here a couple of days," the guy said.

Lucky grunted and raised a piece of slivered chicken to his mouth, rolling his eyes up and pretending interest in whatever ballgame played out on the big screen TV above the bar.

"I'm Jerry." The guy thrust out a hand.

Lucky glared at the hand as well as the guy's face, and Jerry withdrew the handshake. Guys like him were a dime a dozen and had swarmed around Victor like fruit flies. Some had hoped to gain money, others basked in the glow of a rich and powerful man, and still others simply wanted to fit in. Far too many found a place in Victor's bed, briefly. If it suited his purposes, Victor used them, chewed them up, and spit them out. Some adapted, hardening into the kind of man Lucky had become. Others didn't make it. No need dwelling on them, they'd made their choices and were beyond anyone's help now.

Someone called his name, and the overeager gnat beside Lucky said, "Gotta run. Nice meeting you," and buzzed off.

"Fuck off," Lucky growled, too low to be heard.

He returned on Monday and so did Jerry. "What do you do?" the kid asked the moment Lucky deigned to turn his way.

"A little of this, a little of that."

The guy propped his elbows on the bar, leaning into Lucky's space. "I can get you a job running errands, if you know what I mean."

"How in the hell would I know what you mean?" Lucky gave the kid his best *leave me the fuck alone* growl. No need seeming too overeager. Besides, all posturing aside, the kid annoyed the hell out of Lucky. How stupid could one be to get caught up with a bunch of drug traffickers? Oh, wait. Yeah. Okay, they both came from less than stellar backgrounds and hung around with the wrong people, but no way was Lucky that annoying or gullible at the kid's age. No fucking way.

Lucky glanced around the bar, hoping to catch sight of Bo or Reyes, anyone but the kid. Oh, right. Ricky Getsinger, ex-con in need of a job. Time to play nice. "What you got in mind?" Act bored, like the offer didn't matter one way or the other. He reached down deep to pull up the man he'd begun creating in O'Donoghue's classroom if not long before, on his knees in front of Victor, awaiting his judgment.

"Nothing big. A few deliveries, maybe."

"I've done some errand work before. Got my CDL," Lucky drawled, in his best county bumpkin voice. In his youth, Lucky'd dreamed of becoming a long-haul trucker, and he'd gotten his first Commercial Driver's License a few weeks after signing onto Victor's payroll. Only, the loads he'd hauled weren't what he'd expected at fourteen, when he'd eyed car haulers full of shiny new Mustangs with envy.

"Cool. I'll talk to my guy and see what he says." The kid dashed off, "easy target" written all over him. Reyes merely took the misguided hero worship the kid didn't even know he offered with every doltish smile. And fuck if Lucky hadn't once worshipped Victor the same way.

A few days later, when his patience neared an end, the kid showed up again. "Mat... my friend has a job for you."

Thanks to a contact younger than most of Lucky's socks, and probably half as smart, Lucky headed south the next day, though he still hadn't met up with Reyes. Or Bo.

CHAPTER THIRTEEN

Asphalt crunched under Lucky's footfalls as he crossed the parking lot to a shiny black F-150. What a beauty, and identical to the one he'd driven here and parked a few feet away, clear down to the tags, registered to a fictitious construction company, this week. Last week the twin Fords had been the property of a restaurant, according to O'Donoghue. Lucky clicked the key fob, opened the door, and climbed inside the waiting truck, tossing his backpack onto the front passenger seat. If bound for Hell, what a classy way to get there.

Somewhere within this marvel of metal, fiberglass, and leather nestled a small fortune in contraband, undetectable by drug dogs or any device currently in use by law enforcement. A rich customer had once brought a Mercedes into the body shop where Lucky had worked while in his teens, asking for a modification to stash valuables. The shop owner installed a safe in a faux floorboard. As impressed as Lucky had been at the time, the hidey-hole in the Mercedes didn't come close to the work he'd overseen for Victor on far less deserving cars.

Nowadays, retrofitting vehicles equaled big business, and lucrative business at that. And the worst part? Even if they tore the truck apart, the cops likely wouldn't find a thing.

Gone were easily found hidden compartments. And hiding was only half the battle. The new designs meshed with the vehicle's existing systems, varied sequences acting as sophisticated combination locks. The stash box on Lucky's old Mustang required using the cruise control at 60 miles per hour, rolling down the right window, and hitting the eject button on the CD player. The F-150's systems likely put the Mustang's security to shame.

Lucky twisted the key in the ignition and fired up the engine. A sweet purr vibrated through the dash. Eyes directly to the front, he eased the truck out of the rest stop parking lot and onto the highway. Checking out the locale too thoroughly wouldn't go well for him, a supposedly dumb ex-con, and he might be watched as part of his test run. Bad guys were a suspicious lot. But any shady characters now starred in one of Keith's many recordings. The asshole did have his uses.

An hour later Lucky turned west on I-10 toward Louisiana. How'd he love to stop for some crawfish or boudin, maybe a praline or two. No time. With fourteen hours and his every move likely monitored, he'd best stay on schedule. Rolling down the window let in the cool night air: the slap of the breeze kept him awake.

Shortly after filling up the truck and his belly at a truck stop, Lucky sailed past Atlanta, riding I-85 and battling early morning shoppers at the outlet park once he turned off the interstate. Another half-hour's ride put him near Athens. Reyes' apartment sat a few miles from the drop-off point, but Lucky's new employer didn't trust him yet. Better to do an anonymous drop, and have someone more trusted collect the truck later. Still no sign of Bo. Worry squirmed through Lucky's gut. It'd been two weeks since Art's accident. Two weeks of an agent twisting in the wind alone, and strict instructions against direct contact with the bureau. Anything could have happened by now. And what role did Bo fill in the trafficking ring? Lucky's briefing said only that Bo had gained Reyes' confidence, nothing more.

Lucky parked the truck behind a convenience store at the junction of 441 and 15, left the keys in the ashtray as instructed, grabbed his backpack, and locked the door on his way out. He wandered across blacktop, eyes peeled for his unknown ride. A loping *whop, whop, whop* reverberated against the building, a vision in black and chrome pulling to a stop a few feet away. Oh hell yeah! A 2011 model Harley Road King gleamed in the sunlight. Damn, what he wouldn't give for such a ride.

Despite his situation, he couldn't help admiring the machine of his dreams. Judging by the added rumble, the pipes weren't stock, and neither was the wide touring seat, complete with passenger backrest. A pair of studded Mustang saddlebags hung down on either side of the back wheel. A journey bag fitted over the backrest rounded out the extras.

The driver toed the kickstand down in a practiced move and hiked a leg to dismount the bike. *441 Cruisers* stood out on the back of his jacket. A black helmet with tinted shield hid the rider's face, and black leather enveloped his body from the neck down, save at the crotch where faded denim peeked through a pair of chaps. Definitely a male, and a well-hung specimen. Sturdy boots completed the outfit. Walter's intel suggested thirty-two members of the motorcycle club. Lucky's count at the bar brought the number up closer to forty.

At another time in life, Lucky might have climbed the biker like a tree for how well he filled out his leather. Now, the chaps merely reminded Lucky of Bo. The biker dug another jacket and helmet from his saddle bags and didn't say a word as he offered them to Lucky. Get on a bike with a stranger? Lucky's withering glare didn't melt the face shield's tint, and earned him a shrug from the stranger. Yeah, being watched. Another fucking test to pass. Better to risk his life in the hands of a jackass than blow a case.

The jacket fit perfectly, and the temperature rose the moment Lucky zipped the padded leather closed. Next came the helmet. A few more weeks, and they wouldn't need leather to keep warm, but April had been unseasonably cool in Georgia this year. The biker climbed back on the beast, straightened up, kicked the stand back against the bike, and turned his helmeted head toward Lucky while firing the engine. *Damn, I'd love to drive this thing.* According to Jameson, an undercover agent should always take his or her own vehicle, but if pressed, should at least insist on driving and never relinquish control. But hell, if Lucky owned that bike, he wouldn't give up the keys either. He braced a hand against the seat and climbed behind the driver, making sure to leave distance between them. Shoving his groin against a stranger's backside wasn't an option.

No sooner did he prop his feet on the foot pegs than the bike shot across the parking lot. Lucky grabbed the firm body in front of him. The driver patted his leg with a gloved hand and he let go. *Don't go getting too friendly on me now, dude.*

They leaned into a curve, the bike, biker, and Lucky in perfect accord. Fighting the natural motion might get them both killed, and many times Lucky'd nearly lost control of his old dirt bike by a squirming brother on the backseat, struggling against gravity's pull. A few more curves, and he relaxed. Whoever drove handled the bike well.

He leaned back to enjoy the view. Pastureland whipped by, a riot of greens, pinks, and blues from wildflowers. The scent of fresh mown hay hung heavy in the air. They left 441 for back roads. Athens lay the other way. Either they weren't going to Athens, or the driver had another agenda.

The asshole got to ride one hell of a bike, and probably never did an honest day's work. Might as well make him earn his keep. Lucky leaned up, putting his mouth near the driver's ear. He launched into a song his Grandma used to sing about a singing cowboy, complete with lots of off-key yodeling. The driver didn't even flinch, merely reached down and turned on a stereo. Country music blasted from front-mounted speakers. Lucky sang louder, the driver turned the volume up until Lucky couldn't hear his own voice.

He collapsed against the backrest and folded his arms across his chest. *Spoilsport.*

Twenty minutes into their ride, the biker leaned back into the V of Lucky's thighs. What the hell? The backrest cut off any escape. Next, a hand reached down and squeezed Lucky's thigh. Oh, hell-the-fuck-no. Lucky wrapped his fingers around the hand and tugged, only to find his fingers enmeshed in black leather. He jerked his hand, but the biker held fast. He leaned up to growl into the driver's ear, "Let go of my fucking hand." The bike hit a bump, bringing Lucky's nose into the warmth of the biker's neck. He inhaled the clean, fresh scent he'd only smelled one other place. Oh, dear God. With the cupped palm of his free hand he reached down past the top of the biker's chaps to cradle the ample swell of a bubble butt.

Bo's fingers tightened on Lucky's, dragging them down to the tiny flaw responsible for the chaps being reduced to

Lucky's price range over a year ago. His first gift to Bo. He buried his nose in Bo's neck, whiffing in the comforting scent of his lover, soaking up what contact their leather-clad bodies allowed. Bo. Here. In his arms. Sort of.

When farmland gave way to neighborhoods, Bo let go of Lucky's hand and put distance between their bodies. Lucky dismounted the bike in front of the rented house he refused to call home. The Harley roared away, leaving Lucky with the helmet and jacket, hoping to use them often.

Damn. The man stayed so in character that his own lover hadn't recognized him until late in the ride, and then only because Bo dropped the mask. O'Donoghue would be proud.

On his way into the house, Lucky rifled through the jacket's pockets and found a scrap of paper with Bo's handwriting. "Happy Birthday. I hope you like the jacket. Sorry about what happened to your last one."

Oh shit. It was April eleventh, wasn't it? Another birthday and not even at home to get his sister's annual card. Lucky hugged the jacket up tight, the scent of leather filling his nostrils along with a faint hint of Bo's cologne.

***

"Here you go." Jerry dropped an envelope onto Lucky's table. He slithered into the opposite chair without waiting for an invitation.

Lucky ignored the money and the minion for the time being, content to chew a roast beef sandwich, the one non-heartburn inducing item on the whole bar's menu.

"The boss says since you did well, he's got more work for you."

"You don't say," Lucky paused eating long enough to reply.

"Yeah." Jerry beamed ear to ear, ignoring the *fuck off* vibes Lucky aimed his way. "In fact, Cy's on his way over to talk to you."

"Cy?" Shit. Was the somersaulting in his gut the beginning of another bout of indigestion? He'd finally get to talk to Bo, even if the worst annoyance this side of Texas would be sitting in.

The kid's face lit up, eyes gleaming. "Cyrus Cooper, one bad-assed motherfucker. When he first came here, the guys," he jabbed his thumb in the direction of the pool tables, "gave him a hard time. After he kicked their asses, they learned to leave him alone."

Be the meanest motherfucker around, and no one will dare mess with you. Good thing Bo took Lucky's advice to heart.

The squawking jukebox and raucous laughter from the pool tables drowned out any lesser noises. The pool players snapped to attention, announcing a new arrival of importance. Lucky wouldn't look until he had to. A vision in black stopped by the table. His eyes roved upward, taking in the chaps, the faded T-shirt, and leather vest. Further up he saw tousled helmet-hair, penetrating dark eyes, and neatly trimmed facial hair, framing full lips. Lucky's wet dream come true. He swallowed hard. Bo had shorn his hair nearly to the scalp, erasing any traces of highlights, and the moustache and beard were new, but something about his eyes...

Bo inclined his head to Lucky, showing not the slightest bit of recognition. "Well, Jerry, you gonna introduce me to your friend?" The faintest hint of a smile creased Bo's lips, but his eyes remained cold. Yep, one hard-assed motherfucker.

"Oh, yeah. Sorry, Cy." Jerry scrambled to his feet and pulled the chair out for Bo to sit. Bo plunked down, ignoring the fawning young man at his elbow. "Cy, this here's Ricky Getsinger. Ricky, meet Cy."

Lucky brought his hand up to take Bo's. Again, the man displayed no signs of recognition. Damn, he was good.

"Nice to meet you... Ricky." Bo tilted his head to the left. "That'll be all, Jerry."

"Oh yeah. Sure, Cy." The kid stumbled over his own feet on the way to the pool tables where he stood by the wall, eyes never leaving Bo. Uh-oh. Lucky'd noticed that look plenty of times on the faces of Victor's hangers-on. Totally smitten.

Back off. He's taken, kid.

The man in front of Lucky appeared chiseled in stone. A perfect likeness of Bo, but with something missing. Cyrus Cooper sat ramrod straight, elbows resting on the table. "You

The kid's shoulders slumped. "I could stay here and help you. You don't need him." Jerry aimed a hot glower in Lucky's direction. Uh-oh. He'd already sniffed out his rival, had he?

"I'm paying him anyway. Might as well get my money's worth." Bo gave the kid a smile. The affection might not have been for Lucky, but his cock rose anyway.

Jerry straightened. "I'll see you tomorrow, won't I, Cy?" Lucky imagined him as a dancing puppy, tongue lolling out, prancing on its back legs while begging for attention. Yet, in a few years, if he kept on his current course, the naïve kid might turn into the kind of man Lucky hunted down for a living. Best not to underestimate him. Even the most vicious fighting dogs started out as harmless puppies.

"Sure," Bo drawled with a distracted half-smile as he divided his attention between his conversation and the iPad. "I'll be right here."

Oh good Lord. The man dropped fuel on Jerry's fire, like the young 'un needed encouragement. Jerry beamed ear to ear. "Okay, man. Catch you later." He darted out the door. A moment later, a bike lacking the rich timbre of a Harley sputtered to life. A Honda. Had to be a Honda.

"Well, well, well. Just the two of us. All alone. Whatever shall we do?" Lucky took a step closer, Bo took a step back.

"Follow me," Bo said, touching a finger to his lips.

Yeah, the hair was different, the beard and moustache were new, but the face and body belonged to Bo. The eyes, though. The same dark brown flecked with gold stared out from the man's face, but nothing in them said Bo lived there, or even made regular visits.

Lucky followed Bo's leather-covered back to the far side of garage, passing a familiar F-150. Through the open door he peeked into the backseat area at an open panel. Shit! The entire sidewall of truck bed made one huge compartment, complete with a false bottom on the bed itself. No doubt the other side matched. He spotted several smaller caches as well. He must've hauled up one hell of a lot of shit.

Bo slid a panel on the far wall out of the way to expose another door, and keyed in a number sequence on a control panel. The state of the art lock seemed out of place in the rundown garage. "Here's what you brought up from Texas," he said.

"Are you sure we can't be heard here?"

"Yeah. If Mateo wants to record what's going on, he takes folks into the office. If he wants to speak privately, he comes out here."

Lucky stepped inside a vault. Shelves lined the four walls of a closet-sized space, most of them filled to capacity with cardboard boxes similar to the one Bo'd brought into the office.

"They're making the rounds of the clubs tonight with what we brought up last month, but here's your haul, still untouched. And plenty more where that came from." Bo reached a hand into a case and extracted a handful of packets, each filled with gleaming crystalline powder. "We're still building our local customer base."

Lucky took a packet from Bo's hand. Yep, the same stuff from the SNB conference room. He stuffed the evidence back into the box and added a transmitter, slipping the device into the corrugation of the cardboard. "Where's Reyes?" he asked. "And why do you appear to be running the show?'

"Mateo prefers to stay behind the scenes, trusting me to do the dirty work." Bo's formerly manicured nails now sported jagged edges and showed a rind of black underneath the tips. *Dirty work* might be literal.

Wait. *Mateo*, not *Reyes*. Normally Lucky would scold Bo for getting too close, but in this case, the closer Bo got, the quicker they'd disband Reyes' outfit and go home. "Exactly how close are you and Reyes?"

"Closer than I thought I'd be at this point. By the way, how's Art doing?"

"Well enough to be moved, last I heard, and on his way to Atlanta."

"Good. Too bad about Jack, but rumor says I took him out to get his job. I never thought being accused of murder would ever win me so much clout and put me closer to my target." Bo dropped a bombshell. "It happened fast, but I've been promoted to Sergeant at Arms."

"Jack?" *Sergeant at Arms?*

did good, Ricky. My partner and I have more work for you, if you're interested."

Partner? No telling who might be watching. "What you got in mind?" Lucky took another bite of roast beef and moaned. Bo didn't respond with cutting comments about cancer or heart attacks.

A server appeared and placed a beer on the table. Eyes never leaving Lucky's, Bo said, "Thanks, Brenda. I'll have my usual." The woman scampered off. "Can't talk business on an empty stomach," he told Lucky. She returned a few minutes later with a burger on a plate, or rather, what looked like a burger, but with no meat showing beneath the bun.

Bo took a bite before resuming the conversation. The Bo Schollenberger Lucky knew wouldn't dare talk with his mouth full. "We have a few smaller vehicles, like the truck you brought back from Texas, but I understand you drive big rigs too."

"I've done a few cross-country hauls."

"Good. I also heard that you've got reasons to make sure you're careful."

"Twenty years for a second offense makes a man cautious." He wondered if Bo had checked up on his fake profile to impress the partner, or if the comment merely fit the script.

A brief smile flitted across Bo's face. The way he carried himself, the confidence, the danger. Fuck. He wasn't merely pretending to be Cyrus Cooper, he *was* Cyrus Cooper.

"I need a man I can trust, Ricky. Are you that man?" Bo ran a finger around the top of his beer bottle, dipping the tip of his finger into the hole. The flirt.

Back in class again, denying being a cop. No need to answer "I am" to whoever might have tuned in. Any asshole could lie. "Time will tell," Lucky replied instead. He saluted Bo with his glass of Coke.

Bo cocked an eyebrow and returned the salute, reaching into his pocket to pull out a scrap of paper. "Be at this address tonight at six o'clock." He raised his Bud Light to his lips and guzzled down half the bottle in one go without flinching. Bo didn't like beer, preferring wine. Oh yeah, right. Cyrus probably bought brew by the case.

But a light beer and meatless burger in a biker bar? How many times had some jerkoff laughed, only to find a bottle jammed up his nostril? Judging from the wary-eyed bikers huddled around the pool table—not laughing, and staring at Bo with a pall of dread hanging over them—no one called Cyrus Cooper out on anything. *And what does a bad-assed vegetarian biker eat? Any damned thing he wants.*

Lucky lifted the card from Bo's fingers. Mateo's Garage. Bingo! Yeah, time to meet the rest of the folks he'd soon put behind bars.

At five minutes before six, Lucky pulled up to a mechanic's shop. A half-dozen motorcycles stood clustered together near the bay doors, engines pinging as they cooled. A few cars sat off to the side. He'd brought his helmet and jacket, left in the trunk, in case an opportunity presented itself to curl into Bo's back again. While Lucky wanted to drive, riding did have its advantages. Free range motion for roaming hands being one of them.

Music blasted from inside the building, sounding like a party in progress.

He passed the assembled Harleys; Bo's sticking out like a sore thumb. Not a speck of dust marred the glossy black fenders, and the leather seat gleamed from a recent oil treatment, no doubt. Lucky smiled. No matter how good the man was at pretending to be someone else, parts of Bo's character still shone through. Good. Maybe he wouldn't lose touch with himself.

No one could fault Lucky for pausing to admire the leather and chrome masterpieces, right? And if they didn't like it, well, Lucky hadn't been in a boxing ring in a while and could use the practice. He bent down to inspect the pipes on the closest bike. Damn, what he wouldn't give to own one of these bad boys.

He spotted a tear no bigger than the width of his thumb in the seat. With a discreet stroke, Lucky flipped a tracker into the hole. Another device found its way into a saddle bag. Even if found, the gizmos could pass for broken rivets. He made note of which bikes he tagged. In all likelihood, Bo's bike already carried a few devices, both from the department and the outfit he currently worked for. So much for honor among thieves. Lucky'd borrow one of Keith's fancy toys later and do a full sweep.

Jerry appeared in the opened office door the moment Lucky stepped into the bay. The music blasted louder. "C'mon in, Ricky. Everybody else is already here." He stared past Lucky to the Malibu. "Damn, man, you actually let people see you driving that piece of shit?"

Insolent pup. "Don't laugh, it's paid for," Lucky shot back, failing to add, *by somebody else*. The mouthy brat reminded him of Daytona. *Nope, don't go there*.

He drew in a deep breath and crossed to the door. About a dozen men milled around inside the cramped office, ranging from a bearded ZZ Top lookalike to a buzz-cut cop wannabe. Three, maybe four, carried themselves like ex-military.

Biker, biker, skater boy. Yup. They needed their token redneck. Lucky could do that. He stalked into the room, head high, feeling the eyes of the men on him. Several passed him off as inconsequential and turned away, while others sized him up. His lack of height caused many to underestimate him, and he wasn't above exploiting their stupidity. Chihuahuas might be small, but the little suckers bit hard.

A few men in leather vests stood around a refrigerator sucking down brews, while the clean-cut guys formed their own group, sprawled around a rickety table. They snapped to attention when Bo strolled into the room, a cardboard box hoisted on one shoulder. All eyes followed the box to the countertop by a grease-smeared computer. Dressed in black again, Bo could have shown up at the SNB office and not be recognized. The way he carried himself and the hardened steel in his eyes was far removed from the caring, save-the-world Bo Schollenberger. No. Not Bo. Cyrus Cooper. Completely different men.

And yet, the man's newfound confidence jolted Lucky to the core. A niggling discomfort in his belly that might have been his conscience scolded him for lusting after another man. Was this another man or was Bo's alter ego simply another so far unseen facet of an intriguing personality?

Bo, or Cy, rather, shifted his eyes from biker to biker. Lucky almost heard the *click, click, click* of wheels turning in his head. He gave nothing away when his gaze slid past Lucky without lingering.

"What about him?" a wary-eyed cop-type asked.

"That's Ricky, our new driver," Cy replied. "He stays." He pulled a box cutter out of his back pocket and slit the tape on the carton, holding the lid high to avoid nicking the contents. Inside, tiny clear packets held white powder, the black skull logo impossible to miss even from a distance. Cy motioned Jerry over with a wave of his hand. "Count them out," he ordered.

Arms folded across his chest, Cy stepped off to the side, keen eyes taking in the count. The barest tip of a pistol grip poked out from a bulge beneath his unzipped jacket, concealment probably the only reason he wore padded leather on a seventy degree day while not on the bike. Jerry formed twelve piles on the table and then pulled an iPad from under the counter to punch in numbers as each man claimed his goods. The men scooped the packets into anything from bank deposit bags to backpacks. Damn, what a lot of drugs. Plenty of folks would lose their minds tonight. Had Bo managed to tag any of those bags yet?

One by one the men left the warehouse, leaving behind beer cans and the empty box. A few cast suspicious glances at Lucky in passing, but no one spent much time staring at Bo except for Jerry, who needed a few lessons in hiding the obvious. Bo didn't even seem to realize he had a fan. If Lucky didn't know better, he'd swear Cyrus Cooper left the garage every night to go home and bang women, yet there Jerry sat, his adoring eyes on someone he didn't stand a snowball's chance in hell of getting.

Bikes thundered to life in the parking lot, the grumble of pipes fading once the bikers rounded the building.

"You better get home, Jerry," Bo said.

The kid's shoulders slumped. "I could stay here and help you. You don't need him." Jerry aimed a hot glower in Lucky's direction. Uh-oh. He'd already sniffed out his rival, had he?

"I'm paying him anyway. Might as well get my money's worth." Bo gave the kid a smile. The affection might not have been for Lucky, but his cock rose anyway.

Jerry straightened. "I'll see you tomorrow, won't I, Cy?" Lucky imagined him as a dancing puppy, tongue lolling out, prancing on its back legs while begging for attention. Yet, in a few years, if he kept on his current course, the naïve kid might turn into the kind of man Lucky hunted down for a living. Best not to underestimate him. Even the most vicious fighting dogs started out as harmless puppies.

"Sure," Bo drawled with a distracted half-smile as he divided his attention between his conversation and the iPad. "I'll be right here."

Oh good Lord. The man dropped fuel on Jerry's fire, like the young 'un needed encouragement. Jerry beamed ear to ear. "Okay, man. Catch you later." He darted out the door. A moment later, a bike lacking the rich timbre of a Harley sputtered to life. A Honda. Had to be a Honda.

"Well, well, well. Just the two of us. All alone. Whatever shall we do?" Lucky took a step closer, Bo took a step back.

"Follow me," Bo said, touching a finger to his lips.

Yeah, the hair was different, the beard and moustache were new, but the face and body belonged to Bo. The eyes, though. The same dark brown flecked with gold stared out from the man's face, but nothing in them said Bo lived there, or even made regular visits.

Lucky followed Bo's leather-covered back to the far side of garage, passing a familiar F-150. Through the open door he peeked into the backseat area at an open panel. Shit! The entire sidewall of truck bed made one huge compartment, complete with a false bottom on the bed itself. No doubt the other side matched. He spotted several smaller caches as well. He must've hauled up one hell of a lot of shit.

Bo slid a panel on the far wall out of the way to expose another door, and keyed in a number sequence on a control panel. The state of the art lock seemed out of place in the rundown garage. "Here's what you brought up from Texas," he said.

"Are you sure we can't be heard here?"

"Yeah. If Mateo wants to record what's going on, he takes folks into the office. If he wants to speak privately, he comes out here."

Lucky stepped inside a vault. Shelves lined the four walls of a closet-sized space, most of them filled to capacity with cardboard boxes similar to the one Bo'd brought into the office.

"They're making the rounds of the clubs tonight with what we brought up last month, but here's your haul, still untouched. And plenty more where that came from." Bo reached a hand into a case and extracted a handful of packets, each filled with gleaming crystalline powder. "We're still building our local customer base."

Lucky took a packet from Bo's hand. Yep, the same stuff from the SNB conference room. He stuffed the evidence back into the box and added a transmitter, slipping the device into the corrugation of the cardboard. "Where's Reyes?" he asked. "And why do you appear to be running the show?'

"Mateo prefers to stay behind the scenes, trusting me to do the dirty work." Bo's formerly manicured nails now sported jagged edges and showed a rind of black underneath the tips. *Dirty work* might be literal.

Wait. *Mateo*, not *Reyes*. Normally Lucky would scold Bo for getting too close, but in this case, the closer Bo got, the quicker they'd disband Reyes' outfit and go home. "Exactly how close are you and Reyes?"

"Closer than I thought I'd be at this point. By the way, how's Art doing?"

"Well enough to be moved, last I heard, and on his way to Atlanta."

"Good. Too bad about Jack, but rumor says I took him out to get his job. I never thought being accused of murder would ever win me so much clout and put me closer to my target." Bo dropped a bombshell. "It happened fast, but I've been promoted to Sergeant at Arms."

"Jack?" *Sergeant at Arms?*

"The informant, and the last guy to hold the position." Bo fumbled with a few boxes and lowered his voice. "By the way, I owe you another birthday spoiling when all this is over. Does the jacket fit? I had to guess the size."

Last year, Lucky had fought against acknowledging the passing of time. This year, he held his tongue. If Bo owed him a spoiling, he'd have to stay around long enough for Lucky to collect. "Yeah, just fine. And thanks." Though the dragon statue from last year's birthday had grown on Lucky, he'd get much more use from a jacket, particularly if they did a lot of riding this assignment.

Bo locked up and led Lucky outside. "Did you bring the jacket and your helmet?"

Lucky nodded and trotted over to dig the requested items from the Malibu's trunk and put them on. Once the sun set, he'd be grateful for the padded leather's warmth. Strange how an outlaw biker gang conformed to helmet laws. They'd likely be laughed out of the gang, though, if arrested for no helmet instead of racing, fighting, drug dealing, or another hardcore pastime.

Bo climbed onto the driver's seat of the bike like he'd been born there.

"I could drive," Lucky ventured. Hell, until he saved up enough for a down payment on his own, driving a bike owned by the SNB would work.

"I've got a motorcycle license. You don't."

"I do too. Had the thing since I turned twenty." He'd acquired his first license during one of Victor's indulgent moments, and even after losing his bike he'd renewed it for wishful thinking. Though Lucky wouldn't admit now to having once owned a Kawasaki.

"Does your license say 'Getsinger'?"

"Well, no, but—"

"Got it on ya?"

"Well, no, but—"

"It's my bike."

"No it's not."

Bo grinned, teeth gleaming beneath his open face shield. "Says so on the registration."

"Ah, come on. Have a heart." Lucky put all of his acting skills to work on a convincing pout, and apparently fell short. Chances were cameras watched their every move, but while Reyes might think him an annoying asshole, not knowing the history, he wouldn't get the subtext.

"You don't know where we're going, I do. I don't let other men ride my bike, no way, no how."

Lucky pulled out the big guns, mouthing "I'll blow you."

Bo answered with an eye roll. "You'd blow me anyway," he mouthed back.

Well, yeah. Lucky would. "Then I'll—"

"Ricky?"

"Yeah?"

"Get on this damned bike before I leave your ass."

Grumbling, Lucky climbed on the passenger seat. Good thing Cyrus's driving beat Bo's, because Bo drove like a grandma heading to Sunday school. Cyrus had better appreciation for speed and the joys of a well-leaned curve.

Before pulling away, Bo popped a CD into the bike's player. To the strains of Billy Ray Cyrus' *Achy Breaky Heart*, they headed off into the evening. "They're playing our song," Bo said.

Lucky wriggled a hand under Bo's ass. Hey, he'd insisted on driving.

CHAPTER FOURTEEN

They pulled up to a barn in the middle of nowhere. Two men wearing Cruisers' colors stepped from the shadows to open the doors, allowing Bo to drive inside. "That stash at Mateo's—" Bo's words echoed from the helmet he pulled off over his face. "Just the tip of the iceberg."

The doors closed and the lights came on. Holy shit. Boxes sat on shelves as far as the eye could see. Though merely a dilapidated tobacco barn from the outside, inside the building rivaled many pharmaceutical warehouses Lucky'd been in. "Those guys at the garage are being tested. If they prove themselves loyal, they move up in the ranks. Feel privileged to be here. Most of the gang would give their eyeteeth for the honor."

Yeah, Victor had used similar methods for selecting his inner circle.

"She's loaded and ready to go, boss," one of the bikers said, a grizzled man with too much gut and too little hair.

"Good. Now, Ricky, you're about to find out why we hired you."

They stepped out a back door. A shiny Kenworth sat idling, a trailer hooked up behind. A tractor-trailer? A whole trailer worth of goods? Damn!

"Now you get to drive," Bo said. "Follow me. And trust me, if we weren't desperate for a driver who can manage thirteen gears and a splitter—" Bo cocked an eyebrow at one of their escorts, who flushed and turned away. The guy must have made that transmission howl with pain. "Anyway, if you couldn't make this baby go quiet, you wouldn't be here."

Lucky climbed into the cab. Listen to those horses run. A shiver raced up his spine. Damn. Nothing like being in the cab of a diesel. He familiarized himself with the interior, then shifted into gear and rounded the barn to fall in behind Bo. They drove south, down I-85 to Atlanta, and pulled up outside an apartment complex on the outskirts. Lucky rolled down the window when Bo came alongside. "Get out," Bo commanded. Lucky turned off the engine, locked the Kenworth's doors, and placed the keys in Bo's outstretched hand.

"Stay here and be quiet." Bo, or rather, Cy, hopped off the bike and disappeared behind an innocuous looking seven-story building. Lucky kept his eyes on the side mirror, watching the action without appearing to.

From the garage front to the freelance delivery boys, the main warehouse and even the distribution routes, the whole enterprise reminded Lucky of Victor Mangiardi setting up a new operation in a small town. Yet Victor was dead and had never dealt with non-pharmaceuticals. Coincidence? Or did everything illegal simply remind Lucky of Victor?

He sent off a text message to Walter. Somewhere in the department, pinpoints lit a map, tracking the position of the goods. Right now the SNB probably had enough evidence to bring down a few dozen people, but that wasn't Walter's style. He'd mentioned a huge operation and DEA involvement, but nothing in the intel folder mentioned a warehouse. The team needed to bide their time, let the perpetrators dig in deep, and then swoop down to round them all up. Inter-agency cooperation also meant time lags to pass the word and get everyone into position, whereas Walter could assemble a team and have them on site in a matter of hours.

A loud cough brought Lucky out of his musings. A moment later, Bo took his place under the bike's handlebars. "This was our only stop," he said. "Now to go make payroll."

The crew had already assembled by the time they arrived at the garage, most of the leather-set well on their way to drunk. Bo held court at the head of a scarred table, tallying up sales. A man Lucky recognized from photos stood at Bo's back. Ah, the head honcho himself. Though Bo didn't flinch when the man's hand fell to his shoulder, he held himself far more stiffly than normal.

Reyes missed Lucky's height by an inch or so, but his naturally stocky build more than made up for his lack of stature. Pure evil lurked in the intelligent eyes that darted this way and that, never missing a single detail, no doubt. Lucky felt those eyes upon him more than once, even if, upon glancing up, he couldn't catch the guy in the act. One butt-ugly as hell motherfucker, inside and out. And more mean per inch than Lucky.

A hatchet-like face, complete with a vivid scar across one cheek, marked Reyes as someone who'd seen his fair share of dangerous situations. The fact he'd lived to see another day indicated he wasn't a man to take lightly. Coal-black hair, shot through with gray and tied at the neck, spoke of Spanish ancestry, and his blue eyes and pale skin stood out among the others in the room who boasted Hispanic roots.

Nothing about Mateo Reyes seemed familiar, except for the pinched cruelty of his mouth that brought Stephan Mangiardi to mind. Here was a man who'd just as soon kill you as look at you. And Bo'd managed to ingratiate himself with a hardened criminal.

Lucky observed Bo with a mixture of pride and concern as he counted out the proceeds of the night's sales and handed a portion to each man.

Once the errand boys left, Bo said, "Be ready for another trip on Wednesday. When we're more comfortable with you, we'll give you your own route." He stepped closer to murmur, "Meet me at the bar," then strode across the garage, Reyes on his heels.

Bo shouldn't be alone with a suspect, no telling what might happen. "Hurt him and die," Lucky growled under his breath.

Lucky picked at a pile of sweet-potato fries, one of the few items offered after midnight at the bar, trying hard not to stare at the door. He let loose a heavy breath when the door swung open and Bo strolled in. "Gimme a beer," Bo called, stepping up to the bar. He chatted with the barmaid a moment, perusing the surroundings, and did a double-take as if only then noticing Lucky's presence. He made his excuses and drifted over to Lucky's table.

"What you doing out so late?" he asked, folding himself down into a chair across the table.

"Ah, couldn't sleep," Lucky replied. "How 'bout you?"

A slow grin spread across the man's face. "Taking care of business. I'll be heading home directly." He dropped his voice and added, "Pull your car around back. I'll be there in a minute." After stopping by the bar for another chat with the barmaid, he dropped a few coins into a gaming machine, a study in casual indifference.

Lucky paid his check and wandered out into the night, hiding his car as Bo instructed. He dug the helmet and leather jacket out of the trunk and readied himself for whatever Bo planned. A few minutes later a quiet *chuk-chuk-chuk* announced the bike's approach.

Bo pulled to a stop, not saying a word while Lucky crawled on the back of the Road King.

The bike roared into the night, the pipes making sweet music. Somehow the sound seemed purer at night. Now if only a few bills could be rearranged, making a visit to the local Harley dealership doable once this case ended.

They sped around a curve and out of sight of the bar. Time to relax, though Lucky's hold on Bo didn't ease. Any excuse for contact. The temperature rose a few degrees as they sped down West Broad, past Steak 'n Shake, KFC, a Pizza Hut/Taco Bell combo, and Checkers restaurants. The lingering scents of fried chicken, barbeque, and burgers crept under Lucky's face shield to tease his nose. Soon enough, they left the street lights of town for the darkness of country, the headlight's beam providing the only light.

For about twenty minutes they rode, eventually leaving asphalt for a dirt road. "Hang on," Bo said, "the ride's about to get rough."

Boing, boing, bump, clack! Damn! Lucky's teeth clicked together on a bounce over a vicious rut. Dry red clay filled his nostrils. He tightened his hold on Bo and ducked down closer to anchor them together and use his partner for a windbreak.

The juddering evened out onto a smoother path, and the Harley's headlights fell on a log cabin that sported a garage. The door rose, and Bo eased the bike inside.

He parked and held the beast still for Lucky to dismount, then shucked his helmet. An overhead light illuminated his smile. "It's not much, but it's home. For now." He held out his hand for Lucky's helmet and placed them side by side on a shelf.

A moment passed, then two. Lucky held his ground, uncertainty rooting him to the spot. He'd waited months for this moment. Any more clenching and his heart might burst. Alone, Bo within easy reach, nothing stopping him. Did Bo still want him? The moments ticked away. A few feet in front of him, Bo waited, arms folded across his chest. His normally expressive features offered no hint of what he might be thinking.

One minute Lucky stood alone, the next, they came together in a flurry of lips, tongues, and roving hands, the tickle of Bo's moustache and beard adding an unfamiliar thrill. Oh God! How good to hold the man again. Lucky's heart double-timed.

"I missed you," Bo murmured between rounds of reacquainting himself with Lucky's mouth, sounding more like the Bo Lucky knew and loved than the criminal Cyrus.

Bo, he's Bo. I have my Bo back. "I missed you too." An ache bloomed in Lucky's chest for both the lost time and the sweetness of the moment. The scent of Bo's cologne filled Lucky's nostrils, and the strands of his short hair were goose-down soft beneath Lucky's fingertips.

Lucky dragged the zipper down on Bo's jacket. Their eyes met and held when Lucky slipped the jacket from Bo's shoulders. Lucky shrugged out of his own jacket and tossed it on a workbench to join Bo's.

With trembling fingers, he rolled Bo's T-shirt up, skating his fingertips over taut abs while peppering kisses up the man's pleasure trail. The bulge in Bo's jeans matched the cramped swell in Lucky's own. Still, he took his time. One false move might end things before they'd properly begun. He re-familiarized himself with the freckles splashed across Bo's chest, easing the shirt up higher to expose more skin, welcoming each new revelation with a brush of his lips.

They parted to remove their boots. Snaps popped open, and buckles and loose change jangled to the floor when Bo stripped off his chaps and they both shimmied from their jeans.

Bo moved to fold the chaps. Lucky stopped him. After too many hours of waiting, time to fulfill a fantasy. "On. I want those on." Bo's eyebrows rose toward his hairline, but after a moment he chuckled and re-zipped and snapped the chaps over bare skin.

Finally, Bo and Lucky stood naked in the garage, except for Bo's chaps. The dull glow of an overhead bulb painted Bo with shadows and light, accentuating each dip and curve of his torso. He'd filled out some; hoisting engines and carting around equipment had added mass to his lean build. Somewhere along the way, he'd stopped trimming his chest hair. The sparse yet unruly mass of dark curls tempted Lucky's finger to play. The sight of Bo's fully erect cock framed by black leather turned Lucky's insides to mush—his legs were none too steady either. Dropping to his knees and worshipping the uncut length seemed like a good idea. A very good idea.

Lucky knelt, grasping the base and sliding the purplish head between his lips to suck on the tip. Above him, Bo moaned and palmed the back of Lucky's head, holding, but not pushing. Yet.

The taste of the man burst on Lucky's tongue, familiar and new all at the same time. His discomfort from kneeling on concrete faded away. Nothing mattered anymore but the cock in Lucky's mouth, and the man gasping so sweetly above him. He ran his hands along the edge of the chaps, where leather framed Bo's crotch, following a path of stitched leather to an ample swell of ass. Lucky grabbed a double-handful of firm glutes, using a little force to encourage Bo closer. He opened wider, taking all he possibly could into his mouth. Oh hell yeah.

Bo bucked and squirmed, panted gasps warning Lucky when to back off, pleading whines telling him when to pick up the pace. How well they fit together, understood what the other wanted by a mere glance, a moan, a touch.

Bo swayed, brushing his leather-covered leg against Lucky's cock. Oh damn. Lucky clamped down on the urge to grab a shin and hump until he came. *Deep breaths, in, out. Control. Make the moment last.*

He climbed slowly to his feet, anticipation squirming in his belly.

Bo turned and leaned over the still-pinging bike, keeping his legs away from the scalding pipes. Oh dear Lordy in heaven. Bo's incredible ass pointed skyward, framed by black leather.

Good thing Lucky came prepared this time. Ramming his hand into the pocket of his discarded jeans, he located the tiny bottle he'd filled last night just in case. He slicked his fingers and ran them over the tight pucker of Bo's hole. The dark pink skin glistened from the slickness, beckoning. Lucky slipped a finger inside. Oh hell, Bo was tight. He reared back against Lucky's hand. Ah, someone was impatient. A good thing.

One finger became two, and Lucky stroked his free hand down Bo's back. He took a nip from the firm globe of Bo's ass cheek. Bo hissed in response.

Now wasn't the time to push boundaries or rehash old arguments. Lucky sheathed himself and slipped into welcoming warmth. He gripped Bo's hips and gave a series of shallow thrusts. A familiar whimper told him, "Oh, God that feels good."

He whimpered in kind, intense pleasure robbing him of speech. He braced his hands against Bo's back, taking care not to topple the bike while he worked to join them more completely. Months of abstinence and loneliness, gone in a flash. Ah, the sweet union of flesh and the scent of man on man sex.

Their breathing roared in Lucky's ears in the enclosed space. He pushed in and held. Oh, God. How had he survived without this? He dug his fingers into Bo's hips as much to hold himself up as to cling for dear life.

The pinging bike, Bo's grunts, groans, and garbled, "more", "harder" and "please", the faint traces of man, cologne, sex, leather, and motor oil. Heaven.

Lucky withdrew until only the head of his cock remained buried, then drove back in, angling to peg Bo's gland. In, out. Letting go of his self-control, he set a steady rhythm, brain fizzing out and instinct taking over.

"Oh God, oh God, oh God," Bo chanted. He humped against the bike seat, the play of muscles in his ass and back giving away his actions. Lucky bent down, trailing kisses up and down Bo's spine. "I'm gonna come," Bo choked out.

Lucky gripped him harder, picking up the pace. Bo's muscles clenched and unintelligible sounds marked his release. He shuddered in Lucky's grasp, and Lucky let loose, holding tight and burying himself to the hilt. Liquid warmth filled the condom, fluttery feelings deep within pulsing. Lucky's knees weakened, and he arched across Bo's back to keep from falling down.

"Now I know why that seat looks so supple," he couldn't help but jibe. "Come makes a pretty good leather conditioner, doesn't it?"

Bo joined him in a laugh, the echo rumbling through his chest and up into Lucky's ear. "There's a reason folks call Harleys the world's biggest vibrators."

Once they'd recovered, they gathered up their clothes and made their way to Bo's bedroom. They lay in bed, Bo's head on Lucky's shoulder.

"How are you, really?" Lucky stroked his fingers over Bo's ribs.

"Not as good as I'm making out," Bo replied.

Lucky stayed quiet. Best to let the man speak on his own terms. He didn't have long to wait.

"In ways, pretending to be someone else helps with some issues, because Cyrus didn't have my upbringing, though he did have to watch buddies die in the Marines. Seems Reyes served in the military, and swapping war stories helped me get into his good graces."

"Go on." Lucky stopped stroking and pulled Bo tight against his chest. *Reyes* now, not *Mateo*. Good. Bo needed the distance.

"Since I'm not going to counseling at the moment, the pressure builds. Sometimes I have nightmares about my time in Afghanistan and about my father. I hear Drew screaming, and I go back to the night I thought the house was burning down."

Bo'd only been a kid when his daddy had tied him and his brother to their beds and gone out drinking. A neighbor's house fire had traumatized both boys, convincing them they were going to die horribly. Man, but the senior Schollenberger's ass needed kicking.

"I wake up the next morning and have to put my panic aside to play a role. While it works during the day, the anxiety gets me at night."

"I'm here now," Lucky assured him. "As much as I can be without raising suspicion, I will be."

A pat on the arm gave Bo's answer, saying thanks more than words could. "The strange part is, the more I'm Cy, the more the dreams fade. I find myself depending on my alter ego to give me a good night's sleep." He nestled more snuggly against Lucky's chest. "I mean, I know Cy isn't real, but at times I find myself seeing him as a separate person that I want to emulate. At other times, I'm so totally him I forget who Bo is."

Not good for the lines to blur completely. Or for Bo to grow addicted to his created persona.

"Wanna hear the strange part?"

It gets stranger? "What?" Lucky braced for the worst.

"I've met Cy before, or rather, not *Cy,* but the disassociated part of me playing the role."

Bo squirmed before resuming his tale. This Lucky had to hear. "I was a different person when I enlisted, cocky, full of myself. Watching a few buddies die changes a man." Bo shivered. "Cy is who I might have been if I'd not learned a few valuable lessons on how precious life is."

While Lucky would gladly spare the man the past pain, he couldn't help but be grateful for how Bo turned out.

Bo continued, "As Ricky, I see you as you might have been if you'd never met Victor Mangiardi. Oh, you still have a bit of sarcasm, but you're less sure of yourself, more willing to listen."

He was?

"Aren't we a fucked up pair? With no idea who we really are?"

Oh shit. Now Bo sounded depressed. A change of subject might do them both good and pull Bo out of the dark spot in his head where he sometimes disappeared. Besides, Lucky didn't want to dwell on the *less sure of yourself* observation, a product of O'Donaghue's lectures, which added to the new situation he found himself in. "Have you met anyone else besides Reyes and the guys from tonight?"

"Just Cruiser members. He trusts me, but not enough to talk about his supplier. You know pretty much what I do. The goods arrive in about five vehicles that get rotated. He'd hired a trucker who made a few trips up from Texas and then disappeared. I never even knew his name or what happened to him, and none of our guys handle a rig worth a damn. I've been looking for a replacement for a while, laying the groundwork in case Walter sent you."

Being out of touch with the department, Bo might not know what they'd turned up on their end of the investigation. "No one else has managed any better. Searching turns up nothing, and any attempts at tracking the trucks ends at the border. Whoever we're dealing with has a nice little assortment of trackers in a barn somewhere, and surveillance cameras can't get a good image." Victor had taught Lucky to perform periodic sweeps on cargo to minimize tracking. However, trackers were more sophisticated now, and so were criminals. He'd take the camera issues up with Keith the next time he reported to the office. "What's Reyes like?"

"Quiet. He rides his Harley, works in his shop, sends money home to his mother. He's got to be loaded, but he lives in a cheap apartment and, other than his bike, doesn't seem to spend much money on himself, though I've seen him carry over twenty thousand dollars at a time. Each truck returned to Texas takes back more cash than I ever imagined seeing in one place. He claims to come from a small village in Mexico, but he builds vehicle traps you wouldn't believe."

Back in Lucky's day, Victor paid top dollar for body work. Even without the smuggling, in all likelihood Reyes' mother lived like the queen.

"It looks like you got a nice setup for yourself," Lucky said.

"Getting close to the man was tough. Took a full month for him to trust me after he hired me on at the garage, and he pitted me against his men. I literally had to fight my way to the top. Thanks for the boxing lesson, by the way. I've quoted your 'I'm the best' speech on more than one occasion. Then when Jack died, leaving his position up for grabs, I took advantage. Laid a few guys out too."

So, the kid's tales were true. Bo actually had kicked ass to gain position.

"Once Reyes makes up his mind about a person, he doesn't look back, though he keeps an eye on me. It's hard to hide a biker wearing colors, and I've been followed a few times."

"How about relationships? Anyone else he's close to?"

"I've seen him out with women, but they're never at his apartment when I'm there. The one time a girlfriend showed up at the shop, he yelled at her in Spanish until she went away. I have a feeling he uses them and doesn't want them hanging around." Bo let out a yawn. "The only pictures on the walls of his apartment are of his mother and sisters. He's a real lone-wolf type. I'm surprised he tolerates me, since he doesn't seem to have any other friends."

Friends. Uh-oh. "And you're his friend now?"

"No," Bo replied. "Cyrus is. Cy can stand toe to toe with the guy and not flinch. Personally, he scares me. Sometimes he gets creepy quiet, like he's listening to my thoughts. I've watched him call the guys out on things and wonder how he knows."

"The women he sleeps with might be sleeping with his men too." Victor certainly had no qualms about planting spies in a rival's bed. He'd never asked that of Lucky, but he'd asked it of others.

"Yeah, maybe."

"What about the kid? He's got a bad case of hero worship going on."

Bo's chuckle reverberated through his chest. "He's not a bad kid. He's never had a positive role model in his life, no one to look up to. He fell in with the wrong crowd. Besides, the little booger reminds me of my brother Drew. "

Lucky squinted down at Bo, who peered up through his lashes. "I know, Lucky. You're going to tell me not to get too close and remind me that the guy could face serious charges when all this is over, but I can't seem to convince him to get out without raising suspicions."

"Well, hell. What good am I if you're going to deliver your own lectures?"

"A few things come to mind." Bo reached down and grabbed Lucky's groin. His hand retreated way too soon. "Anyway, don't think me ungrateful, but working without you staring over my shoulders, ready to catch me when I fall, is making me more cautious. Yes, I like Jerry. In other circumstances, I might call him friend. But I'm well aware of the lines I can't cross. It's a dance. One misstep, and the whole assignment comes crashing down."

That's one way to put it. "Crashing down in this case could be a body found in a dumpster."

"I know that too." Bo ran his fingers over the scar from Lucky's near miss in an alley. "How's your foot?"

"I'm not ready to enter marathons, but I'm getting there." So like Bo to change an uncomfortable subject. "And yes, I went to physical therapy." *Twice.*

They lay in silence, Lucky soaking up the feeling of his arms around Bo, and of Bo's breath gusting across his chest. "I'll make a deal with you," he finally said. "I won't turn up dead in a dumpster if you won't."

"Now, Lucky." Bo tightened his grip around Lucky's waist. "I said before that you'd never lied to me when it mattered. Don't start now."

CHAPTER FIFTEEN

"Here, Jerry, make these go away." Bo slid his bowl of fries over in front of the kid, whose eyes had followed each crispy strip from bowl to ketchup to lips.

"Uh, okay." In all the time he'd been coming to the bar, Lucky had never once noticed the guy ordering anything, though he accepted any handouts from the bikers. And now he munched Bo's castoffs like they were his first food today.

Trust Bo to see the guy was hungry. Trust Bo to do something about it without calling attention to the guy's plight. Trust Cy to accomplish Bo's goal by stepping on the guy's foot to make his mouth open like a trashcan. But did either Bo or Cyrus see how Jerry's eyes begged for a lot more than food?

After two months of waiting and several more trips in pickup trucks, Reyes finally called Lucky in for a meeting. Lucky wanted behind the wheel of the big rig in the worst possible way.

"Mr. Getsinger, do I know you?" Cold, blue crystals stared out of a battle-hardened face.

Lucky forced his breathing to remain steady, feigning nonchalance in the face of one of the most dangerous men he'd ever met. One wrong move and Lucky's parents would be right in thinking their son dead. "I don't reckon." He kept his eyes on Reyes, though instinct commanded him to seek out Bo, lounging in a chair by the door. True to Bo's word, Mateo Reyes lived in a tiny walk-up apartment, belying the vast amounts of cash passing through his fingers. Lucky sat on a ratty couch with threadbare fabric, patches of stuffing visible in spots. A coffee table adorned with water rings and scratch marks separated him from his host, who reclined against a heavily padded loveseat.

"You served time for trafficking? Where?" Reyes might have put the department's best interrogators to shame. His unwavering gaze demanded the truth, his casual attitude merely a deception. Hawks didn't study their prey with such brutal intent.

"Conspiracy to distribute," Lucky clarified. "Earned myself a ten year stay in the Durham Correctional Center."

Reyes studied his fingernails, or appeared to. Lucky had little doubt that the man took in his every breath, every blink. "Did you meet someone there named Paco?"

"At least two, maybe three. Can you be more specific?"

Reyes scrutinized Lucky a moment. "It's of no matter. Who did you work for before?"

Stick as close to the truth as you dare. If this guy had been close to Victor, Lucky would have known. "I worked for Victor Mangiardi's outfit." Damn, even saying the name aloud hurt. *Wherever you are, Victor, I'm sorry.*

A muscle twitched in Reyes' jaw. "I've heard of Victor Mangiardi. He had a home near the village where I grew up."

According to Reyes' profile, he grew up in Abilene. Interesting, and a tidbit of intel he might not have intended to give. Lucky needed to let Walter know of the slip.

"Were you working for him at the time of his arrest?" the felon persisted.

"Nah. I'd struck out on my own by then, and got busted a few weeks after I'd heard about Victor's death."

"How... unfortunate for you, and for him." The muscle in Reyes' jaw jumped again. "And he trusted you?"

"You didn't work for Victor long if he didn't." True enough.

"You've not let me down yet. But demand is increasing. I need someone I can trust, not only with small quantities, but with large ones."

"How much are we talking?"

"Two tractor trailer loads per week."

Holy shit. The man wasn't playing.

"We'll also be expanding more up the East Coast. Chapters of the Cruisers are forming in North Carolina, South Carolina, Virginia, and Tennessee. Are you familiar with those areas?"

"I've driven from Texas to Virginia and never even got pulled over."

Reyes watched with mistrust in his eyes. "How long did you drive a big rig?"

"Five years, give or take a few months." Not to mention the classes Lucky'd taken in the meantime to keep his skills sharp and his license valid.

For the longest time Reyes simply stared, giving Lucky the creepy feeling that the man read his mind as Victor had once been famed to do. It dawned on him then—Victor and Reyes instinctively practiced the techniques Lucky'd been taught in a classroom. They didn't read minds, they merely allowed their quarry time enough to give themselves away. No way in hell would Lucky let the man see him squirm.

Tension grew, sending uncertainty through Lucky. He kept his breathing even. At last, Reyes barked out a laugh. "You're one cool son-of-a-bitch, aren't you?" To Bo he said, "He'll do."

Lucky yawned to keep from letting out a relieved sigh.

"Do you ride?" Reyes asked, dropping the businessman act to portray genuine interest.

"Ride?"

"A Harley."

Deliberately keeping his eyes from darting toward Bo, Lucky replied, "I can, but I don't have a bike right now."

"If you're with us, one day I expect you to wear our colors."

Bo escorted Lucky from the building, still in Cy mode. "I believe Mateo likes you. He doesn't usually invite guys to join the club until he knows them well."

Lucky waited until they were out of sight of Reyes' apartment to answer. "Did you ever have a doubt?" Because Lucky sure had.

The man loosed a grin. Not Bo's lopsided number, but Cyrus'. How odd for two men sharing the same body to have different smiles. "A bit. He's pretty suspicious of everyone. Liking you doesn't change that."

"Yeah? Well, I want you to make me a promise."

"What?"

"If he gets too suspicious, and it comes down to me or you, I want you to throw me under the bus to save yourself."

"What? I couldn't—"

"You're the one he trusts, and you're the one who can get what we need. If giving me up will get you closer to Mexico, I want you to do it."

Every trace of Cy fled, leaving behind a torn-looking Bo. "I won't. There'd have to be another way."

"You can and you will." Lucky faked a smile. "You know me. I'll be okay."

Lucky got in the Malibu and drove away. About halfway home, he realized Bo hadn't promised.

The phone on the nightstand rang. Lucky pulled himself out of the first good sleep he'd gotten all week, his fuzzy brain clearing at a strange number on his phone. "Hello?"

"It's me."

Lucky shot upright in bed, knowing better than to mention names on an unsecure line. "Is everything okay?" Bo certainly didn't sound okay. He sounded shaky.

Silence, then. "Yeah. I... I needed to hear your voice. Look, I'm sorry, but I haven't told you everything I know. There's things I've seen that I can't talk about yet. I hope you understand."

No, Lucky didn't understand, but biting Bo's head off wouldn't bring him back if he'd strayed off the straight and narrow. "Have you compromised the case?"

"No."

"Have you broken the law?"

Silence.

"Okay, have you broken any *major* laws?"

Bo hesitated before answering. "Not personally."

"You believe telling me specifics might put you in danger?"

"Not just me, but you."

"Why are you telling me now?" *And do you need a quick trip back to Atlanta?*

"Those nightmares I'm having? They're not only about my dad and my time in the service. I just...I don't like keeping things from you."

Lucky didn't like it either, but he trusted his partner's judgment. "Are you keeping records? Can you justify your actions in a court of law?"

"Yes."

"That's all I ask. That and for you to keep yourself safe."

Another night, another drug deal, and no time alone with Bo to find out specifics on their phone call. Lucky followed the route he'd been given, hauling another load to the apartment singled out as their biggest customer. Over the past few weeks, the boxes had gotten bigger and bigger for the crowd in the garage, too, and Lucky made two weekly runs to Texas. Soon, he'd deliver his first full tractor trailer load.

While Lucky fed the supply, Landry, Johnson, and other newbies took down the end users under the watchful eye of O'Donoghue. Meanwhile, Cyrus Cooper received word of Art's undercover persona dying, though the real Art now rested at home. Reyes didn't flinch at the news. What did he care if a former neighbor's heart gave out?

With a few hours to kill, Lucky drove out toward I-85. He pulled into the Tanger Outlet Park, weaving his way through maze-like parking, and pulled up to a Cracker Barrel restaurant. Always in a public place. This close to closing on a weeknight, most tables stood open. Lucky headed straight for the back, waving off a hovering hostess.

His chair legs scraped across the hardwood floor as he sat down at a table.

"I ordered chicken and dumplings for you. Does that meet with your approval?" Walter folded and placed aside the newspaper he'd been reading. *Walter, not O'Donoghue. Thank God.*

"Works for me." Not that Lucky would eat much tonight. Too much adrenaline flowing through his veins. He'd planned to order bacon, but perhaps Walter's choice worked better with a queasy stomach. The thrill of the chase, oh how he'd missed it, even if he worked for the good guys now and didn't get to keep the nice pile of hundreds currently bulging out his wallet.

"Reyes claims he comes from a village near Valle Hermosa."

"Oh really?" Walter blinked thoughtfully behind the lenses of his glasses. "Two major cartels operate in the Valle Hermosa area, and bath salts aren't a part of their normal product line. But there's no guarantee that we don't have a new player in the game. Since the introduction of the substance in Europe, it was only a matter of time before Mexico got in on the act. Are you familiar with the area?"

"Victor Mangiardi had a home there."

"Have you been there? Do you know the lay of the land?"

"No. He always went without me." Hell, Victor'd never even gotten Lucky a passport until too late. For a minute the niggling doubt resurfaced. Maybe there was something or someone in Mexico that Victor hadn't wanted him to know about.

"It's probably better that way," Walter replied. "His enemies wouldn't have hesitated to use you against him."

That's something Lucky hadn't considered. Some countries Victor visited weren't kind to gay men, and Victor even traveled with hired women on occasion, a smokescreen when dealing with homophobic dealers. Besides, some of the women doubled as spies. Secrets some men vowed to take to their graves were easily offered up to a pretty face and a willing body.

"You would have made a useful hostage. One with too much information about Victor's dealings."

Yeah. Victor could've admitted weakness for a male lover, paid ransom, and probably have gotten pieces of Lucky back for weeks. Suddenly Lucky didn't mind so much having been left behind.

Not wanting to linger on old ghosts tucked in the back of his closet, Lucky shook the irrelevant thoughts from his head and fixed Walter with a steady gaze. "You get anything?"

"Only a handful of trackers found in a truck stop trashcan in Harlingen, Texas. Whoever we're dealing with has access to state of the art equipment. Few in the States would have been able to detect the devices." Walter took a bite of what appeared to be fried catfish.

Lucky's dumplings arrived, and he picked at his meal, waiting for Walter to speak again.

Walter swallowed a mouthful and resumed the conversation. "How's Bo?"

"Deep into his assignment. I'm worried about how in character he gets. He's gotten close to Reyes, though not close enough to find the supplier."

"Give him time," Walter replied, patting his mouth with a napkin. A buzzing sounded from his side of the table. "Excuse me," he said, pulling out a cell phone and bringing it to his ear. "Smith," he answered. If Walter wanted to, he could shield every emotion from his face. That he chose to show his wide-eyed shock to Lucky spoke volumes. "When? Are you sure?" Walter swore, "Damn it! What a clusterfuck!"

Lucky jumped in his chair. Walter? Swearing?

Walter ended the call, closed his eyes, and blew out a cheek-bulging breath. "I'm sorry, Lucky, but I'm afraid you need to get back. The shit, as you say, is about to hit the fan."

"What happened?"

"Local law enforcement was warned to keep a distance, but a fight broke out at a club tonight. A member of the 441 Cruisers, a local man by the name of Joe Clinkscales, has been arrested, and his motorcycle searched."

"I don't need to ask what was found, do I?"

"No, you don't. Do you have any idea how Reyes may react?"

"No."

"Get back to Athens, make up a cover story of where you've been, and keep a watch out for Bo. If things get messy, I want you both out of there."

"Yes, sir." Walter didn't need to remind Lucky to stay as long as possible. That's what the SNB did. They rode out storms.

Lucky barely made it home before Bo showed up, wearing only his helmet, jeans, a T-shirt and boots, the night being far too warm for leather. "C'mon. Reyes wants us. The shit just hit the fan."

"I know, and so does Walter."

Bo gave a curt nod. "Let's go." He fired up the bike. Lucky donned his helmet and hopped on.

Lucky clung tighter to Bo than normal all the way to Reyes' apartment. It might be his last chance for a while.

Reyes shouted into a telephone in Spanish. Lucky sat on the man's ragged couch, catching every third word. Although Victor had owned property in Mexico, among other places, he'd been of Italian descent. However, he'd occasionally entertained Spanish-speaking guests, and Lucky had picked up a word here and there. The Spanish he'd learned in prison couldn't be repeated in polite company. As fast as Reyes blathered, though, Lucky couldn't keep up.

Bo stood at alert in his usual spot by the door, but his attention was focused on a newspaper. He turned the pages at too-even intervals to actually be reading. Reyes didn't seem to notice.

"Take care of it," Reyes barked in English before flinging his phone to the loveseat. He turned to Lucky and Bo. "Gentlemen, it's late. Take the rest of the evening off and tell the men not come to the garage until I say so. There's a matter requiring my complete attention."

"I'll take Ricky home," Bo said, in full Cy mode.

The brief flicker of a smile crossed Reyes' face. Affection? For Bo? Oh shit. "You do that. Take care of yourself, my friend." He shut the door behind them, but before Lucky and Bo were out of hearing range, he'd started yelling again, either to himself or someone on the phone, Lucky wasn't sure.

"Come," Bo said, grabbing Lucky's arm. "We don't need to be here right now."

"Do you know what all that was about?" Lucky double-timed, trying to keep up with Bo's longer strides.

"Yes. Remember the truck driver I told you about that disappeared? Now he's back, and Mateo's accusing him of conspiring with the cops. The guy was a sneaky little prick, and used more than he sold most days, from what Mateo just said. I picked up a name too. Travis Eubanks."

"Wait. You speak Spanish?"

"*Hablo muy poquito español,*" Bo replied. "Very little, but enough to get by. Now, let Walter know to put a watch on this Travis guy."

Damn, but Bo kept pulling out new facets of himself on a near-daily basis. Lucky texted Walter while Bo fished Lucky's helmet out of his saddle bags. "C'mon. Let's get out of here. The further away we are, the better."

Bo led the way to the cabin's front door, signaling *wait right there* with his hand before disappearing inside.

Lucky discarded his helmet on the front porch. He breathed deeply, drawing in pine and something sweet—honeysuckle, maybe?—while night critters whirred and chirped. Overhead, a million stars lit the heavens, a reminder of the night when Lucky had huddled on a mountaintop alone, wondering if he'd ever set eyes on Bo again. Wow. It'd happened in June. A full year ago. Just thinking about that hellish ordeal caused his chest to constrict and made breathing difficult.

A few moments later, a helmetless Bo skipped down the steps, arms loaded. "Follow me," he said, "but watch your step."

By the light of a nearly full moon and the soft glow of Bo's flashlight, Lucky followed a trail through the trees. He stepped out into a clearing and... Damn. The moon reflected off the glassy surface of the Oconee River, if he wasn't mistaken. He'd been too busy his last trip out to notice water nearby. Bo set down his burdens and spread a quilt on the ground, plopping down on top. "Come on, get comfortable," he said, taking off his boots and tossing them aside.

Lucky eased down on the edge of the quilt to take off his boots, keeping his eyes on Bo's barely visible form and letting his eyes adjust to the dark. The click of a pop top sounded twice. Bo handed a can to Lucky. Beer, not wine. So Cyrus and not Bo.

Lucky swigged down a mouthful of some pigswill Bo would never drink. He murmured, "Bo," to double-check and received no reaction. Yes, definitely Cyrus then.

They sat in silence for a while, sipping beer. Being close enough to reach out and touch stiffened Lucky's cock, but if he acted on his impulses, would he have Bo in his arms or Cyrus Cooper? Was wanting them both wrong?

"What do you want with me?" he asked.

"I want to kick your ass to prove I'm the bigger badass, mostly." Cy's grin gleamed in the faint light. "And another part of me wants to fuck you till neither of us can walk."

Sounded mighty damned good to Lucky.

Cy murmured, "Ricky" and sealed the deal. Tonight they'd be Cyrus and Ricky, with no SNB to worry about, no case, no do-we-use-condoms-or-don't-we. For the next few hours, they were two horny men getting some action. However, Ricky and Lucky weren't two distinct people like Bo and Cy. Ricky was merely an earlier incarnation of the current Lucky or, as Bo had said, the man he might have been if not for Victor's influence.

Who moved first? Who cared? Cyrus met Lucky midway, and they tumbled to the quilt together. "God, you're hot," Cy breathed against Lucky's ear. Then he put his tongue to good use, delving into Lucky's mouth. They wrangled each other out of their clothes, breaking the kiss long enough to deal with T-shirts and jeans, and came together again like their lives depended on the connection.

Cyrus wound up on top, demanding a place between Lucky's thighs. Where he wanted, not where Lucky wanted him. A double handful of that round ass let Lucky thrust and shove from below until their cocks rubbed together. Cy chuckled low in his throat and pinned Lucky down, making him squirm for position. Relenting, Cy lifted enough to slide one callused hand between them, holding their stiff lengths in his grip. Lucky moaned. Those weren't Bo's soft pharmacist's fingers; this wasn't Bo's tender handling.

The soft scrape of whiskers also didn't belong to Bo, and they rasped against Lucky's "been too long since I last shaved" growth. Lucky pulled away, only to roll a lot farther than he expected when Cyrus disappeared.

Cy made a Bo-shaped silhouette against the sky, with something in his hand. The small shriek of ripping foil warned Lucky to brace for the chilly squish of latex over his cock. Instead, a slick finger found his hole. How long had it been since Bo had breached him? And it wasn't Bo touching him now. Cy wanted in.

"Put this on me," a gruff voice demanded. In the back of his brain, Lucky complained, *Who the fuck does he think he is?* But he merely nodded and complied, sliding the condom down Cy's erection. Hell, yeah, Cy would top. No switching around there. Lucky lay back on the quilt, legs spread, honing his attention on the fingers working him open.

Cyrus caught Ricky's face in one hand. "Answer me this, first. Who am I to you? Are you fucking Bo or Cy?" The question was pure Bo; Cy wouldn't even ask. Cy's gesture would be a handful of hair, yanking back.

"I'm fucking whoever the hell you are, 'cause you're all the same to me." And he? Who was he? It was the truth. It was a joke. "And you can consider yourself *fucking Lucky*." With that he spread his legs wider and welcomed Cy inside. The expected, "Are you okay" or "I'm not hurting you, am I?" didn't come.

Cy fucked like he rode a bike, the master of his own universe. He hit Lucky's prostate, nothing gentle in his penetration. Work-roughened fingers wrapped around Lucky's wrists, pinning them to the ground. *Oh dear Lord, yes!*

A moan escaped, followed by a tightening in Lucky's groin. He wrapped his legs around Cy's waist for added leverage. Cy plunged into his body, forceful and passionate. He shoved in once more, twice more, sliding into the confines of Lucky's ass.

Driven on by need, Lucky bucked up, garbled pleas and barely discernible moans harmonizing with the crickets and whippoorwills. They rocked together in a whirlwind of lust and barely held tension.

Faster and faster they came together and drew back. Not one for tender kisses, apparently, Cy nipped on all of Lucky's available skin within reach. A moment of panic clenched

Lucky's insides. Soon he'd blow while giving himself totally and completely over to another man. But who? Whose cock filled him now? And who did *that* man think *he* was fucking? Did it matter how many men were inside when they all wore Bo's body?

Cy shifted his weight to one hand, freeing the other to grip Lucky's shaft. So close. So damned fucking close. Lucky's fingers slipped and slid off Cy's sweat-slickened biceps. Cy's cry of completion carried out over the water. *He's coming. Inside me.* Fire shot through Lucky straight to his groin. Whoever he is. Whoever I am. *Oh dear Lord in heaven.*

Cy's plunging faltered and Lucky added a hand to his cock, speeding up the stroking. He stiffened and cried out. Cy buckled a moment later, falling on top of Lucky and sucking in mouthfuls of air. When Lucky would have squirmed out from underneath, Cy's brought his arms up around him, holding him in place. "I love you, whether you're Ricky or Lucky."

I don't know why you do, but please don't ever stop came out as, "Love you, too, whoever you are." Bo loved him. No matter what he'd done, where he'd been, or how badly he fucked up on occasion, Bo still loved him. Lucky didn't deserve the love, could never be good enough to deserve it, but he'd try like hell to come close, because without that love? Without Bo? Well, he simply didn't want to dwell on such.

And then it occurred to him. *I'm Simon Harrison, and I can make Simon into anyone I want him to be. If I fuck this up I really will kick my own ass.*

Lucky shifted in Bo's embrace, wrapping the quilt tighter around them. The unmistakable thundering of a Harley echoed through their valley from the main road. Goose flesh formed on Lucky's arms. Damn, but he loved the purr of a big bike. Someday. Someday. Him and Bo and the open road. Bo dreamed of backpacking the Appalachian Trail. Lucky dreamed of cruising to Spokane, Bo nestled against his back. "Are you ready to tell me about your strange phone call the other night?"

Bo sighed. "Yes, but I have to do it as Cyrus."

Not good. "Whatever works."

Hauling himself upright and stretching his legs out on the blanket, Bo drew an aura about himself, sitting up straighter, shoulders back, donning the mantle of dead drug dealer Cyrus Cooper. "Reyes runs a tight ship," he said in the distinct, gravelly growl that meant Cy.

"And?"

"Someone stepped out of line. Some of the guys got to comparing notes, figuring out who made more money. You remember a skinny kid named Demarcus?"

"Not really."

"Wore a red bandana and drove a Sportster."

A face came to mind, seven kinds of ugly and missing a few prominent teeth. "Oh, yeah. Toothless."

"He has a name, Ricky: Demarcus Sutton."

Ricky, not Lucky. Damn, Bo dug down deep for this confession.

"Now that you mention it, I haven't seen him around lately."

"You won't."

Lucky's hackles rose. "Why not?"

For a fraction of a second, Bo peered out of Cyrus's eyes, their brown depths glistening. Cyrus blinked rapidly a few times. "Like I said, a few guys got together and started making demands. They sent Demarcus to the garage as their spokesman. You were in Texas at the time."

Oh shit. "Please tell me you didn't kill him." Walter might defend his men from a multitude of sins, but murder wasn't one of them.

"I... I never touched him. Not directly. I watched the door while Mateo took a tire tool to him."

"It killed you not to interfere, didn't it?"

The man across from him swallowed hard. "No. And that's what bothers me. As Cyrus, I felt the guy deserved what he got, and I wouldn't have helped him even if I could."

No way Bo could disassociate his compassion to such a degree. "To stick your neck out wouldn't have helped either of you, and would have compromised your position."

"Yes."

Damn, Lucky'd never considered such a possibility. "Are you all right?"

"Not really." Cy shrugged. "But what can I do? I'm two different men, and the stronger is taking over the weaker."

A comment best filed away and saved for the experts. Man, but Lucky wished he'd studied psychology. "Is the guy still alive?"

"Probably wishes he wasn't, but he'll live. If he's capable, he'd make a good witness in our case against Reyes, but it might take a while for him to recover."

"Understood."

"Lucky?"

"Yes?" Good, "Lucky" meant he hadn't lost Bo completely.

"Jerry was there too. Mateo made him watch. I could tell he didn't want to, but he's under Mateo's sway. In the end when Demarcus lay bleeding, Mateo ordered Jerry to kick the guy a few times." Cy squinted his eyes shut, as though trying to block the unpleasant image. "I didn't like the look in his eyes when he finished. I want Jerry out of this before Mateo turns him into another version of himself. He thinks it's a game, watching the boy trying to win the affection and respect of the guys. They tease him, tell him they'll give him colors one day if he does what they say. They won't. They laugh at him behind his back. Which is why I protect him. I want him out." Even as hard-assed Cy, Bo took care of the people he'd claimed.

But untangling Jerry from the web might cost them their case. "Thanks for telling me."

"Don't mention it again, please. I'm not dealing well."

No, he wasn't, and Lucky saw a few extra counseling sessions in Bo's future. But he'd done good. He'd endured, and he hadn't blown his cover. "I'm proud of you."

"I'm glad, 'cause I'm not too proud of myself right now."

"Why?"

"I hurt a man, or rather, stood by and let one get hurt."

"We haven't talked about it, but didn't you ever pull the trigger on someone in the service?"

"Several times," Bo replied, "and I still see their faces, their slack jaws and staring eyes. If I channel Cyrus, they leave me alone."

Cy was a cold, prickly fucker and could handle pretty much anything, but Bo had a warmer heart. Lucky scooted across the blanket to take Cyrus or Bo or whoever into his arms. Bo let out his breath in a rush, collapsing against Lucky's shoulder. No tears fell, but the strangled noises from his throat sounded like dry sobs. Lucky held him and rocked him, so many things growing clearer, like his compassion and the way he lived his life. Bo wasn't a light-weight, and he took up for himself when it mattered, but like Lucky, he'd done things he'd never forgiven himself for. He excelled at being someone else because he'd hidden behind a false identity before. The badass who'd taken a swing at his father wasn't the same terrified kid who'd screamed for his life while tied to a bed. Whenever Bo felt uncomfortable in a situation, he ran and isolated himself. If he couldn't run physically, he disappeared into his mind.

"You've talked to your counselor about this?"

"Yes. Long before Cyrus Cooper, I pretended to be someone else when the going got rough. When I stripped during college, my alter-ego helped me out. In Afghanistan, 'Schollenberger' took over. Do you think I'm evil?"

"No, why would you think that?"

"Because I have the backbone of a jellyfish unless I'm pretending to be someone I'm not."

"Those parts are all in there somewhere. You just don't use 'em all the time. The three eighths inch socket don't disappear out of the toolbox when you're not tightening bolts."

"But then I get... You know how I can't sleep..."

Lucky's shoulders rose two inches with the air he needed to admit this. "I can't say I would've handled matters any better had I been in your shoes." He took another deep breath and made a confession of his own. "I've been in rough places more than once, but I've never had to shoot a man, and the mere thought gives me the screaming shivers."

"Really?"

"Really. Now, don't get me wrong. If someone threatened you or Charlotte and the boys, they'd be road kill, but I'm not sure if it came down to them or me, I could pull the trigger to save my own skin." He shrugged the shoulder that'd taken a bullet not too long ago. "While I had no problem holding a gun on the woman who shot me, and faulted the guards for not dealing with her better, when it came down to it, I hesitated. She didn't."

Neither one of them spoke after that. Bo lay back down on the quilt, allowing Lucky to cover them up in an attempt to shield them from the mosquitoes who'd recently noticed their presence.

Eventually Bo asked, "Can we stay here forever, and never go back?"

Go back. *No, I never want to go back.* "Someone might miss us." Only a handful of someones, but they were out there.

"But I'm happy here with you," Bo grumbled, all traces of Cyrus gone.

A cabin by the river in the middle of nowhere, with Bo, and a Harley Davidson to take them wherever they wanted to go. Could it get any better? Bo planted a kiss on Lucky's forehead.

"How long you reckon we can stay out here before they miss us?" Lucky asked.

Bo sighed. "I gotta be at the garage at eight in the morning."

"What time is it now?"

"Not sure. Midnight, maybe?"

"Any objection to walking funny and being tired tomorrow?"

Bo paused a moment before replying, "No, none at all."

Lucky bent down for another kiss, then tucked them both back into the quilt. A buzzing a bit louder than a Georgia mosquito had him grabbing his phone out of his jeans pocket. A text message from Walter said, "Travis Eubanks dead. Gunshot to head. No witnesses, no suspects."

CHAPTER SIXTEEN

Lucky spent the day lying low and surfing the Net for information on Travis Eubanks and Joe Clinkscales, and watching his phone like a hawk lest Bo call. He asked Walter to increase surveillance on the garage.

Whoever Reyes had spoken to last night had to be in the area to get to Eubanks so quickly. Bo could be in danger. Lucky also hinted at using Jerry Wilkerson as a possible witness. He might not be able to promise immunity, but having Walter in the kid's corner was the best he could do that this point. Bo wanted the kid out, so Lucky would do his best to make that happen.

He came out of his bathroom after a shower, towel around his waist, and stopped in his tracks. Mateo Reyes sat on his couch. Bo stood by the door and Lucky finally understood what even Bo hadn't yet figured out: Reyes planned to use Cyrus Cooper as an enforcer. Sergeant at Arms wasn't merely a symbolic position. No wonder he'd given his trust. But Bo couldn't have possibly taken out Eubanks last night; he'd been with Lucky. Or had Eubanks died before the heated phone call, while Lucky met with Walter? Had Cyrus been a party to murder? How much disassociation was Bo capable of?

Bo wouldn't have hidden such a thing. Cy would.

"What can I do for you?" Lucky asked, channeling Ricky Getsinger and pretending dangerous men showed up at his house uninvited on a normal basis. Well, they had eleven years ago.

"I have a problem," Reyes said, adding a silken purr to his voice. "And when I have a problem, everyone has a problem."

"Is that kinda like, 'when Mama ain't happy, ain't nobody happy?'" Lucky quipped.

167

"Mr. Getsinger, yesterday I had my bike cleaned. Know what they found?"

Lucky longed to snap a glance to Bo, but he didn't dare. "Since we're in Georgia, I'm guessing a windshield full of dead June bugs."

"Not that kind of cleaning." Reyes remained deceptively calm while tossing over one of the gadgets Lucky'd been planting like radishes.

Lucky squinted at the tiny fleck of metal. "What's this? Did you break a rivet or something?" He poured his entire self into being a good-ole-boy hick, too country to know what he held in his hand.

"That's a tracking device," Reyes said, crossing his legs and leaning back on the couch like he owned the place.

Lucky willed his wildly thudding heart to calm, stepping back into character. "Who the fuck did this? Tell me! I'll hurt 'em for you."

Reyes visibly relaxed, lips pulling back in a smile. "Cyrus tells me I can depend on you. I should have listened sooner. But you see, a man in my position can't trust lightly."

"I understand," Lucky said. He didn't give his trust lightly either, if at all.

"Good. I hope you also understand why I had you followed last night."

Oh shit. For the first time since he'd joined the SNB, Lucky'd been unaware of being followed. *Stupid, stupid, stupid.*

"And?" Lucky kept any waver from his voice.

"I called my man off when I realized the two of you intended to spend the night together." He chuckled, turning a fond gaze on Bo. "I didn't realize you swung that way, *mi amigo.* Although I'm sure you could have found—how do I say this?— a prettier companion. If he's loyal to me, we don't have a problem, yeah? Any port in a storm, I've heard."

"Beauty's in the eye of the beholder," Bo replied, appearing nonplussed. Did he have to add, "And in the dark, who can tell?"?

"That is true, my friend. So true." Lucky began to relax enough to almost forgive the jibe about his looks, until Reyes added, "However, when my man was leaving, he spotted a bike parked back from the road. He wasn't the only one watching."

Holy shit. Please say it wasn't Keith.

"I have a traitor in my midst who means to harm me and my friends." Reyes plucked the tracker from Lucky's outstretched palm. "His name is Jerry Wilkerson. It seems young Jerry hasn't been entirely honest with me." Reyes' tone remained unconcerned, as though he merely discussed the weather. "He's been a busy guy. This isn't the first time I've caught him nosing around where he didn't belong.

"This was a friendly visit, to warn you." Reyes rose from the couch. "If you should see our little friend, I'd very much like to talk to him."

Bo dropped the Cy persona long enough to exchange a flash of eye contact with Lucky before following Reyes out the door. Lucky got the message loud and clear: *watch your back.*

How fucking stupid not to guess that his and Bo's every little move would be scrutinized. Only, until last night, Lucky hadn't a clue how important Cyrus had become to Reyes. Yet, even months ago Bo had referred to the man as "partner." Shit, when Bo went deep, he went deep. *Batten down the hatches, folks, there's a storm coming.*

At six o'clock, Lucky made his way to Mateo's garage. Normally relaxed, tonight the crew eyed each other with suspicion, an extra measure thrown in for Lucky. "Like what you see?" Lucky growled at a clean-cut man giving him the stink eye.

They played a dangerous game, and one had followed him and Bo last night. No telling how much the guy had seen. How much had Jerry witnessed, and why had the little twerp been spying in the first place? At least in character as Ricky and Cyrus, Bo and Lucky had kept SNB talk to a minimum.

As of yet, other than Reyes, Lucky hadn't met any of the supplier's people. He picked up a truck in Texas and drove it to Georgia, returning the vehicle on the next run. So far he'd counted three different F-150s in rotation, though Bo'd mentioned five. The trucks never crossed the border. The drugs came up from Mexico and were loaded into the trucks somewhere near Harlingen.

"He gets the truck keys through FedEx delivery," Bo had said, "from a Harlingen address." As much as Reyes seemed to trust Cyrus, he still kept his right-hand man in the dark about much of his business.

Harlingen, Texas. Close enough to the border that a stiff wind might send the whole town across the line. Victor's old home lay a little over six hours from there. The US confiscated Victor's domestic holdings. What became of his foreign real estate?

Whoever was behind the deal certainly kept a low profile in the States. Warning bells sounded in Lucky's head. Victor's parents were dead, and his sister and brother had turned blind eyes to their brother's shady dealings. There was the nephew, Stephan. Nah, couldn't be. Stephan didn't have enough of his uncle's brains and business savvy to pull off an operation of this size, though he'd been smart enough to avoid charges during Victor's takedown. A coincidence, maybe? It wasn't like Victor's methods hadn't become common knowledge. Even Bo mentioned the organization's exploits being used as textbook examples. Walter mentioned two cartels operating in the region. So many little things about this case reminded Lucky of Victor.

Bo arrived, and Lucky couldn't help notice the absence of Jerry nipping at his heels. *"Can I get that for you, Cy?"* or *"You know I'll make deliveries, right? You know you can trust me, right?"* Maybe it was better that the kid wasn't here. If he'd shown up, in a few short hours Bo would have to turn him over to Reyes. Lucky didn't want to even imagine what might be left after the encounter.

Okay, maybe Lucky was going soft, but somehow they had to get the kid out of there without tipping off Reyes.

He sat in a chair at the back of the garage, watching Bo distribute the evening's goods. A few eyes fell on Lucky. He pretended not to notice. Maybe he should distance himself from Bo. The men were getting suspicious, and if whoever'd followed them last night turned out to be a homophobic ass-hole... *Damn, I'm getting as paranoid as Reyes.*

"We need to hurry. The guys will be back soon." Bo opened the door wide, letting Lucky inside the vault.

"These are the last I brought with me. I've asked for more." Lucky held out his hand to show a dozen transmitters. They'd have to make damned sure to get the goods out before Reyes had the bright idea to check the boxes and not just his bike.

"These'll have to do." Bo captured Lucky's gaze, his brow wrinkled, questions in the depths of his eyes. "How much longer?" he asked, so softly Lucky scarcely heard.

His stoic veneer showed signs of stress. Six months was a long time to be someone else, separated from your own life. Doubly so for someone barely past training. Triply so for someone who fell too deeply into character.

"Do I need to tell 'em to pull you out?"

Bo scrunched his eyes closed and shook his head. "No. It's... I'm not sure how much longer I can hold on. I'm already growing too close to some of the guys. I'd never do anything against protocol, but it's hard, you know? Donnie has a wife and two kids, but doesn't make enough at the warehouse where he works to give them the things they need."

"So he gets them by peddling shit to secretaries who flip out and shoot people. Go on."

Bo shot him a threatening glare. "Javier can't find work other than what I... what Cy gives him. Hell, and to watch Reyes beat a man. And there's Jerry..."

"What about Jerry?" Other than the fact that Reyes intended to have him for breakfast.

"Well, he's a sweet kid. Misguided maybe, with no positive role models. He's balls deep in this, and if Reyes gets his hands on the boy, thinking he's the traitor..."

"Technically he is, if he's snooping around behind Reyes' back. He just doesn't have any high-level info. Also, he's damned near too stupid to live." *Much as I used to be.*

"That isn't going to change if he doesn't have a chance to grow up," Bo growled from between clenched teeth. He stared at the gadgets in Lucky's hand, head hanging down. Lucky'd only been on the job two months, and already this assignment threatened to swallow him whole. How much more so for Bo?

"And..." Bo continued, "...and I miss you. I see you here and there, whenever we can, but I can't touch you. At the end of a hard day, I can't sleep with you and forget."

Uh-oh. Bo seemed to be losing his grip on Cyrus, and Cyrus was who he'd soon need. Time to break the downer mood. "What? You don't miss my amazing prowess in bed?"

Bo quirked up the edges of his mouth. "Yeah, the whole shebang."

"Hang on a bit longer. They're trying to get their hooks into the operation south of the border, and we've got folks under surveillance as far north as Virginia. The other Cruiser chapters are small yet, but growing. Once enough folks are in place, we'll wrap up here." It was the right move. They were close, and Lucky couldn't do this job without Bo. But Bo needed out. Soon.

Bo nodded without lifting his head.

"You're not feeling temptation, are you?" Free access to drugs and a former addict weren't a good combination.

"Not my drug of choice. Hallucinogenics and a crappy past don't mix well. Remember, Cyrus leads lemmings to water but doesn't join them when they drown." The slumped shoulders and the utter defeat were cracks wide enough to split Bo's cover in half. Lucky stepped closer. One quick hug wouldn't hurt. The moment skin touched skin, Bo gasped, wrapping his arms around Lucky's back. Lips met lips, and someone moaned. The shock wore off after a moment, and Lucky plunged his tongue into his lover's mouth. Locked together in the middle of a storeroom full of drugs, he clung tightly to his lifeline. *God, get us out of here together.*

The kiss ended, and Lucky buried his face in Bo's neck, the warmth of his body an anchor. They might have held each other for an hour or mere minutes, but when they parted, Lucky felt whole again.

"Thanks," Bo said. He pulled his fabricated character around him like a coat, iron-willed Cy once more in control. "We need to get a move on," he said. "The guys'll be here soon."

They'd no sooner tagged the merchandise when the man Lucky privately called *Dusty Beard* barged through the bay doors. "What in the hell got into Jerry?"

"What do you mean?" Cy asked, snagging himself a beer from the fridge in the office.

"I was coming in and met him on the road going the other way, driving like a bat out of hell, and all over the damned road. Acted drunker'n shit."

Oh fuck. He'd seen.

"Damn little son-of-a-bitch. Why the hell did you call out a search party for such a worthless little piss ant?" Lucky groused, because Ricky would. They'd all be a hell of a lot better off if the kid fled the county, out of reach of Reyes. If they were lucky, Walter's crew would find him first. Lucky's frantic phone call had better pay off.

"He's not hurting anyone." Bo drove past the bar one more time, having commandeered the keys to the Malibu. "Besides, he doesn't have anyone else but us."

Lucky narrowed his eyes at his partner. "Better watch it there, Cy. For a moment you sounded like a guy I know named Bo."

Bo pulled his eyes away from the road long enough to glare at Lucky. "Asshole."

"He's old enough to take care of himself. He's probably pissed about something or another, maybe someone looked at him wrong, I don't know. But the further he stays away from here, the better." Lucky no longer saw an earlier version of himself in Jerry, for even without Victor's influence, Lucky had started stealing cars at Jerry's age. No, instead of a younger Lucky, Jerry favored Daytona: good-intentioned, but far too gullible for his own good.

Bo sighed. "You're right. I'll head back to the garage. Maybe he showed up there. As long as we find him before Reyes does and ask why he's been following the guys."

The truth dawned on Lucky. "You don't get it, do you?"

"Get what?"

"He's not following Reyes' men. He's following you."

"Me?"

"The kid's got it bad, though I can't blame him."

Oh shit registered on Bo's face a split second before the words came out of his mouth. "Then we have to find him. He may have seen or overheard something he wasn't supposed to. If Reyes corners him, there's no telling what he might say."

Somehow Lucky doubted Reyes would go looking. He'd put someone else to the task.

Sure enough, a beat-up Honda sat in the garage parking lot. "Thank God," Bo breathed. He ran across the parking lot and through an open bay door. Lucky would've had someone's ass for leaving the door unlocked. Sirens sounded in his head, and sirens called for guns. He banged the dashboard; the glove box popped open. Walter'd told him long ago to listen when his gut told him something wasn't right. Armed and ready, he took off after Bo.

"Jerry?" Bo called, stopping to flip on the lights before bounding across the floor.

The hidden door stood open, a flashlight's beam cutting the darkness within. "Oh shit." Bo ran and Lucky tried to keep up.

While Bo barreled on in, Lucky held back, gun at the ready. He took up a defensive stance outside the door and peered inside to find the kid sitting on a low shelf. An open box sat in front of him, packets dumped out on the floor. A misting of powder covered his hands.

"My God!" Bo fell to his knees. "Jerry? Jerry! Are you okay?"

Jerry lifted his chin, too much white showing in his eyes like a crazy horse. "I saw you," he said, voice low and the accusation clear. "I saw you."

"Saw me what?" Bo ripped the open packet from Jerry's fingers. White lined the kid's nostrils. "Good Lord, Jerry. How much of this did you snort?"

"You treat me like a kid," Jerry growled. "I'd do anything for you. Anything. You won't even notice me."

"That's not true. I do notice you. I'm sorry if I haven't told you how much I appreciate you, but I do."

Had anyone been watching but a high-as-a-kite kid, Bo's cover would be blown. Nothing about the man kneeling down, trying to wipe away tears and drugs, resembled a hardened criminal. No, Bo Schollenberger, bleeding heart extraordinaire, scrubbed the guy's face with the back of his hand.

"No, you don't. You used to have lunch with me, hang out. Until *he* showed up."

Pure hatred raged in Jerry's eyes when he lifted his head and glared past Bo, straight at Lucky. "I saw you. I came out to your place last night, hoping to talk to you. You were fucking *him!*" He might have meant to point an accusing finger at Lucky, but he pointed at the wall instead. Even from a distance of a few feet, Lucky noticed the kid's pupils blown wide. The contents of at least four packets covered the box. No telling how much the kid had sniffed. He needed help about five minutes ago.

"Cy?" Lucky kept his voice low. "We need to get the boy to the emergency room. I know what that shit can do."

"I ain't no fucking boy!" Jerry shrugged Bo off and staggered to his feet. A cloud of white dust swirled from his lap down to the floor. "I'm a man, and I love you!" he screeched at Bo. "You don't want me. You want him." Again with the finger pointing. "And... and..." Jerry's eyes flew wide. He took a step backwards, hitting the back wall. Nowhere to run. And Bo now standing between him and the only exit.

"B... Cy, you need to step away." Lucky tightened his grip on his .38. *Don't make me do this, kid.* "This might get ugly quick."

"No, it's fine," Bo argued. He faced Jerry. "Jerry, you've got too much of that shit in you. How much did you use?"

"What the fuck do you care?" Jerry huddled in on himself, eyes riveted to a spot above Lucky's head.

Holy hell. Here's where the space aliens and crap show up.

Jerry began to shake. He backed further into the corner, crouching down.

Bo approached, hands out in front of him. Having seen a similar performance not too long ago, Lucky voted for conking the kid on the noggin and hauling him off to the nearest emergency room in restraints. Let the paid professionals deal with the aftermath.

"Stay back!" Jerry wailed.

"I'm not going to hurt you," Bo murmured. "Please. You've had too much. I need to get you to the hospital."

"But you don't want me. You want him," came out in a whimper.

Lucky started to lie, but the wild eyes said Jerry had passed beyond logic's reach.

Bo took another step forward. "Lu... Ricky? You're upsetting him. Why don't you go wait by the car? I've got this."

How much Corruption did it take to shoot someone past hallucinations into cardiac arrest? "No."

Bo whirled, spitting out, "Damn it, Ricky!"

A *snick* sounded unnaturally loud. Oh fuck. Jerry upped the ante with an ace of cold, hard steel.

Hands out to his sides, Bo took a slow step toward the kid. "Put the knife down, Jerry. I ain't gonna hug you with a knife in your hand."

What the fuck? Bo wanted to hug him?

Jerry stared at Bo, a momentary flash of hope replacing his angry scowl. The knife dropped two inches, but rose again. "You ain't gonna hug me! You fucked him!"

"Didn't know you wanted that." Bo tossed his head toward Lucky. "He holds still for about anything."

Okay, I'm not in your league. I fucking get it already.

White crystals stood out in vivid contrast to the mottled red of Jerry's face. "You gave it to him! When I—"

Bo put himself at eye level with Jerry. "Hey, buddy. Remember how we went hiking out by the river? It's been too long. Maybe we should go again sometime. What do you say?"

A furrow formed between Jerry's eyebrows, and he cocked his head to the side. "I don't remember that."

"Oh yeah, sure. We went to the caves, saw the bats. And the old railroad bridge."

Bo stood three feet away, hands still out in a "see, I'm harmless" pose. Jerry's white-rimmed nostrils flared. His chest rose and fell with each breath.

Lucky took a step closer.

"You fucking bastard!" A glint of steel flashed an inch from Lucky's nose. He dove and rolled. A shower of cases rained from a toppled rack.

"Jerry! No!" Bo screamed.

Time slowed. Lucky struggled out from under a mass of cardboard. "No!"

Two hands, overhead. A blade plunging straight down at Bo.

Lucky aimed and fired.

CHAPTER SEVENTEEN

"Can't you go any faster?" Bo sat in the Malibu's backseat, cradling Jerry to his chest.

"This is as fast as the car'll go," Lucky shot back. Why the hell hadn't he insisted on driving his own Camaro? At least Jerry quit hollering about three miles ago. "How's he doing?"

"Going into shock."

Lucky glanced in the rearview mirror, watching Bo wrap the kid tighter in a blanket they'd found at the garage.

He gripped the steering wheel in one hand, hitting a speed dial number on his phone with the other. The call picked up on the first ring. "Athens Regional, twenty minutes, gunshot wound to right shoulder, possible overdose." He hung up and tossed the phone onto the front passenger seat. *Please let us make it, please, Lord, please.*

Why the fuck did the kid have to develop a crush on Bo? Why did he have to invade the stock? How the hell had he gotten in there to begin with? Oh yeah. He'd been spying on Bo, and possibly Reyes too.

They arrived at the hospital to find a gurney waiting. Bo ran in with Jerry while Lucky parked the car. Before he could get out, his passenger door opened. The car leaned to one side when Walter got in. "I won't ask you if you needed to fire that round. You wouldn't have unless necessary."

Good thing Walter believed Lucky's innocence. For the entire drive, Lucky had envisioned the scenario from every possible angle, like a training film, trying to find better options. He hadn't found any. "He nearly stabbed Bo."

"How is Bo?" Walter sounded more like a father worried for a son than employer and employee.

179

"A bit shook up. Took a scratch." Thank God for small favors.

They remained quiet for a time. The rich scent of coffee filled the car, tinged with Old Spice. At the moment, Lucky couldn't care. Quietly he said, "I've never shot anyone before."

"Never?" Did Walter really find the news shocking?

"Never."

"I remember the first time I shot a man," Walter said. "I was eighteen years old and had started my first tour."

"Kill him?"

"I'm not sure. I didn't stick around to find out."

The silence grew oppressive. Bo waited inside the hospital, but Lucky had no idea what he'd face the next time they met. Would he look into accusing eyes and keep saying "I'm sorry"? 'Cause he was, and yet he wasn't. If he'd been given more options, he'd have chosen differently, but with a split second decision between his lover or a hopped up maniac, he'd done what he had to, and he would again. "Does it ever get any easier?"

"I'm afraid not." Walter placed his hand on the console, covering Lucky's. "Do we need to pull you to out? Have they figured out who you are?"

"I don't think so on both counts. Reyes suspected the kid of planting trackers and spying on the guys. That's why I'd asked you to have him picked up. Then he got into the goods, flipped out, and pulled a knife." No need to mention the jealous rage over Bo and Lucky's night together.

"We'd hoped to flush out the Mexican supplier, but after seven months, we're no closer now than we were. It's the DEA's call, but I recommended that we close our fist and take out the connections that we have. We've put nonstop surveillance on the barn and garage on our end, and have enough evidence to issue warrants. A few phone calls to neighboring states will put them on alert."

Lucky wholeheartedly agreed with closing the fist now. "Whoever's down South knows the game."

"What will you tell Reyes about the man you shot?"

"The truth, or all he needs to know. The kid got into the goods, and we don't allow that."

"Good answer." Walter's big mitt came into view, clutching a Starbucks cup. "We'll make the arrangements and issue the warrants. To keep your covers intact, you and Bo will have to stay, I'm afraid. Expect a call from me soon. In the meantime, we'll post a guard on Jerry Wilkerson."

"You do that."

The car dipped again when Walter got out.

Lucky sipped his Starbucks, trying not to close his eyes. Every time his lids drooped, he saw Jerry's wild eyes, and the knife plunging down. Next, he'd see a frightened kid, looking much younger than his years, tears streaming down his face and staring down at his bloodied shoulder. In the next moment, Bo yelled, "Oh fuck!" All in slow motion, on endless loop.

While Lucky had always carried a gun when he'd worked for Victor, and considered it a privilege to have one with the SNB, he'd never actually considered having to shoot someone he knew, not even while taking aim at man-shaped targets at the firing range.

What if the kid died? Bo might never find it in his heart to forgive Lucky. Hell, Lucky might not forgive himself.

He slunk out of the Malibu to enter the hospital and face the music.

"How is he?"

Bo sat in the emergency room waiting area, head buried in his hands. "Stable. His mother's on the way. I suppose we need to get out of here."

They shuffled in silence back to the car. "What happens now?" Lucky asked. "Your call." Lucky voted for getting the hell out.

"Now, we go back to work and pretend nothing happened, though the guys'll be even more suspicious after this. You know how it is, all fun and games until someone gets hurt." Bo opened the passenger door and got into the car.

Lucky didn't buy the calm act for a minute. Sooner or later, Bo would explode. He slid behind the wheel, glad to be driving 'cause it kept his eyes open and on the road instead of reliving shooting a man.

Bo stayed quiet until they'd made it halfway to Lucky's house. "What did Walter have to say?"

"That they're moving things up."

"Even without the supplier?"

"Yeah, the supply chain's getting too big. Tomorrow I'm scheduled to bring up my first rig." A whole damned tractor trailer load of Corruption. One hell of a lot of drugs. And like the smaller trucks, whoever placed the load in the parking lot would disappear somehow.

Staring out at the night sky, Bo mumbled, "When this is over, I'm going to ask for some time off. I need to get away for a while. Maybe go hiking."

For the first time, Bo didn't include Lucky in his getaway plans. "I didn't want to shoot him."

A glance to the right showed Bo's nod. "I know. It was him or me. Sometimes it's a fucked-up choice."

If they didn't discuss the matter now, they likely never would. "Come home with me?"

"Can't. Take me back to the garage. I need to clean up the mess and make sure Mateo hears our side of the story. Then I want to go home."

At the garage, Bo said, "I need to get my head together, okay?" He didn't have to add, "See you later, Ricky."

"Sure." How the hell did a man get his head together when he wasn't himself to begin with? Lucky sat in the car and watched a near-stranger named Cy stalk away into the night.

It seemed Cy and Bo both agreed on how to handle emotional extremes. When most in need of a hug, they ran away to lick their wounds in private.

Yeah, but what about me? I need a hug too. And about a million years to hold him and make sure he's okay.

That night Lucky fell asleep. Eighteen different times.

***

He drove an F-150 to Texas, slept overnight in a fleabag motel, and picked up a loaded Peterbilt new enough to be a joy to drive and old enough not to draw undue attention. All the while he kept his phone close, hoping for word from Bo.

He didn't dare call and ask about the kid, and couldn't risk calling Walter for a non-emergency. After far too long spent driving, Lucky staggered out of the truck at the usual drop-off point.

A handful of men Lucky didn't know stepped from the shadows, led by Reyes. He scanned for a familiar Harley, but Bo was nowhere in sight. The men came closer. *Vrroomm...* Bo appeared from behind the building, pulled up in front of Lucky, and tossed him his helmet. "C'mon," he said. "Let's get out of here" As they pulled away, Lucky watched in the bike's mirrors. Three panel vans pulled up. Damn, that was one hell of a lot of drugs, and a whole hell of a lot of men Lucky hadn't known about, chatting in Spanish as they off-loaded cases.

The fact that they no longer hid the goods in a truck's interior sent up red flags. Reyes knew his business, and his mystery boss didn't strike Lucky as stupid or incautious. Money might be crossing palms to ensure safe shipments. He'd be sure to let Walter hear his suspicions.

He'd hoped to spend the night with Bo, but Bo drove straight to Lucky's rented house. "Who were those men?" Lucky asked.

"Mateo's making some changes. He's getting nervous." Bo flipped his helmet visor open so Lucky could see his eyes. "Ricky... I mean, Lucky, he's getting crazy and paranoid. We need to end this soon. Watch your back. He's been asking a lot of questions about you, like where you're from, and keeps saying how he's not a homophobe. Methinks he protests too much." Without so much as a kiss, Bo roared away into the summer evening, leaving Lucky all alone once more.

As he unlocked the door, his phone rang with an unknown number. "Hello?"

"Ricky?" Damn. How did Mateo Reyes get his personal number?

No help for it now. Holding his voice steady, Lucky replied, "Yeah."

"My friend, I have a job for you." Oh shit. He'd been afraid of that.

CHAPTER EIGHTEEN

Crumbling bricks dug into Lucky's shoulder, and he exhaled into the warm summer air. A blinking neon sign flashed the message "Vacancy" from a rundown rat trap across the street. He'd not been to this part of Athens for a long, long time, and he was dead on his feet from driving the rig non-stop from Texas.

Two fucking a.m. Either way too early or way too late to be making connections.

This isn't my world anymore. Even so, a steady pulse of excitement thrummed through him, squirming through his veins and urging him to action.

Though he projected outward calm, inside his heart thudded against his ribcage. He'd never cared much for the meet-face-to-face-in-the-wee-hours-of-morning thing. Back in the day, Victor used to hire lackeys for that kind of work, considering Lucky's skills too valuable to risk on a drug deal gone wrong. He'd kept Lucky more of a behind-the-scenes kind of guy, but desperate times called for desperate measures, and staying in Reyes' good graces meant doing whatever the guy asked.

The prickly fingers of anxiety caressed Lucky's spine, his nerves jangling on an adrenaline high as they always were when neck deep in drug deals. It didn't help that his contact was late and each precious moment ticking away put him further and further in danger. Time was running out. This deal needed to be over and done by sunrise. Where the fuck was Bo? Not that he dared risk a phone call if this little exercise amounted to some kind of paranoid test.

He'd tagged himself with a tracker, though, and clued Walter in to his location. He didn't need a visual. Keith had him under surveillance. The bastard might be a card-carrying asshole, but he did his job. Somewhere in the big scheme of things, Walter and O'Donoghue readied the troops.

Lucky finally spotted a coal black sedan easing down the nearly-deserted street, pulling to a stop on the opposite side. Glancing right and left to ensure he wasn't being openly observed, Lucky crossed the road against the light. Another quick look-see, and he opened the driver's door. The hard thumping of a bass beat elicited a wince as he slid behind the wheel, the former driver having relinquished the driver's seat in favor of the passenger side. There was no need to check. The cloying stench of cheap cologne gave away the guy from the garage that Lucky'd growled at during their last meeting.

The man yelled to be heard over the loud rap music blaring from too many speakers. Lucky fucking hated rap. "Drive up I-85, and cross over to 385 to Spartanburg. I've got the GPS programmed. When you get to Church Street, pull into the Krispy Kreme Doughnuts parking lot. Call Mateo, and he'll tell you where to go from there."

Nodding agreement, Lucky stared straight ahead as his contact slipped from the car. Lucky jabbed the button on the disk player, silencing the too loud music. Ah, blessed silence, though his whole body still vibrated with the memory of the pulsing beat.

He reached into his pocket and turned off the recorder, hoping the sensitive mic hadn't blown up and had caught the voice even over the background noise. Technology was his friend. One down, a few more to go. The guy he'd relinquish the car to would be next. Reyes made this job sound important. If it wasn't a test, Lucky might get to meet someone higher up the food chain.

He locked the doors and adjusted the seat for his shorter stature. Five foot six wasn't exactly tiny, but the previous driver was at least six-five. Fucker. After fastening his seatbelt, Lucky put the car into drive and eased away from the curb into the night. The muscles in his jaw clenched.

Gut wrenching unease persisted, no matter how much he chanted, "Nothing's wrong, nothing's wrong."

Maybe he should throw in the towel on the SNB, since he'd paid his dues. The older he got, the more he cherished life. The thrill of the chase drove him on, but what would his existence be like in the normal world, coming home to Bo every night, talking about their days? Maybe he'd lost his nerve. Or maybe he hadn't lost anything. Instead, he'd gained a reason to keep his miserable hide free of bullet holes, and to keep his bullet holes out of others. Perhaps the time had come to cut his losses and move on.

Bo wanted a home and a family. Well, maybe Lucky did, too, but he couldn't see that happening with him and Bo away for weeks at a time, unsure if they'd ever return. But even a tamer job didn't offer too much protection. Look at the woman on the SNB memorial page. She'd been an accountant, taken out by a drunk driver. And Art nearly made the page, thanks to a freak accident and a bunch of birthday balloons. There were no guarantees, no matter what path Lucky chose.

What of Bo? By his own admission, all was not well in his mind right now. No matter how exciting Lucky found Bo's newly discovered dangerous side, if the man adopted a hard-assed attitude for real, he'd lose the qualities that made him who he was. He'd be someone else entirely. Someone with absolutely no use for a two-bit, ex-con narcotics agent, a white picket fence, kids, and a family dog.

A smiling face appeared in Lucky's mind, honey and chestnut hair, crooked, shy smile, and dark brown, gold-flecked eyes, irises rimmed in a deep, deep green. In spite of the tension, he couldn't help smiling back at the image. Bo. His Bo.

He eased to stop at a red light. *Sccreeeech!* Car tires squealed up the street, a dark blur fast gaining ground. What the hell? Holy shit! His eyes glued to the rearview mirror, he tucked and covered as the speeding car slammed into him from behind with the unmistakable crunch of metal on metal. *Cheeeeeesh!* A shower of glass fragments rained down, biting into Lucky's skin. Like a rag doll, Lucky whipped forward, banging his head on the steering wheel and then back, to pound his head against the headrest. Stars danced before his eyes. His nose stung from the stench of burning rubber. Despite both feet holding the brake to the floor, the tires groaned in protest as the car behind him pushed him out into the intersection.

More glass shattered and he ducked, a baseball bat smashing the driver's side window, missing his temple by mere inches. Rough hands grabbed at him, and he scrambled on his belly across the seat to get away.

"Oh no, you don't," came the same sinister bark from before as a hand latched onto his ankle. So, the rap lover wasn't as dumb as he looked and had at least figured out that Lucky wasn't on his side. He flipped onto his back, dislodged the grip and kicked out, landing a shoe to the nose of his attacker. The man howled and grabbed his face. "Get the li'l faggot!" the injured man yelled, "he's getting away."

At least that solved the mystery of who'd followed Lucky and Bo. Lucky fumbled the passenger door open and barreled toward the sidewalk, fumbling to start the recorder in his pocket. If he went down, he'd gladly take others with him.

Damn, but his leg still wasn't up to running, even a year after being injured. He gave it his best shot, his smaller, more agile body ducking and dodging his larger, ungainly pursuers. Down the road he ran, darting into shadows. Fuck! Why did his leg choose now to start aching? If they'd found out about him, his cover was blown. He merely played mouse to Reyes' cat.

Ducking into an alley, he pressed himself flat against the wall, willing his heart and breathing to slow. One man thundered past, but Lucky'd counted at least three, though Broken Nose might still be incapacitated. Served him right, the bastard. The minutes ticked by, and Lucky strained his ears for sounds of pursuit. Only the occasional passing of a car or muffled curses from Rap Lover reached his ears. The waiting might kill him, figuratively speaking, but not waiting would kill him literally.

He barreled blindly down the alley. Hallelujah! An opening at the other end. Running hell-bent-for-leather, he pushed as hard as he could. He easily scaled the chain link fence barring his way, but once on the other side, the telltale rattling behind him proved he'd been made. Side and ankle screaming in agony, he continued his mad dash with no idea where he was or where he was going.

Lucky pulled his gun out, ducking between two more buildings and trying to watch both ends of the alley at once.

Energy fading, feet slowing, by the glow of a street lamp he watched in horror as the silhouette of a handgun descended on him. The blow connected. He loosed a grunt and fell, blackness crowding his vision. Bo appeared in his mind. Oh shit! Had they made Bo too? "I'm sorry," he whispered before reality slipped away.

Blinding pain, his body jostling. A trunk. Lucky rode in a car trunk. He squeezed his eyes shut and patted his pockets, coming up empty except for the recorder made to double as a key chain. All gone. His gun, his cell phone, his watch, his wallet, the tracker. With any luck, he'd merely dropped the tracker and no one found it. Or if they found it, they'd think someone planted the device on him. If they used his work phone, who would answer? The department all knew the drill, and would pretend to be someone associated with Ricky Getsinger, Walter's name having been entered into the memory as Uncle Walter.

The car hit a bump, jostling Lucky again. Damn, but his head hurt. He closed his eyes and knew no more.

The car stopped. Lucky rubbed his head. Whoever'd clobbered him had gotten him good. A car door slammed and he lay still, hoping whoever opened the trunk might think he was still out cold. They hadn't killed him outright, but might simply be waiting for the right moment. There had to be an emergency latch in here somewhere, but he couldn't escape. No telling what waited for him outside the car.

Hard-soled shoes clicked across concrete, and Lucky squeezed his eyes shut when the trunk lid popped opened. The night grew lighter for a moment, until shadows darkened it again. Someone leaned into the trunk, close enough to waft breath on Lucky's ear. Expensive-smelling cologne teased his nose.

A deep chuckle sent a spike of fear plunging through Lucky's innards. "You have the wrong man," a cultured voice said. "I can promise you, he is no narc." A finger trailed down his cheek and Lucky fought back a flinch. "Keep searching. You'll find who you're looking for."

Lucky's heart thudded so hard he feared being heard. Keeping his eyes closed might possibly have been the hardest thing he'd ever done.

"Are you sure?" Rap Man asked from further away.

"As sure as I've ever been about anything. For old time's sake, take him back where he belongs and let him go. I want to talk to him later, but not tonight. Now, what have you brought me?" The trunk lid slammed shut.

The voices faded, the men moving away from the car. Lucky lay petrified, replaying the last words he'd heard before his dubious savior walked away. "Hello, Lucky." He reached into his pocket and clicked off the recorder.

CHAPTER NINETEEN

Lucky lay in the trunk, afraid to move. It couldn't be. It simply couldn't. And yet... The car started moving again, which helped jolt Lucky from his shock and back into survival mode.

There had to be a logical explanation. Dead men didn't come back to life. Well, Lucky had, but only because of Walter Smith. He played dead again when the car stopped and two pairs of hands dragged him from the trunk. He landed in a soft bed of grass. Something hard hit his side, but he held perfectly still. Something softer grazed his hip.

"If it was up to me, I'd kill you for the hell of it," a voice spat, a broken nose making it sound like the guy had a cold, "but the boss has spoken."

Rap Man had seen the big boss. Interesting, and something Lucky would capitalize on if at all possible. The car sped away into the night, and Lucky patted the ground for the things that had hit him: his gun and wallet. A passing car's headlights reflected off his cell phone, lying a few feet away. The car didn't stop. His watch. Shit! They'd kept his Christmas present from Bo. Fuckers.

Lucky rolled to his back, staring up at the heavens. Stars twinkled overhead, and in the distance, a bullfrog sent out a plea for a mate. Lucky sure wouldn't mind his own mate showing up about now. Crickets chirped and, across the road, a cow lowed. He closed his eyes and breathed in grass, clover, and wildflowers. For a moment, he imagined himself back at his parents' farm, on the hill overlooking the tobacco fields, Charlotte beside him, sharing his dreams.

Ah, to be young again, with his whole life before him. He'd sure as hell make better choices. Choices that didn't lead him into the arms and bed of Victor Mangiardi. Victor might still be alive if not for Lucky. Would Charlotte and Bo one day come to regret knowing him, as Victor had?

A red light flashed on his phone, taking him from his thoughts. If he ignored the outside world, he could lay right here, take a breather. But Rap Man and He-Lucky-Dared-Not-Name were gunning for a possible narc. Bo stood right in their line of fire.

He picked up his phone and stared at the screen at a string of messages, all from Bo. "Where are you?" and "Are you all right?" and "Damn it! Talk to me." The last message said, "It's going down." Thank goodness the last incriminating message came through only minutes ago and hadn't been seen by his abductors.

Wait! *Going down? Now?* Damn. Couldn't let the party start without him. Lucky rose unsteadily to his feet, one hand on his aching head. His fingers came away sticky. Oh well. Wasn't the first time he'd been bashed over the head, and it probably wouldn't be the last. He stared at the horizon, surprised to find himself only about a half-mile from the garage. A quick check of his gun showed all rounds in the chamber. Idiots. Never leave someone you've pissed off armed. Checking the safety before tucking the gun into his waistband, he aimed his feet toward the garage. "Damn leg, you better hold out." He took off at a trot.

A quarter mile in he met a car, unmistakably an SNB issue. Show time!

Loud voices rang out through the open bay doors, a group of men gathered around, cheering and catcalling. In their midst, two men squared off. Oh shit. Rap Man and Bo. Clenching his teeth against his leg's protest, Lucky ran.

Rap Man threw a wild punch, and Bo ducked, coming up fast and slamming a fist into his opponent's kidney. The man went down to his knees.

"Get up! Get up!" someone shouted.

Too involved in the fight, no one noticed either Lucky creeping up to the door, or the other shadows gaining ground in classic stealth mode.

"Son-of-a-bitching narc!" Bo shrieked, lunging at Rap Man with a roundhouse right. He connected hard. Lucky rubbed his jaw in sympathy.

Another man came at Bo, who jumped back, sizing up his opponent. Damn, but the former rookie had gotten good. He no longer held himself stiffly, using only his arms to swing. The way he rocked on bended knees, he'd easily deflect or dance away from blows. Heh. Lucky'd taught Bo something with that first ass-kicking in a boxing ring after all.

A shadowy shape flitted from the building next door and disappeared behind the garage. Lucky divided his attention between the agents getting into place and the agent creating a distraction in the garage. *Just a few more minutes, Bo.*

Dusty Beard raced forward out of nowhere, a tire tool raised high overhead, aimed straight at Bo's back. *Oh hell the fuck no!* Bellowing like an angry bull, Lucky elbowed men out of his way, charging toward his partner. Bo glanced up, the relief on his face short-lived. *Crack!* Right across the back. Bo stood still for a moment, all expression draining from his face. And then he fell.

Lucky grabbed Bo, easing him to the ground, then spun and caught Dusty Beard before the tool came down again. With both hands wrapped around the man's wrist, Lucky shoved, gritting his teeth and holding his ground. *Hurry the fuck up!* he mentally ordered his team.

He never thought he'd see the day when he'd be glad to hear, "Hold it right there. Put your hands on your head. All of you." Johnson stepped into the light from outside, gun at the ready and a take-no-prisoners attitude. If Lucky ever kissed a woman, it'd be her.

Dusty Beard dashed toward the back exit, but the door opened ahead of him. A grim faced O'Donoghue barred the way, flanked by two members of the Athens police department. Lucky froze, discreetly checking Bo out from the corner of his eye. Bo moaned but placed both hands on top of his head. "You too" came from behind Lucky.

He laced his fingers together, assuming the frisk position. "Try not to enjoy yourself too much." He glowered at Landry. As soon as he could, Lucky was gonna take the young pup down to the gym and teach him a valuable lesson: Lucky could kick his ass. In that case, he'd enjoy the hell out of training, but nobody else had better lay a hand on one of his rookies.

A snarl sent Landry back a step or two, indecision in his eyes. Oh, that'd cost him if Lucky'd been an actual felon. Still a felon. Officially. Whatever. Johnson took over, kicking Lucky's feet further apart and patting him down. The gun he'd gotten back ten minutes ago didn't survive the search.

Panic seized him when Johnson grabbed his wrists and locked them behind him. *It's all for show. I'm not going back to jail.* Lucky's heart didn't believe him, pounding to beat the band. The only one he wanted cuffing him was Bo. The last thing he saw before leaving the garage was O'Donoghue sliding back the hidden panel and whistling at the contents within the vault.

"Nice to see you're still with us," Lucky told Johnson on his way across the parking lot. He meant it too.

"Seeing your ugly mug again ain't too traumatizing either," Johnson shot back, in the same tone she'd used to say, "You've got the right to remain silent" earlier. She manhandled Lucky into the backseat of a car, and Lucky didn't put up too much of a fight. Ankle throbbing, smacked over the head, and excitement giving way to exhaustion, he didn't feel up to the effort.

"Who'd you piss off to draw this detail?" he asked.

"Piss off? Honey, I'll have you know I had to arm wrestle some jerkoff named Keith for the honor of arresting your ass."

"You won?" Lucky couldn't wait to rub Keith's nose in defeat.

Johnson snorted. "Was there ever any doubt? Southeastern's gotta get with the program, 'cause I can whoop everyone here, 'cept maybe him." She nodded toward Bo. "I hear he's one bad motherfucker."

"And me." She'd doubtless make Lucky earn his victory.

"Keep dreaming." After settling Lucky, she slammed the door and stalked away into the night to a soundtrack of crackling police radios and the flickering of strobe lights. Of all the scary things out there in the dark, he'd just met up with the scariest. Damn, but he was glad she was on his side.

The faint scent of Old Spice tickled his nose, signaling the boss's presence in the front seat. "Hello, Walter."

"Hello, Lucky." Walter's greeting came out a yawn. It'd been a long day for everyone. "My apologies, but the local Starbucks isn't open at this hour."

"You can owe me." Lucky's love of Starbucks brew was legendary, although he stopped wearing his *Will Work for Starbucks Coffee* T-shirt to the office when one of the accountants suggested taking him up on the offer.

Lucky struggled into a more comfortable position, or as comfortable as he could get with his hands locked behind him. He stared out the window at the flashing lights and cops leading men away. Hey, what did you know? Even the DEA sent a car. But with all the manpower focused here... "How about the barn and the customers?"

"The gentleman who took the rigs was arrested an hour ago, and DEA agents secured the barn. Four other Cruiser chapters are being raided as we speak. Arrests are being made from Atlanta to Athens. Most larger cities in the South Carolina pipeline are rounding up suspects: Clemson, Greenville, Anderson, Spartanburg, as well as a few smaller busts, and I've yet to hear from North Carolina, Tennessee, and Virginia. At last count, we've captured seventy-five suspects, which puts this operation as one of the largest in the South in recent history."

Looked like another one of Lucky's cases might make headlines. "Did you get Reyes?"

"Not yet. He fled. Local officers are in pursuit."

Lucky took a deep breath, blowing it out slowly. "We may have a bigger problem." He really didn't want to say the words, as though speaking evil might somehow manifest the boogeyman.

"Oh? How so?"

"Someone thought I had 'narc' written on me and tossed me into a trunk. I might have met the man pulling Reyes' strings."

Walter turned as much as the confining front seat allowed. "Keith lost you, and we'd wondered where you'd gotten to."

"Nearest I can tell, I was in a warehouse, but I'm not sure where. I had a recorder, but lost the tracker somewhere while getting away."

"Was this man anyone you recognized?"

"I didn't actually see him, I only heard his voice. And yes, I believe I know him." *Please let me be wrong, please let me be wrong.*

In his best kind-old-uncle-you-can-tell-anything-to voice, Walter asked, "Who, Lucky?"

"Victor Mangiardi."

CHAPTER TWENTY

"Are you sure?" Walter stared hard at Lucky, making him squirm.

"I'd been hit over the head, and I was out of it, but, yeah. Sounded like him."

Part of Lucky wanted so badly to believe Victor Mangiardi still lived and breathed, if only to remove his own guilt for the man's death. However, the "works for the SNB" part of him said the world was better off without Victor. What a fucked up life.

The last of the cars marked *Athens Police Department* pulled away, leaving only an ambulance and two SNB vehicles.

"You're bleeding," Walter said. "You can tell me the rest after the paramedics check you over."

A few minutes later, Lucky sat in the back of the ambulance, cuffs removed and sipping coffee someone had gotten from somewhere while a paramedic dabbed stinging shit on his head. It wasn't Starbucks, and it wasn't decaf, but Lucky needed all the help he could get to stay awake. It's not like his head could possibly hurt worse without splitting in two.

Bo stood a few feet away with Johnson, one hand covered in gauze while a uniformed man examined his shoulder. Damn, but that tire tool left the bruise from hell. Thank God Bo caught the blow too high to crack ribs and too low to bust his skull.

Lucky's scalp stung, snapping him back to the here and now. "Ow, damn it."

"Now, Lucky." Walter sighed. "Don't take your frustrations out on the innocent."

"Hey, dude. You innocent?" Lucky asked Tall, Dark, and Ham-handed. Anything to keep his mind off his partner. Why weren't they loading Bo into the ambulance and rushing him to the hospital? He needed attention.

"Depends on who's asking," the guy responded.

"I'll take that as a no, you careless..."

"Lucky!"

No one snatched Lucky's leash faster than Walter Smith.

"Don't blame me, blame the head injury." Truth was, here Lucky sat, being treated like he'd lost his mind, while out there a man he'd once loved, who now gave him nightmares, might roam free. There was no way in hell the Feds had faked Victor's death, was there? Lucky'd seen the medical reports and papers himself. Victor hanged himself following his sentencing, after Lucky's testimony helped to cement a guilty verdict.

Of course, the newspapers also said Lucky Lucklighter died in a car wreck, saving another agent. Even the SNB website proclaimed Richmond Eugene Lucklighter dead. Lucky wasn't the only one capable of faking a death, and Victor Mangiardi had the clout, connections, and money to do anything he wanted.

Lucky waited until the paramedic stepped out of earshot to ask, "Check the records for me, will ya? Make sure no one cut a deal. If you can make Lucky Lucklighter disappear, who's to say someone didn't work the same kind of magic for Victor?" He sipped his coffee. Maybe acting normal would help shake the heebie-jeebies.

"I will, but only to make you feel better. Believe me, if Victor had cut a deal, I'd know."

Walter didn't know every damned thing. He couldn't know how Victor always had one more trick up his sleeve than even Lucky suspected, and Walter sure as hell hadn't lived within earshot of that voice. Lucky knew what he'd heard and could prove it. He reached into his pocket and fished out the recorder. "Listen to this." He pushed a button and nearly retched coffee.

"You have the wrong man," a familiar voice said.

Ice water formed in Lucky's veins.

"I can promise you," the man continued, "he is no narc."

"Are you sure?" another voice asked.

"As sure as I've ever been about anything. For old time's sake, take him back where he belongs and let him go. I want to talk to him later, but not tonight. Now, what have you brought me?"

More mumbled words, then a distinct, "Hello, Lucky."

Lucky clicked the recorder off. The voice didn't change on second hearing. "Sounds like Victor Mangiardi to me."

He snuck a peek at Bo, who stared at his bandaged hand. He had to have heard. What was he thinking? Surely he didn't believe Lucky would desert him and run back to Victor. Even if Victor somehow managed to survive, Lucky's heart had found a new home. He'd tell Bo at the first opportunity. Until then they had a job to do.

"Boss..."

The color fled Walter's face, and one meaty hand gripped the ambulance door. The man swayed on his feet. He opened his eyes and stared straight at Lucky, opening and closing his mouth, but nothing emerged.

Johnson broke the awkward moment. "Who's Victor Mangiardi?"

Before Lucky could answer, the radio in Walter's car squawked. Walter wobbled away, relief in his eyes. Oh, no. He wasn't getting away. Sooner or later, he'd be answering Lucky's questions.

Lucky rushed to Walter's side. "They've spotted Reyes' motorcycle," Walter said. "Approximately five miles from here, heading east."

"Let's go." Lucky jumped into the driver's seat, shouting to Johnson and Bo. "They spotted Reyes. Let's move!"

Johnson trotted over to her car while Bo ran to his motorcycle and grabbed his helmet off the seat. "If he goes off road, I can follow."

Walter took his place in the passenger seat, and Lucky fired up the engine. The hunt continued.

A few taps on the GPS pointed out Reyes' location. Ha! So the guy hadn't found all the trackers. Lucky peeled out of the parking lot, heading on an intercept course. Bo flew around him a minute later. Johnson's headlights shone about a quarter mile back.

Lucky tore up the back roads, fast gaining ground. His heart pounded, and he clutched the steering wheel in a white-knuckled grip. Closer, closer... He rounded a curve, and his headlights fell on two motorcycles barreling down the straightaway, neck and neck. In the distance sirens shrieked, approaching from another direction.

A dark shape appeared from nowhere, heading right for the bikes. The darkened car barely missed the first. A wobble left, then right. RPMs roaring, the Harley straightened.

The car swerved, ramming the second bike. Rider and machine tilted sideways, trailing sparks across the asphalt. Lucky stomped the brakes, folding Walter over the shoulder harness. The car skidded to a stop nearly on top of smoldering wreck.

Oh, fuck no!

The luckier of the two bikers spun his bike and hauled ass after the fleeing car.

Tires squealed behind him. Johnson spun a one-eighty and hit the gas, chasing the car and motorcycle.

Lucky fumbled open his seatbelt with fingers that didn't work right. Walter already barked orders through the radio to an emergency dispatcher.

By the light of the car's headlights, Lucky darted across the road, his heart lodged in his throat. The coppery scent of blood overlaid burnt rubber. "Oh God, please. Not Bo."

He hunkered down beside the still biker.

Reyes.

Lucky closed his eyes and huffed out the breath he'd been holding. Reyes. Not Bo. And he hadn't been wearing leather or a helmet. Bo's argument for wearing leather hit home. A mangled mass, bits of denim clinging to flesh, stuck out from under the bike. Two fingers to the man's neck didn't turn up a pulse, and with one side of his head caved in, resuscitation wouldn't help.

Not Bo, not Bo, not Bo. Lucky's eyes burned, and he blinked hard to clear his vision. *Not Bo, not Bo, not Bo. Thank you, dear Lord in Heaven.*

Thank God Bo's not here to see this. No telling what the grisly visual would do to his PTSD. Blood puddled out from beneath Reyes' still body.

Within seconds, squad cars descended. Lucky's long day got longer.

After sunup, an ambulance hauled Reyes away and clean-up crews washed away the evidence before the God-fearing folk of Athens needed that stretch of road to get to work.

Lucky leaned against the hood of Walter's car, giving a statement.

A uniformed cop, a rookie by the looks of him, ran up, mumbled to Walter, cast a wary glance to Lucky, and faded into the background after slapping a gun into Walter's hand. "I believe this belongs to you?" Walter extended the .38 to Lucky, grip first.

Damn, but Lucky had to stop letting people take his gun. "Thanks, boss man."

"Don't mention it. You seem to be making a habit of losing that gun." Walter gave a weary smile.

"Yeah, well someone took my watch, and I want it back."

"I'll make a note on the report."

"What about the car that hit Reyes?"

"Unfortunately, the driver seemed familiar with local roads. We lost the vehicle somewhere in the Commerce area."

"Tag?"

"No tag or other identifying markings. Bo couldn't get close enough to make out the driver."

Bo. Safe. Hallelujah. And this time he'd get hugged whether he wanted to or not. In fact, once Lucky got his arms around the man, he might never let go.

Lucky collapsed into the passenger seat of Walter's car, weary beyond belief. Walter drove him to the garage to retrieve the Malibu.

"Now, Lucky." Walter straightened to his full impressive height, or as much as the car allowed. "Take care of yourself out there. Get some sleep. I'll expect you at the office within the next day or two for a full report."

"Will do." Lucky rubbed his tired eyes and made his way to the ugliest Malibu in Georgia, now a welcome sight. After a quick trip to Starbucks, he headed away from town, cruising along a country road with the windows open to let in the morning breeze.

Soon the bumping, banging, and scratch of low limbs on the roof of the car told him what he needed to know. He was home.

Bo waited for him on the cabin's front porch.

Lucky ran appraising eyes up and down his partner, pausing long enough to study bumps and bruises acquired during the night. "Bo...I..." Words failed him.

"I know." The shimmer in Bo's eyes said he did too.

The back of Lucky's throat burned, and he blinked hard to drive the sudden onslaught of moisture from his eyes.

Then his arms were around Bo, and Bo's around him, and oh damn, how right. He clung, willing Bo to understand how he was needed, how nearly losing him cut like a knife to the heart. This time, Bo didn't run away.

They made their way into the cabin and Bo's room. Piece by piece Lucky stripped off Bo's clothing, examining each injury. In the middle of a creaky four-poster bed, he wrapped his body around his lover's, afraid to let go or Bo might disappear.

Lucky woke often over the next few hours, bolting upright from visions of Bo lying bloody on the pavement, no light shining from his deep brown eyes. A dream, only a dream. Each time he stayed awake a while, listening to the steady in/out of Bo's breathing, resting his head on a rising and falling chest to hear the *thumpa, thumpa* of a strong heartbeat. He held a bit tighter until sleep claimed him again.

CHAPTER TWENTY-ONE

Lucky searched the SNB archive, as he'd done before, for any mention of Victor Mangiardi, though nothing new had been added since his death over eleven years ago. Lucky closed his eyes, seeing Victor as he'd been in the courtroom, gaunt, disheveled, a man without hope. And he'd smiled at his betrayer.

But Lucky hadn't betrayed him, not really. He'd had no hand in Victor's arrest; he'd merely offered honest answers to pointed questions during the trial. Chances were the jury would have returned a guilty verdict even without his testimony.

No use dwelling on shoulda, woulda, coulda. It wouldn't change one damned thing. He clicked on an icon on his laptop, listening to the voice again, determined to hear something, anything, to prove the words didn't belong to Victor. Eleven years was a long time, and memories faded. Maybe he only wanted the unknown voice to belong to Victor. That's what his prison counselor would have said. Maybe he should go see Bo's counselor, convince himself he wasn't losing his mind.

The phone on his desk rang and he snatched up the receiver. "Harrison."

"Lucky, could I see you in my office, please?" Walter's matter-of-fact delivery gave away nothing.

"I'll be right there." Lucky guzzled the last of his coffee and made his way to his boss' office, grateful O'Donoghue wasn't sitting in front of Walter's desk. With what they had to discuss, he didn't need anyone else knowing the details about the time he'd spent as a drug lord's boy toy.

"You wanted to see me?" His chair squeaked as he settled into its padded depths.

"We've analyzed the recording you gave us, but unfortunately, media wasn't allowed at Victor's trial, and comparisons with any other recordings are inconclusive."

Fuck. And here Lucky'd hoped for a return to normalcy.

"However, Victor Mangiardi hanged himself in his cell. I've received copies of the coroner's report. The man you suspected might be Victor didn't know you were with the SNB?"

"You heard him. His exact words were, 'I can promise you, he is no narc.'"

"He mentioned wanting to talk to you at a later date." A furrow appeared between Walter's fluffy gray brows.

"That's what he said." Lucky could recite every word on the recording by heart.

Walter leaned back in his chair, stroking his chin. "Ricky Getsinger and Cyrus Cooper are about to escape justice on a technicality. Chances are, whoever's behind this operation will want to rebuild." Lucky noticed he didn't invoke Victor's name. "Who better to help him than an old friend?"

What the fuck? Oh, hell no. "Boss, I don't know if I can." What if Victor still lived? Or maybe someone who'd associated with Victor? What if they found out about the SNB connection, or worse, what if they found out about Bo? If they wanted to talk to Lucky, Bo would make damned good leverage. Then again, no matter who the mystery man was, if he dealt drugs on Lucky's turf, he'd have to go down.

Victor. His heart clenched. Another face pushed aside Victor's in his mind. Bo. He needed Bo.

"Lucky?"

Lucky snapped to attention. "Sorry, boss." He rubbed a hand over his aching head. "I'm getting over a nasty pistol whipping, you know."

"The paramedic said you'd be fine. Now, I want you and Bo to lay low but stay where we can find you, and V... and whoever too. Any contact, and you call me."

Ah. So unlike Walter to slip up and nearly speak the name.

"Stay together as much as possible. You've both dodged a bullet, so it won't be out of character to team up in defense." Lucky could practically see the wheels turning in Walter's mind, spinning out a viable scenario. "A condition of your release is that you not leave Georgia. If someone wants to find you, they will."

Lucky swallowed hard. "And if they want to kill us?"

"I'll have full surveillance on the cabin. Move your things out there. Like I said, it's not uncommon in your circumstances to combine forces."

Full surveillance. Oh shit. Looking, but not touching, minding every word.

"Outside," Walter clarified. "I trust you to record what needs recording, but I'll not invade your privacy any more than absolutely necessary. I don't expect you to live on one of those damnable reality shows where the world pries into your every move." Lucky watched as one shaggy eyebrow rose slightly before snapping back into place.

"What about the kid?" *The one I shot.*

"Jerry Wilkerson should make a full recovery, and is now in protective custody. He claims to have dealt with no one higher than Reyes, and we've about exhausted his usefulness, though he's come in handy for identifying gang members and translating coded distribution records on Reyes' iPad."

Lucky chewed his lower lip while mulling over Walter's words. "With me and Bo gone for months, where does that leave the department?"

"You'll be happy to hear that Art's made a full recovery and has assumed your role of training supervisor for the foreseeable future. We've retained Owen Landry for the time being, and Loretta Johnson is transferring from Southwestern. Seems she's quite taken with Atlanta."

Loretta, huh? Maybe Lucky shouldn't keep calling her Johnson.

"And the guys that tossed me in a trunk?"

"Have added kidnapping to their extortion, trafficking, and money laundering charges. However, none will corroborate your story about our mystery man. We can't reveal the existence of the recording without compromising your position. "

"After what happened to Reyes to keep him from talking, do you blame them for shutting down?" No way in hell would a man like Mateo Reyes have cut a deal, but someone hadn't taken any chances. They'd not found hide nor hair of whoever'd assured his silence.

"No, I can't say that I do. The Athens P.D. hasn't yet identified a suspect in Travis Eubanks' murder."

Figured.

"Joe Clinkscales and Demarcus Sutton are being questioned. Now, finish up the day here and get back to Athens."

Lucky'd nearly made it to the door when Walter's, "Lucky?" stopped him.

"Yes, boss?"

"Be careful. I don't want to have to rush to the emergency room in the middle of the night again." Though spoken with authority, Lucky didn't miss the affectionate undertone.

"Aren't I always?" Lucky stepped into the hall and closed the door behind him before Walter could answer.

"You can stop your infernal yowling, it's not gonna change a thing."

Cat Lucky howled again, stepping into the open duffel on Human Lucky's bed. Lucky scooped the tomcat out and tossed in a shirt. "You can't go, and that's final. Although you'd be great at sniffing out rats, wouldn't you?" He paused long enough to deliver a chin scratch. The cat stropped against his hand, then leapt from the bed and pranced away.

A few more shirts and another pair of jeans filled up the bag. Next, Lucky trudged into the kitchen for his coffee maker. Whoever owned the cabin didn't have one, the slacker. He tossed a few cans of tuna into a bag for his landlady. While technically the cat belonged to her, it wouldn't hurt to help her out with feeding Cat Lucky. The critter liked to eat.

After one last look through his home, Lucky loaded up the Malibu and let the cat out.

"Nice car," his landlady remarked from next door.

Lucky approached, placing the bag of tuna on the porch near where she sat swinging and smoking a pipe. Cat Lucky hopped up to stretch across her lap, dislodging two more felines. "It serves the purpose."

She'd never asked, and he'd never told what type of work he did, but the old lady kept an eagle eye on the neighborhood and not much escaped her notice. "You've already been gone two months. How long you going for this time?"

"A few weeks, maybe."

"I'll keep an eye on your place, and your cat." She scratched Cat Lucky's ear.

"I'd be much obliged," Lucky replied, using the same words his granddaddy had taught him years ago.

He didn't look back. What lay ahead was all that mattered.

CHAPTER TWENTY-TWO

Lucky stared out over the water, checking the river for stray boats wandering too near. Two weeks and no contact from the supplier. A cabin by the water, down a lonely dirt road. Plenty of fish to catch, no one bothering him... and Bo. Life didn't get any better than this, if Lucky ignored the surveillance cameras posted around the property. While Walter assured him of no recording in the house, nothing took the wind out of a man's sails faster than knowing some asshole coworker might have gotten overzealous and installed a bug anyway. An asshole coworker with an ax to grind.

"Hey," Bo said, coming up behind Lucky, two coffee cups in hand. Lucky accepted his, Bo's coffee coming in a close second to Starbucks. He tilted his head back to better study his partner. The shorter hair suited him, as did the ball-brusher facial hair. Felt pretty good against Lucky's cock too. Casually leaning against a tree, Bo appeared at ease, though traces of Cy still clung to him. Perhaps they'd always been there, to be summoned as needed.

How else would Bo have taken a baseball bat to his worthless drunk of a father when the old man went too far on Bo's kid brother? At eighteen, he'd gone to war to make something of himself, and he'd stripped to help pay for college. He'd stood in the middle of a group of bikers and picked a barehanded fight. If the meek inherited the earth, like Granddaddy used to say, most folks who didn't know him better might believe Bo stood to claim a nice chunk of real estate. But Bo had a lot more in common with Cyrus Cooper than Lucky would have imagined a few months back. Different facets of the same man.

209

"I'm getting antsy sitting around waiting for something to happen." Bo took a sip of what had to be green tea. Cy hadn't yet convinced him to guzzle coffee.

"What you got in mind?" Lucky asked. He turned up his cup, swilling down perfect brew.

"We're supposed to act normal, right?"

Lucky gave Bo a squint-eyed glare. "I don't reckon either one of us has acted normal a day in our lives."

Bo snorted. "Speak for yourself. Anyway, Cy and Ricky can't be expected to hang around and do nothing all summer, can they?"

"Our release calls for us to stick around. Whatever you're planning, we can't go too far."

"We won't. Come on. Help me pack the bike."

Inside the cabin, Bo dug two sleeping bags out of the closet along with a miniature gas stove in a bag and an old fashioned coffee percolator. Next, he raided the kitchen for coffee, almond butter, and bread, carefully arranging the supplies in the bike's saddle bags and strapping the sleeping bags to the back. "Where're we going?" Lucky asked.

A smile peeked out of Bo's facial hair. "Somewhere I always threatened to take you. We're going camping."

"Okay, but I'm driving."

"No, you're not."

"Am so. No one's watching, and at the moment you're not being Cyrus Cooper. There's no reason in God's green earth that I can't drive the hog."

"I have a motorcycle license."

"I have a license too."

"In Simon Harrison's name?"

"Well, no."

"Then you're not driving."

"Yes. I. Am."

"No. You're. Not." Bo grinned. "I have the keys." He held the ring aloft.

Lucky made a grab, but Bo held the keys higher. "Give it up, T-Rex."

"Oh yeah." Lucky dug his fingers into Bo's sides.

Bo immediately doubled over, shielding as best he could. "Not fair! I'm ticklish."

"Poor widdle boy. Didn't hear me say 'not fair' when you were poking me."

"That's 'cause I was poking you with my dick."

"If that was your dick, I'd be complaining. Felt like a finger to me." Lucky feinted left and grabbed right, getting the keys. He grinned in triumph, brandishing the ring. "You were saying?"

Bo gusted out a sigh. "I'll blow you for those."

Twenty minutes later they pulled away from the cabin. Bo drove. Funny, Lucky didn't remember "Bo gets a blowjob too" figuring into their earlier negotiations.

They'd made it ten miles when Lucky signaled Bo to stop.

"What?" Bo shouted over the engine roar.

No way in hell could Lucky say what was in his heart. He needed a demonstration that left no room for misunderstanding. "There's someplace we need to go first."

Darkness and shadows, the perfect concealment of mischief in the making. The last time he'd been here, Lucky'd worn a jacket. Now he considered a T-shirt and jeans overdressed for the steamy summer heat.

Amateur night raged on at Spencer's bar; the performers hadn't improved much either.

Shuffling footsteps and a quiet "Uh-hmm" called his attention to the shadowy figure leaning against the wall. A full moon and a streetlight shone into the alley, illumination playing on the lone figure partially obscured by darkness.

"You looking for me?" a sultry voice crooned, sending tendrils of desire curling through the pit of Lucky's stomach.

"What're you offering?"

"Everything." The man stepped farther from the shadows. His eyes sparkled in the low light, and dark whiskers obscured most of his face.

"What's everything?" *And do you really mean everything?*

"You know. Ev-er-y-thiiiiing."

"Tell me what you're offering." The spot at the base of Bo's throat beckoned, and Lucky wrapped his mouth around the pulse point, sucking up a bruise.

Bo sighed, tilting his head back to give Lucky room. On a hissed breath he replied, "Every single inch of me, in whatever way you'll have me."

Lucky's semi-erection sprang to full mast. Bo meant more than sex by the words, but somehow *more* didn't scare Lucky now.

Rising up on tiptoes put him at the right height to slam his mouth over his partner's, and he poured all he couldn't say into the kiss. Bo's jeans didn't stand a chance. In no time, Lucky had him unsnapped, unzipped, and facing the wall.

He reined in the impulse to simply sandwich Bo against the door and do what came naturally. Bo moaned and gripped the same doorframe he had on their last visit. The scream of an electric guitar drowned out all other noises, and Lucky cast a wary eye down the alley. Bo liked sex in public? Bo would get sex in public, and pity anyone with the gall to interrupt.

Lucky teased Bo's hole with saliva-moistened fingertips, preparing the way for something bigger. The music paused long enough for him to hear a muffled whine from overhead. Oh yeah. Bo was ready. He grasped Bo's hips and pulled, plastering himself to Bo's back. Their T-shirts rubbed together, the tang of sweat temporarily overpowering the scent of French fries and burgers from the bar.

Lips close enough to brush Bo's earlobe, Lucky asked, "Does that offer you made still hold?"

"Yes."

He ran his hand beneath Bo's T-shirt, stroking his fingers through a light dusting of hair, clasping his lover against his body. His cock nestled between Bo's cheeks. Lucky's breath caught in his throat. The time had come. He fished the mini bottle of lube from his blue jeans and stepped back, undoing his button and fly. A moan escaped him as he slicked his flesh, and when he stepped back into place against Bo's back, Bo met him halfway.

Lucky positioned himself. "You sure?" he asked. Bo answered by a particularly ambitious backward shove. The head of Lucky's cock breached his entrance. They both froze, Lucky clutching his lover.

Words failed Lucky at the tight heat that welcomed him into his lover's body, and he stopped twice to hold back the urge to come. Sweet mercy! All this time, he'd been denying himself and Bo. Bo thrust back and Lucky took the hint. Hands gripping Bo's shoulders for leverage, he shoved in and withdrew, both of them groaning in time with the music from the bar.

"You feel so right," escaped before he could stop the words.

Bo may have said, "Told you," or perhaps he said, "Just let go." Either way, Lucky lost the fight with his self-control and lunged, burying himself to the hilt in Bo's body. He clung to the man who'd become so much more than a work partner, their closeness a nearly tangible presence.

At last he moved again, hands clutching Bo's hips, setting up a gentle rhythm that nonetheless meant business. Bo gripped the doorframe with one hand, stroking himself with the other and rocking in time with Lucky's thrusting.

What had Lucky been afraid of? Being in Bo, with no barriers... The final barrier to his heart fell too. Love. Bo loved him, without barriers, without boundaries. Unconditionally. Wanted him for the long haul. He loved Bo just as strongly and told the man so with his body.

His caresses were gentle enough to be loving, his lunges hard enough to appeal to Bo's darker nature. He angled his hips, aiming to give Bo the maximum amount of pleasure. A tingling began within, and rather than fight to prolong the moment, Lucky raced for the finish line.

He reached around and joined his hand to Bo's. With moans and whimpers and strangled cries, they made promises to each other they couldn't yet make with words.

Pressure built, and Lucky bucked, willing Bo to come with him. Tightening in his groin heralded his imminent release. No going back now. "I'm gonna come," he warned. Bo thrust back harder. Fingers digging into Bo's hips hard enough to bruise, Lucky let go. "Oh fuck!" Pulse after pulse fired from his body and into Bo, their coupling more intimate than ever before. Lucky held fast, still trembling when Bo cried out his release. Lucky gulped air. God, he loved this man. Laughter burst from his heart and out his throat.

Despite his best effort to stay there forever, eventually he softened and slipped from Bo's opening.

When Bo turned, he met Lucky's eyes, and though they shimmered more than Lucky thought they ought to, Bo's trembling lips turned up in a smile. "Thank y—"

Lucky cut him off. "Don't thank me. You shouldn't ever have had to ask."

The kiss they shared tasted of tears Lucky didn't have to apologize for.

They dressed quietly and returned to the bike. Lucky wrapped an arm around Bo.

"I believe you said something about camping?"

Next week the bottom might drop out of his life, next month he might get shot at again. Hell, it might not even take that long. But right now was a damned fine moment to climb on the Harley behind Bo, wrap himself around his lover, and roar off into the night with someone who didn't want to see him dead.

And if during their camping trip Bo happened to bring up their future together? Well, this time Lucky wouldn't flinch.

ABOUT THE AUTHOR

You will know Eden Winters by her distinctive white plumage and exuberant cry of "Hey, y'all!" in a Southern US drawl so thick it renders even the simplest of words unrecognizable. Watch out, she hugs!

Driven by insatiable curiosity, she possibly holds the world's record for curriculum changes to the point that she's never quite earned a degree but is a force to be reckoned with at Trivial Pursuit.

She's trudged down hallways with police detectives, learned to disarm knife-wielding bad guys, and witnessed the correct way to blow doors off buildings. Her e-mail contains various snippets of forensic wisdom, such as "What would a dead body left in a Mexican drug tunnel look like after six months?" In the process of her adventures she has written fourteen m/m romance novels, has won several Rainbow Awards, was a Lambda Awards Finalist, and lives in terror of authorities showing up at her door to question her Internet searches.

When not putting characters in dangerous situations she's a mild-mannered business executive, mother, grandmother, vegetarian, and PFLAG activist.

Other Rocky Ridge Books: